THE CITY UNSEEN

Book Two of the Unseen

by Andrew C. Jaxson

Also by Andrew C. Jaxson

<u>The Unseen Series</u>
#0.5 The Dark Unseen
#1 The Fire Unseen
#2 The City Unseen
#3 The Truth Unseen (release date to come)

Web: andrewjaxson.com
Facebook: facebook.com/andrewcjaxson
Instagram: instagram.com/andrewcjaxson
Tumblr: andrewcjaxson.tumblr.com
Twitter: twitter.com/andrewcjaxson

About the Author

Andrew C. Jaxson writes stories that scare, intrigue and move his readers. He works across genres, although his novels may be best described as Young Adult Contemporary Fantasy Thrillers (phew!). He's worked a litany of jobs, from wedding DJ to teacher to youth worker and even a very brief and horrifying stint as a street salesman. He hates referring to himself in the third person, because it makes him sound pretentious.

WHAT HAS GONE BEFORE

The tiny town of Ettney, Australia is full of dark secrets. Ari, a sixteen-year-old rural girl is de-facto mother to her younger sister, Skye; as their father left, and their mother is an alcoholic. After a devastating accident, Ari wakes up in hospital. She shouldn't have survived, and while she was unconscious, she was transported to a strange, dark landscape full of impossible things.

A stranger visits Ari during her recovery, claiming she is special, and that she will know everything in time.

The new boy in town, Noah, wants to hang out after school, but his dad makes her uncertain; especially after Mr. Hackman comes to visit her at school. Hackman is the stranger who visited her in hospital, and he also happens to be the new Police Chief at Ettney.

During their date, Noah and Ari are attacked by hooded figures, and Noah is killed in a firestorm.

Ari wakes in a police holding cell. The cops say Noah rolled his truck and it caught fire. She's sure of what she saw, though. The cops are hiding something. They can't be trusted with anything that comes next.

At Noah's funeral Ari meets Rachel, who seems to share a secret with Hackman. Rachel is sympathetic to Ari's plight, and offers to drive her to the accident site. At the site, a strange whisper echoes through the trees, and Rachel panics, driving Ari straight home.

Ari is woken in the middle of the night by a spidery presence on her bedroom roof. It attacks her, and then disappears. In the morning, a black spot has appeared on her stomach. It's cold to the touch.

Josh, Ari's best friend, is pushing for answers, and thinks Noah was a creep. Ari lashes out, hitting Josh, before apologising and kissing him instead. He comes back in the evening, as her mum is working overnight and Ari doesn't feel safe in her house after the prior attack. In the middle of the night, Skye cries out in her sleep. Ari enters the bedroom, and sees Skye suspended in the air by black tendrils. The tendrils speak through Skye in an unknown language, then the house bursts into flames. Josh, Ari and Skye evacuate, surrounded by black tendrils and smoke, and find themselves chased by masked figures. They're rescued by Hackman in his police car, but Skye is taken by the hooded figures, then Ari is knocked unconscious.

Ari wakes in an underground base called the Complex. She's invited to join the Kindred, a secret and ancient organisation whose members can manipulate matter with their minds. Hackman and Rachel are both part of the Kindred, as was Noah until his death. They use the natural resonance of the universe to accelerate and decelerate the particles that make up the world, allowing them to destroy, freeze, or set fire to the world around them. The problem is their power only works when no-one else is watching the same place; only the most powerful Kindred can over-ride the interference generated by someone else's gaze.

The Kindred are the mortal enemies of the Unseen, an organisation as old as the Kindred but with competing aims. The Unseen have taken Skye and Ari's mother, seemingly to use as leverage to get Ari to join them. Josh is safe and being held in the Complex for his own protection. A romance grows between the pair, although Ari feels guilty about betraying Noah - despite his death and their short relationship.

Ari is trained in her power and demonstrates unusual ability. During an outdoor competition, she witnesses a strange sandstone building in the forest that moves when she blinks. A melting figure stands in the doorway, calling to her. Later, Rachel shows Ari a secret entrance to a ledge in the side of the base, where they again witness one of the dark creatures. They're called Shadows, and they seem to absorb energy from the world around them.

Ari is sent out on a reconnaissance mission to an old farmhouse, so they can find her family. On the mission, they overhear an Unseen member mention they have a mole in the Kindred. On return from the mission, Ari overhears Rachel talking to the Unseen on a satellite phone. Ari turns Rachel in, and she is tortured for information.

A mission is launched to recover Ari's family and destroy the Unseen; with the information from Rachel's phone they've located the Unseen safehouses and can wipe them from the region.

During the mission, most of Ari's team are killed, and Ari's family are not located. Ari manages to kill several Unseen in the process.

After the battle, while Ari is alone, Noah reappears. He wasn't killed that night, but rather rescued by Rachel who took him to an Unseen safehouse. The Kindred are the ones who have Ari's family, and now Josh as well. They're using her loved ones to manipulate her into joining them. They are the true villains, and the Unseen are made of up ex-Kindred who defected once they learned the truth about the organisation's goals. Noah and Rachel have been working as double-agents for the Unseen until Ari turned Rachel in.

Noah and Ari mount a rescue mission back into the Kindred complex, rescuing Rachel and her loved ones, but not before a Shadow begins feeding on the Kindred. In the escape, the entire facility is destroyed, and Ari witnesses thirteen Shadows emerging from an altar.

Outside, the team take stock, but Hackman kills Ari's mum and forces Ari and Josh to follow him to the sandstone building called the Chapel. In the process, Hackman cuts off Josh's finger. Inside, Ari has a vision of herself transforming into a Shadow in a street filled with blood. In the vision, Noah dies in front of her, blaming her for everything that's happened. Hackman is convinced that Ari will bring about the Final Day spoken of in the Kindred Agenda. In a fit of rage, Ari uses her abilities to set fire to the air around her, and the resulting fire kills Hackman in the doorway of the Chapel; he looks just like the figure she'd seen during her training session. The first vision had come true.

Get your free Unseen starter library today!

Did you know you can get two extra instalments in the Unseen series for free?

The Unseen starter library contains the prequel to the series, *The Dark Unseen*, as well as a short story that bridges the events of The Fire Unseen and the City Unseen. PLUS you'll get further free short stories and novellas in the series as they're released.

You can get the stories with zero cost or obligation by signing up to the Andrew C. Jaxson readers' club here:

andrewjaxson.com/free

Ad-blockers may make the sign up form disappear, so be sure to switch it off if the sign up form doesn't show.

For Ella, who will always be my light.

ONE

The girl stared at me for a moment, then dove off the boardwalk, disappearing under the black surface of the water. I ran for her, but she was gone. She was a girl just like me, although a few years younger, and this was the second time she had tried to kill me.

The harbour was quiet, a stark contrast to the cacophony carried on the wind from the casino three blocks away. This part of Coleton didn't get much traffic at night, which was why she had planned her attack here. The far end of the wharf was mostly used for tourist boats during the day, and dozens of masts bobbed against the reflection of the water, their constant motion blending into the dark edges of the dock. Standing on the boardwalk, I scanned the area for possible accomplices, but there seemed to be no one else bent on killing me.

For now.

It was a dead end here. Waves lapped against a tiny beach that was accessible only by a small wooden staircase, and the sand was rimmed by imposing houses built by millionaires but owned now by the middle class, thanks to the brutal recession that had hit the city three years before. Despite the seclusion, there were still a thousand ways someone could get to me, so I had to move. Plus, the police might have questions if they found me here, considering a wooden yacht mast was smashed across the boardwalk a few feet away. Thankfully, I had heard the crack when the girl snapped it, and jumped out of its path. If I hadn't, my head would now be crushed into pulpy bits on the boards, ruining an otherwise lovely view for the tourists in the morning.

Last night, on her first attempt, the girl had shoved me into the path of a bus as it thundered down North Avenue. It had braked just in time, and I'd passed it off as an unfortunate mistake, until I saw her glaring from the crowd that had gathered on the pavement. The whites of her eyes glowed under her hoodie, the same one she was wearing tonight, though her face was mostly obscured by the darkness. She had disappeared into the crowd before I'd caught her.

Tonight, though, she had used resonance. She had shattered the base of the mast with her mind and sent it falling my way

My eyes darted to dark windows in an office building to my left. No movement, although I couldn't be sure it was empty.

The only reason I knew she wasn't Kindred was because no one else had turned up to finish the job. The Kindred would never be that sloppy. They wanted me dead, but I'd flown under the radar so far.

I took out my phone and sent Noah a text.

We need to meet ASAP.

My phone buzzed a moment later.

Meet at Location D.

I sent back a thumbs-up icon. If the Kindred were tracking our phones, they wouldn't know where we were going. The scrambler installed by the Unseen techies meant the Kindred couldn't locate us by our signal, but an old-fashioned intercept of our messages might lead to an ambush, if we weren't careful.

Location D was under a bridge in Century Park, a sprawling botanical garden with plenty of entrances. It was easy to hide in the park, which is why it was one of our five emergency locations. The Unseen were paranoid about security, which was a pain at times but also kept me alive. The only reason I had been allowed to stay at Dad's place was because he'd gone to a lot of trouble to buy it under a fake name, with no clear paper trail, in order to keep it from Mum if they got divorced. Lawyers did things like that. She was dead, now, so that ship had sailed, but his trick had come in handy. Either way, Dad's was as safe a place as any for us, and Skye needed the stability after everything she'd gone through back in Ettney. Kidnapping is a traumatic experience by itself, let alone being nearly sacrificed to an impossible Shadow creature, and watching your mum burn to death from the inside out.

I was coping better these days, thinking more like a soldier and a fighter. It helped. Any time the memories of those awful weeks in Ettney returned, I'd ask myself how the soldier version of me would react.

Noah and I had done a couple of missions with the Unseen, little things like reconnaissance of suspected Kindred facilities in the city, but this was the most threatened I had felt in months. The uncertainty was the worst part. This girl had come from nowhere, and if she wasn't Kindred there was possibly another faction out there who wanted me dead.

Despite my best efforts to stay silent, my feet slapped on the wet pavement. A car engine roared, and the hiss of wheels on wet tarmac slithered up on my right.

"Hey, princess," said a gravelly voice, "You look a bit wet. Want to get in?"

The man was in his late twenties, at least, with slicked hair and a manicured moustache. One earring glistened on his left lobe. The car was expensive, black, with custom silver number plates and glowing lights under the body.

His friend leaned over from the back, eyes sunken into their sockets. He had attempted to grow a moustache too, but it was fluffy and weird. He ran his tongue over his teeth. "She's probably hot under all those layers. Maybe we could help her lose a few, you know, dry off."

I didn't break my pace, and kept my eyes fixed ahead.

"What's wrong?" said the moustache man. "You frigid or something?"

I sighed. "Get lost."

He kept driving slowly alongside me. "Come on, you stupid bitch. At least look at me."

He revved the engine, and I stopped walking.

"That's better," he grinned, and leaned over, sticking his head out the window. Slowly, I walked over to him. The leer was awful. I smiled at him, then reached out and slammed his head down on the edge of the car door. He swore, and blood stained the chrome window edge. While he held his head in his hands, I tuned into the car's front wheel, raising its resonance. The tyre melted onto the road, then caught fire, sending black smoke curling into the air. Sunken-eyes in the back stared at me, too surprised to be angry. He couldn't see the outside of the car, so I melted it shut, fusing the car door to the body. Moustache wiped the blood from his eyes, cursing me out. He reached for the handle, but I'd fused his door shut too. He ducked his head out the window to see what was blocking his exit, then, eyes wide, stared back at me.

"She's one of those kids," he muttered to Sunken-eyes. "Look, I'm sorry. I'm really sorry, please."

Kids? I was seventeen, but whatever.

"Don't kill us," Sunken-eyes whined. "We won't do it again."

The fire in the front wheel spread to the bonnet.

I grinned. "I won't kill you, but you should probably climb out the window and run. That fire's gonna reach a fuel line soon."

They swore simultaneously and tried to unclip their seatbelts. Apparently, even creeps care about safety. Moustache clambered out of his car window, falling to smack his shoulder on the pavement. He staggered to his feet, ignoring his friend in the back seat, and sprinted off down the road. Sunken-eyes couldn't undo his seatbelt, and looked at me with sweat running down his forehead.

"Help me, please." His eyes darted between me and the fire, and he let out a little sob.

"Close your eyes," I sighed, feeling a bit sorry for him, despite his earlier actions.

"What?"

"Just look away or something, creep."

He did, tears squeezing out of the edges of his eyes.

I tuned back in to the car body and wheel. The steel rang clear, but that wasn't what I was after. The plastic was a muddy, wet mush of notes, especially now that it was on fire. I lowered the sound, dropping the resonance of the plastic parts until they were cold enough to draw ice from the air around them. The rain froze as it hit the bonnet, and frost crystallised on the wheel edge, drawn out of the air by the icy surface. The fire was gone.

Static broke off my tuning. The creep had opened his eyes. He stared open-mouthed at the frozen wheel.

"Who's frigid now?" I smirked and set off at a jog away from the car. The creep wouldn't follow me. He was too scared.

The street curved to the left so, by the time I reached the end, I'd lost sight of the creep and the car. Hopefully, he would make better choices in the future.

I reached the edge of Century Park as the night turned to drizzle. Coleton had its own weather; the coast had a personality almost opposite to Ettney's inland heat. Coleton was wet, and cold, and wet again.

Century Park was ominous in the rain-mist, and path lights glowed dim as they wound their way across the turf. Black steel fence-posts marked garden beds as off-limits, and huge fig trees grew across the artificial hills, branches woven together at the top to make a canopy that, while thick, failed to keep out the rain. It did, however, keep the sun from reaching the ground during daylight hours, so most of the grass had given way to dirt and fallen leaves.

Something stirred in the cavity of one of the figs, a man pulling his weatherproof jacket tighter across his body. He watched me for a moment from behind his enormous beard, then rolled over to try and keep the rain off his face. I wanted to help him, somehow, but had nothing to give. I didn't even have a coat myself, and my shirt was growing damp in the drizzle.

A tent city sprawled under a large bridge to my right, made up of veterans, single mums, and families who had run out of luck. The recession had hit this city hard. The tents were tolerated by the council as these people had nowhere else to go. The place had become a kind of fixture in Coleton, so much so that locals called it Downtown, because the people were down on their luck. Some were scared of Downtown, but I wasn't worried. In a way, I had been homeless myself for a while, after the Kindred fire that destroyed our family home. These people weren't dangerous, they were just having a rough time.

Besides, Downtown's existence made it an excellent place for Location D, as no-one would think twice about a seventeen-year-old girl wandering Century Park in the middle of the night.

As I walked past the tent city, I scanned it for any sign of the girl. It was unlikely she had followed me, but better safe than sorry.

Towels and clothes hung drying on guy ropes, and the effect was of rows of banners, like flags that signalled the occupants' identities. A row of baby clothes meant a newborn lived inside. Next door a huge black overcoat belonged to an elderly man who was cooking over a small gas fire. He smiled at me as I walked past, but I turned away. I wasn't being rude, but I had to stay under the radar. I couldn't afford anyone remembering I was here. My stunt with the car was dangerous enough. No point adding to my exposure.

Leaving Downtown, I walked slowly across the park, trying not to attract attention. Anyone could be Kindred. I had learned that by now. I couldn't trust a soul except for Noah and my friends. Honestly, I barely trusted the Unseen. I didn't know much about them, and they had played me just as much as the Kindred back at Ettney, leaving me out of the loop and putting my family in

7

danger. Besides, any one of the Unseen could be a Kindred spy. I couldn't trust anyone. Not anymore.

The bridge was small and dark, perfect for a secret meeting. I had to duck under the concrete edges, as it was a footbridge, and was very low at this end. Underneath, the shadows were deep as midnight.

A car horn echoed out across the park from the overpass closer to the city. From here, skyscrapers towered above the trees, lights glaring from windows like eyes against the dark sky. I missed the stars. Back in Ettney, the sky was filled with them, but here only the brightest few remained, drowned out by the light pollution from street lamps and skyscrapers. The clouds covered the stars tonight, regardless, and reflected a dull orange from the city lights below.

In the distance, a man in a dark jacket scurried through the park, darting between the fig trunks and the shadows, a package cradled in his arms. There was something odd about his movements, but then Noah appeared and I turned my attention to him.

Noah looked older, even though it had only been six months since we'd first met. His hair was still cut short, but he'd let it go longer on the top and it was soaked. He wiped it out of his face. The wounds above his left eyebrow and on his cheek had healed, but the scars were still there, a testament to everything we'd been through. He smiled for a moment, then his brow creased.

"Were you followed?" he asked.

"Yeah, totally. I'm just standing here waiting for them to kill me," I snarked.

"Alright, silly question. Why the emergency meeting?"

I told him about the girl who had attacked me.

He frowned. "Strange she had no backup. Operating alone isn't Kindred style. It's not Unseen style, either. There's something else in play. I can put a description out to the intelligence network, but the chances of picking her up are pretty slim. We don't have the same reach as the Kindred."

"She's probably eleven or twelve, darker skin," I described. "She looked Indonesian, maybe? She wore black hoodie both times she attacked me, so I didn't get a good look at her. Her clothes were dirty, though, so she might live on the street or in one of the poorer areas."

Noah peered out into the rain. "Not much to go on, but I'll pass it on."

I paced around the tiny underpass, kicking up dust with my shoes.

"Speaking of the streets," he said. "There's been reports of children going missing. Not that anyone with power in this city really cares. That's why I'm here - most of the missing persons reports are from Downtown. I've been here the last two nights, watching for anything strange."

The idea of kidnapping made me shudder. Ever since Skye was taken, that sort of thing struck a deep chord in me.

Noah stepped forward a little. "I'm sorry, I didn't even ask how you are. I'd be a bit twitchy after two murder attempts."

I shrugged. "I'm fine. Thanks for asking, though."

"I never meant to bring you in to all this," he said, taking my hand in his. It was warm.

"I know."

He paused for a moment. "Have you talked to Josh yet?"

I shook my head. "Not about that. I'm not ready. Sorry."

"It's okay, really. It's just that—"

"Jamie?" someone called, and we both turned to see a woman stagger from one of the tents. "Has anyone seen my baby girl?" she cried, this time with more urgency.

9

More people came out of their tents, glancing around, shaking their heads.

Then the woman screamed her daughter's name into the night, and suddenly I realised what the man had in his arms as he ran across the park. It hadn't been a package. He was holding a baby.

TWO

"I saw the man who took her," I blurted to Noah. "When I first got here."

"Which way?" he asked, urgency in his voice.

I pointed the direction the man had run, towards the tree-line, and we set off across the park.

The rain, although light, had muddied up the ground, so our feet sloshed in the wet grass and leaves. Fortunately, it also meant the man had left footprints behind.

I crossed through the wrought iron gate that marked the entrance to Century Park. An imposing statue glared at me from the front of an old stone bank building across the street. The windows were boarded shut, like many in this part of the city.

I looked left, and then right, up to the ends of each street, to traffic lights that changed from red to green despite the deserted road. In the distance, a walk signal beeped, inviting the empty night to cross.

There was no sign of the man in either direction.

"We need to split up," I told Noah.

"Great idea. That's always such a safe move in horror films," Noah smirked.

"We're not exactly defenceless, though, are we?" I said, staring him down.

Noah nodded, and went right towards the harbour. I ran left, trying to keep my feet from making too much noise. If the man was Kindred, it was best I stayed to the shadows.

Graffiti covered each side of the street, coating boarded windows with obscene messages, mostly suggesting the government have an intimate relationship with itself. For all its small-town boredom, Ettney wasn't like this.

Dead ahead, across the road from me, was a huge wrought-iron fence protecting an imposing brick and sandstone building. The Australian flag fluttered out front. Government House. A uniformed guard eyed me from a box behind the gate. The lights were on inside, so the State Parliament was still in session. Maybe the guard had seen something.

I approached casually, waving like a lost tourist.

The guard frowned.

"Hi," I said, "Uh, I don't know if you saw anyone come past here, but I'm looking for my friend. He's tall-ish, holding a package. Any chance you've seen him?"

The guard shook his head and waved me on.

"Great, thanks for your help," I muttered.

My phone buzzed, and I pulled it out of my pocket. It was wet from the rain, but thankfully the Unseen made sure we had waterproof phones. The text was from Noah.

Found him. Sent you a pin. Approach quietly.

The phone buzzed again, and a screenshot of a map came up with a pin marking a spot three streets over. Eighteen Tymedale Street. I broke into a run now, rain whipping my face and trickling down my neck. After everything that happened with Skye, there was no way I was letting some random psycho take a lady's kid.

A siren wailed somewhere in the distance. Normal people would call the cops in a situation like this, but not me. No chance, not after Hackman's betrayal. The Kindred had wormed their way into positions of power across the world. Cops included. For all I knew, there were probably a bunch of them walking the halls of Government House behind me.

Tymedale Street was run down like all the others, although a few late-night sleaze shops still blared neon lights across the pavement. I followed Noah's pin, slowing down as I neared number eighteen. The sign over the top read "Elements Gallery of Fine Arts." Its windows were dark, in contrast to the glaring screens of the Channel Three television studio next door.

"Hey." Noah's voice came from behind a large stone pillar in front of what might once have been a hotel, but was now a defunct wine bar. I joined him in the alcove. It stank of urine.

"He went in there," Noah pointed to the gallery. "He had a key, so he owns it, or works there."

I clenched my jaw and moved to cross the street, but Noah grabbed my arm. "How about we make a plan first?"

"Fine. But none of our options should involve leaving him alive."

"Hey," Noah frowned, and then his face softened. He sighed. "I know this gets to you. I get it, really. How do you think I feel every time I see someone out having coffee with their dad?"

I looked away, focusing on a cockroach on the pavement that was trying to tackle a scrap of bread.

Noah took my hand. "Don't feel guilty about that. It was the only way."

I shrugged and shook his hand away.

"I'm just saying we need to think this through. We can't go in all guns blazing and get ourselves killed. Besides, he might not even have done anything wrong. He might not even have the kid. He could just be some random guy."

"But—"

"Listen to me," Noah snapped. "You really want to play mistaken identity again? That didn't end so well last time."

I clenched my fists and shut my eyes tight. My face went hot.

"I'm sorry," he said. "That wasn't fair."

Another siren wailed in the night. Maybe they were checking out the car fire I'd started.

"No, you're right," I said to Noah. "They're all dead because of me. You're right to be angry."

Noah shook his head. "No, it's not—"

"Skye, Josh, Rachel and everything that happened to her. Mum..." My stomach turned.

Taking my hand again, Noah looked into my eyes. "It's not your fault. Let's not focus on that right now. We've got to check out this gallery."

I nodded.

"Also, it's still really weird seeing you with green eyes," he smiled, admiring my contacts.

I returned it, weakly. "They match yours."

"They match each other," he teased. "But I like your real eyes better."

My chest felt lighter for a moment, then I turned my attention back to the dark gallery across the street. "Let's do this."

THREE

At the end of the road was a cross-street that linked to an access alley. On the way, I walked past the Channel Three building. The windows were filled with televisions broadcasting the same image; the Channel Three station feed. Right now it was a late-night rant from a bearded guy, who was shouting about something; probably immigrants judging by what I'd seen of him when I channel-flicked late at night. At least the televisions were on mute so I couldn't hear him screaming at the world.

I crossed into the alley, which was a service road that ran behind the gallery. The alley was covered in huge, almost beautiful graffiti. Words and cartoon characters and tags formed an artwork that spoke to years of neglect. It was haunting, though, in its own way. A tribute to angry youth and street life formed over generations. Even the back of the Channel Three studio was covered in paint, sprayed with messages aimed mostly at their news division, a strange contrast to the shiny television screens and polished signage out front.

It only took us a few minutes of research on our phones to pull up photos of the area and piece together a map and a plan. Noah would vaporise the glass in the front gallery window and enter through the foyer. The security alarm shouldn't be a problem, as it would be switched off if the man was inside.

The loading dock was at the back, and that was my way in. I'd picked up a few skills from the Unseen during induction; an intense three months of training that had covered espionage skills, things like hand-to-hand combat, tracking, and—fortunately for us—lock picking. I could have vaporized the lock but melting metal could be noisy, and we wanted to avoid alerting this guy that we were coming. So, I'd break in the old-fashioned way, using the multi-tool I kept in my pocket. I'd stolen my personal motto from the Scouts - 'be prepared'. Except, of course, mine was less about surviving the wilderness and more about surviving a clandestine super-powered organisation with a doomsday fetish.

I'd had to grow up a lot in the past six months. I sighed. Had it really been that long? It was coming up on Mum's birthday. Or what *would* have been her birthday.

I crouched down and wriggled the lockpick, carefully selecting each tumbler until the lock clicked. Then, I cracked open the dock access door. There was no-one inside. Stepping quietly through, I let the door click shut behind me.

The loading dock had a huge truck in it, a big white one with *Blackwood Logistics* written on the side in bold red lettering. My footfalls echoed in the space no matter how softly I stepped, so I took off my shoes and walked in my socks. The floor was cold. There were two doors on each side at the back. The dock was close to the Channel Three studios on the right, so maybe it was a shared space. I took the left door, which was unlocked.

The gallery was bigger than I'd expected, white walls stretching out in front of me. Garish artwork hung on the walls, huge monstrosities of colour and shape and texture. The one immediately to my left was titled *The Death of the Martyr* and featured a line-drawn image of an overweight naked man riding a panther out of a television.

Art was weird.

I stepped forward and froze. Straight ahead, there was someone staring at me. She didn't move, so I stepped forward again, and she copied. I shook my head. Idiot. I was looking at a mirror. In big, hand painted letters around the gold edge of the mirror, the artwork said *Which One of You is Real?*

It was a good question, to be honest, even if the artwork was a little obvious. I stared at myself for a moment, despite the urgency of my situation. These eyes were strange on me, which was funny considering they looked normal to everyone else. Everything about me was different. I'd cropped my hair shorter, because it kept getting in the way during training and I'd finish a martial arts session looking like a ball of fur with legs. Something else was different, too; not just the eyes and hair. I looked darker, even darker than after the accident. Which one of me was real? The one before the Unseen, or after? The Ari from the vision — the one turning into Shadow in a city of blood, or the Ari who had once tried to burp the alphabet at preschool and instead threw up on her shoes?

There was something weird about the me in the mirror. I raised my hand, and the mirror me copied. Only, it was slightly slower. The mirror was a video screen, perhaps, operating on a time delay. I put my hand down, and the mirror me followed a fraction of a second later. It was weird, as if there were really two of us, split apart by the surface of the screen. It made me feel uncomfortable.

In the door behind the mirror me, something moved—a dark shadow sweeping across the wall. I turned to see if it was really behind me, but there was nothing. When I looked back at the mirror, the mirror me was back in sync with my movements. No delay anymore.

Weird.

I wiped the sweat from my forehead and walked towards the mirror, despite the growing rock in my stomach. The question written on the mirror frame was threatening now.

Which One of You is Real?

Six months ago, I would have chalked my anxiety up to a bad cheeseburger, but not anymore. Now, I knew anything was possible, and this mirror was freaky as hell. I half expected the Ari in the mirror to change again, to stop following my movements, to reach through the glass and grab my throat, but she didn't. Stepping around to the back of the mirror revealed nothing. For all appearances, it was an ordinary mirror.

A figure moved behind me, and I whipped around ready to fight.

"You all right?" asked Noah. "You don't look so good."

I relaxed, and nodded. "Yeah, fine."

He grinned. "Well, if you're done checking yourself out, we've got a weird art guy to hunt. Seriously, though, some of this art is freaky. There's a painting at the front of a guy biting the head off a chicken."

"Gross." I should have told Noah about what I'd seen, but I couldn't. Not after I'd had the vision of him lying on the street, bleeding to death from whatever I'd done. I couldn't shake the fear in his eyes when I'd changed. Never, ever did I want to see that look again.

Noah pointed to the front of the gallery. "There's a door behind the front desk, in the admin cupboard. I don't know where it goes, but it feels like it's meant to be private."

"Great. Creepy secret room of a deranged art dealer. That's not going to be disturbing at all."

Noah grimaced. "You know, we haven't entertained the possibility that this is actually just a normal, weird dude, and not a child stealing psychopath. If he catches us in here, I don't want to hurt him."

"You haven't seen *The Death of the Martyr* yet."

"What?"

"Never mind." I thought back to the weird mirror. "But this guy isn't normal, trust me."

Noah led the way to the front of the building. We passed ever darker artwork on the way, which I tried to avoid looking at entirely. Not just because of the freaky mirror, either. Some of it was really explicit, and all of it was violent.

The admin room was basically empty, except for a big steel door that had a passcode.

"You or me?" Noah asked.

"You do it. I'm tired."

I closed my eyes while Noah melted the door off its hinges, and then we dragged it to the side. Cold air wafted up from the basement, and snatches of laughter made their way up from below.

We descended the staircase. I still wasn't wearing shoes, so I could walk silently. Noah's feet were louder, but it didn't matter. Whoever was in the basement, they were cheering noisily, and there were a lot of them.

Someone yelled "Welcome!" and I froze. They weren't talking to me, surely. I stepped to the bottom of the stairs, standing just below the end of the stairwell. If I peeked my head around the corner, I would be able to see what was happening. Of course, they might see me, too. The noise died down, and a gravelly voice spoke.

"We have a new family member tonight, my children. This little one" —a baby whimpered— "has been saved from a life of poverty and crime. Her future is renewed. She has a loving family, now. She has a true home. And I know you will all welcome her with open arms."

I peeked my head around the corner. The basement was huge and dingy, but liveable. In fact, it looked like a lot of people lived here. Beds and couches lay scattered around the floor. Nobody was facing me, but the gallery man stood at the front of a large group. He was in his mid-thirties, with a thin face and blonde, wispy hair. His eyes were a piercing blue, and he oozed charisma. He was still wearing the dark jacket I'd seen at the park. It was definitely the same guy.

In his arms was a young baby, probably six months old. She should have been crying, taken by a stranger like that, but she wasn't.

The man had a strange presence about him. Just looking at him made me feel better, like I had purpose. Like I belonged…

The strangest bit was the crowd. Kids, all of them. Nobody much older than twelve. They looked well fed, and strong, and they all gazed at the man with a kind of reverence. Like he was their father. One of the girls wore a black hoodie. Even from this angle, I could tell she was the girl who had tried to kill me. She began to turn my way, and I ducked back behind the wall.

"We need to go," whispered Noah.

"But—"

"You want to fight a guy in a room full of kids?"

"No," I sighed. "You're right."

Noah frowned. "You know what's weird? Try to tune."

I focused my abilities, trying to tune into the concrete walls. Instead of the sound, though, I was overwhelmed by static. "Too many people in here to tune into anything."

"Let the static stay for a while. Push through it."

Retuning, I winced as the static came back. This time, though, I waited, kept the sound going, and then a single clear note rose above the static. It pulsed, and rippled, and shimmered, and it was beautiful. My mouth dropped open. I'd never heard anything like this before. A tear streaked my face, and I smiled. "What is that?"

"I don't know, but I don't like how much I like it," said Noah. "Being able to break through static like that? Something really weird is going on."

"But it's beautiful," I whispered.

"Maybe," he replied. "It's also impossible. I think it's him." He nodded in the direction of the man in the basement. "Before we do anything here, we need to know more. We need to get in touch with her."

"Noah…" I shook my head.

"You've been putting this off way too long. We need Rachel."

FOUR

We hurried out of the basement and through the gallery, exiting via the empty window this time, which was fine, as I didn't want to go anywhere near the mirror. The man would notice the window was missing, but there was nothing we could do about that now.

Rain still bled from the clouds overhead, a slow but constant downpour that kept me uncomfortably damp. A few shops down, I stopped outside a neon-lit store with an 18+ sign out front.

I grimaced. "I don't want to see her. I can't. Not after what I did."

I hadn't seen Rachel since the Ettney massacre. That's what they were calling it. The massacre. To the Unseen I wasn't exactly a hero. Because of me, their brothers and sisters, friends, and parents in Ettney had been slaughtered.

Noah put his hand on my shoulder. "It wasn't your fault. You didn't know. And Rachel should have trusted you sooner, brought you into the fold."

I shook my head and brushed his hand away. "I should have known."

"It doesn't matter now. What's done is done, but we still need to see her. There's something very weird about that guy, and not just because he has a basement full of kidnapped children. I've never heard someone produce a distinct resonance. Normally it's all noise and static because of the organic tissue. That sound… that was wrong."

"But beautiful."

The neon sign flickered overhead. Noah frowned.

A husky voice yelled from inside the store. "You lot coming in, or just blocking my entrance?"

"Yeah, looks like business is booming!" I shot back. The street was completely empty. Still, the guy inside swore at us, and so Noah and I moved away, continuing down the street.

The Unseen base of operations was across town in an old industrial estate in the suburb of West Hills. The fastest way out there from here was the subway. At one time, there was a working subway station in West Hills, but it was closed now. The whole place had become a ghost town after the recession. The city had once been a hub for manufacturing and trade, but almost nothing of that industry remained. West Hills was dead, which made it a perfect place for the Unseen to set up shop. However, it also made getting there a little complicated, especially with me not having a drivers' license. Noah had one, but he was too broke to buy a car, let alone afford the fuel.

We walked back to Century Park and trudged down the subway stairs opposite the front entrance. I glanced over at Downtown as we descended, but I couldn't see the woman anymore, the one whose baby the gallery man had taken. She was probably out searching the city; the cops wouldn't listen or even care about another

23

Downtown disappearance. My stomach turned. We shouldn't have left those kids with the gallery man.

But there was something so *off* about what I'd seen, despite the beautiful resonance. We had to know more before taking action. Besides, I wouldn't have been able to live with myself if I'd messed up and one of the kids got hurt, or worse, killed. I'd had enough of impulsive decisions. I'd made too many of those back at Ettney, and way too many had paid the price for my bad judgement.

Century Park Station was dirty, old, and hot despite the weather outside. My footsteps echoed off the grey tiles. At one point, they'd been white, but they'd long since been covered in grime. We walked to a bench seat and sat to wait for our train.

I took a breath and tried to regroup.

A shabby, hairy man sat in the corner of the station humming to himself. The tune wasn't discernible, but it struck me as a similar tone to the gallery man's.

Eerily similar.

Noah turned to stare at the man as well, as if he recognised the sound, the clear, beating pulse.

The man stopped humming and stood. Noah looked back at me, meeting my eyes. *Be ready,* he mouthed. The man was covered in rags, as if wearing a jacket made of scraps that hung loose around his legs. They slithered as he moved, creating the impression of a man-sized snake nest shuffling towards us. I took a deep breath, legs on fire and ready to run, but my mind was clear, focussed. I was prepared to kill him, if necessary, if he was somehow connected to the gallery man. His eyes sat in shadows, skulking under deep eyebrows in the faded overhead lights.

"Hey, buddy," said Noah, trying to de-escalate the situation.

Nothing. The pile of snakes continued its slow, halting walk.

"Hey, you okay?" I added, not wanting to seem like I was afraid.

The man tilted his head, keeping one hand in his coat. Was he hiding a gun?

The Unseen had tried to train me in bullet melting, but I'd never been fast enough to disable a firearm. Hopefully, Noah was faster. I tried to tune in to any potential weapons but there was too much static. If the man had a gun, I had no way to stop him. The Kindred didn't bother with guns; this kind of war rendered them basically pointless. I'd never expected to die at the hands of a random man in the Century Park Subway.

A horn echoed in the tunnel. A train was coming. The wheels chanted as the driver slowed to pass through the station. The chanting grew, and the brakes screamed. The man still had his hand in his coat, and he was still advancing. His eyes remained dark, hidden in the shadows. Noah moved in front of me instinctively, but I stepped out from behind him. No way was he going to be a human shield for me. If I couldn't take care of myself in this war, I didn't deserve to be a part of it.

The man was halfway across the station now and stood between us and the exit. We should have run, but until now we hadn't been sure he was a threat. He started to hum again, voice adding to the rhythm of the impending train. The humming grew louder, and louder, ringing across the station despite the background noise. It rose to a crescendo, then stopped. He tilted his head and smiled.

He was so close now, but I still couldn't see his eyes. Despite this, I knew he was staring straight at me.

He spoke, and it felt like he hadn't used his voice for a long time. "I know you."

My stomach dropped. The train blew through the station, blaring its horn. I jumped back, startled, and the wind from the carriages thumped my hair into my eyes. I scratched it out of my face and looked back at the man.

He was gone. There was nowhere for him to have hidden that quickly, but he had disappeared.

Noah looked at me. "Ari, your contact." He pointed to my eyes.

I pulled out my phone and set the camera to mirror. My right contact lens had fallen out, revealing a blue eye instead of green. My left amber eye remained disguised, but if the snake-man was Kindred he could have recognised me. He had said he knew me.

"Did it fall out before or after he left?" I asked Noah.

"I don't know. I was looking at that psycho. Ari, if he was Kindred..."

"It probably fell out when the train blew my hair into my eyes. It's nothing."

Noah frowned. "That sound he made though. The hum."

"If you're really worried, we can take the train from a different station, make sure we aren't followed."

He nodded, and we hurried up the platform stairs and back out into the freezing night.

FIVE

As far as we could tell, we weren't followed to the next station, although it was past midnight by the time we got there. Dad thought I was working late at the Pizzeria, a store owned by an old Unseen woman named Annie. I had never actually worked at the Pizzeria, but Annie covered for me any time Dad called to check up. "Very busy," she'd say. "Such a hard worker."

The Unseen paid us a monthly income to help cover a few basics, but it wasn't a lot. I was honestly thinking about really working at the Pizzeria to make some decent money. I'd dropped out of school after Ettney. Didn't seem much point in going back, as I never learned much there anyway. Besides, considering the Kindred's impending apocalypse, I wasn't giving much thought to my five-year plan.

The next station was simply called "City" and was a little nicer than Century Park. The place was deserted, and our train was late, but eventually we began the halting journey to Greenpoint station, the last stop before West Hills. The doors hissed shut and, as the train picked up speed, the tunnel lights flashed by, illuminating graffiti marks scratched into the train windows.

I sighed. "Noah?"

"Hmm?" he said, not really listening. He'd been staring out the window, lost in his own world. He'd been doing that a lot lately.

"I saw Josh the other day."

Noah turned his head to look at me. "Yeah?" he said cautiously.

"He asked how you were. After, you know, everything."

The carriage lights flickered as we passed through a junction. The driver's voice came over the loudspeaker to announce the next stop, but it was so garbled he may as well not have bothered.

We sat in silence for a moment.

"Why did Josh ask about me?"

"You did save his life," I said.

"That was mostly you, really, but that's not why he was asking." He shifted in his seat and turned his eyes back to the tunnel outside.

I took a breath. "I don't think so, no."

"You have to tell him. If it was me, I'd want to know. Rip the plaster off quick. It hurts less."

Frowning, I fixed my eyes on the subway map overhead. Three stops to go. "That's easy to say when you're not the one who has to do it."

"True."

"And after everything Josh has been through..."

Noah thought for a moment and nodded. "I understand."

"Really?"

"Yeah. I'm not jealous or anything, 'cause you're with me. I mean, we're together... sort of. Aren't we?" He went red, and took a breath. "I guess I just don't want to see him hurt more than necessary."

I looked into Noah's eyes. "I'll tell him next time he's down. I promise."

Noah squeezed my hand and turned his attention back to the scratched-up window. Two stops to go.

I closed my eyes for a second, and Noah nudged me awake only a moment later. "We're here."

We hopped off into Greenpoint station and waited for the driver to swap ends before the train went back in the direction we'd come. There was no security here, not even cameras. Greenpoint was dying, just like West Hills, and soon it would be closed as well. The whole city was rotting from the outside in. Or maybe it had started on the inside, with the politicians and the bankers and the anger of the crowd, the leaders making decisions out of fear, not vision, to appease the bearded guy on Channel Three. No-one could do anything anymore without the online world blowing up into a hate-fuelled firestorm of toxic fury. Maybe that's what started the decay of Coleton: small people keeping smaller people happy, until the city drove itself into the ground as tribute to their tiny, angry lives.

If only they knew what lurked beneath the surface of the world, this secret war that threatened everyone.

Honestly, some days I felt like sitting back and letting the Kindred have them.

But that would be too easy. This city could be better. The world could be better, if only people had a reason.

After we were sure the train was gone, I jumped down onto the tracks and Noah followed. It was more dangerous following the subway line, but infinitely more covert. No prying eyes could possibly spot us down here and report back to the Kindred.

Still, it was really freaking creepy.

It was completely dark two steps in, and I switched on my phone torch. It only lit a few paces at a time, and I stood still for a moment to let my eyes adjust. Aside from the tiny sphere of light around me, it felt like I was lost in an abyss, surrounded by nothing. The tunnel blazed bright for a moment, and I blinked. Noah had switched on his pocket torch, a much brighter LED version supplied by the Unseen. He was better prepared than I was tonight.

Noah's light blared down the tunnel, but somehow seeing our surroundings in more detail was worse. Two red eyes glared at me from the left rail, a rat that blinked and scurried off around the bend. Cobwebs fluttered, suspended over my head, along with a billion tiny particles of dust that twisted and scattered in the air, and a huge black spider pulled itself along a tangled web. I wasn't scared of spiders though, not anymore. There was so much worse that lurked in the night.

We moved quickly, the crunch of our feet on gravel reverberating off the hewn rock walls. Every so often, a locked access door led off to goodness knows where, and spray-painted distance markers told us we were getting close.

Every time those numbers counted down, I felt a bit more anxious. I was heading to a reunion I'd been dreading ever since that awful night in Ettney.

SIX

The Unseen base of operations was in a dirty old shed right at the back of the West Hills Industrial Complex, not too far from the abandoned station. The Unseen were present in Coleton in similar numbers to Ettney, but spread over a city of millions. Not nearly enough to do any real damage to the Kindred, but enough to maintain a presence in the city, disrupting the occasional Kindred gathering or attempting to assassinate key Kindred in positions of power. Mostly, though, we were limited to intelligence gathering, collecting information on Kindred movements and passing it to the other cells to keep tabs on the machinations of the Kindred Agenda. Nothing important had happened while I'd been here, so Coleton seemed a dead end.

As we approached the base, my heart beat faster. I'd been to the base before, but never while Rachel was stationed here. She'd been brought in two months ago, after she was deemed fit to return to service. I hadn't come back since, not even to complete the last stages of my induction. Now, it was time to face her, and answer for what I'd done. Noah gripped my hand, before dropping it as we entered the rusty warehouse. Pigeons warbled overhead. No-one had told them it was night, apparently. My shoes squelched through a big puddle on the floor. Overhead, a section of the tin roof had collapsed, leaving wooden beams exposed to the sky. The clouds had cleared, taking with them the foggy orange glow of the streetlamps, and stars glowed dim above the lights of the city. We trudged to the back of the building, a nondescript security door covered in a spray-painted mural of a little girl holding a balloon. It had been here when the Unseen moved in, probably painted by some local kid with equally too much talent and time.

I slid back a concealed panel above the door handle to reveal a pin code and thumb print reader. If one of us was ever coerced to use our thumb print—or had our thumb cut off and brought here—the pin was supposed to add an extra layer of security. We could enter the distress code rather than the unlock code and warn those inside that they were compromised. There was a back exit that led into the subway somewhere, but hopefully we'd never have to use it.

Punching in the pin, I scanned my thumbprint and the door whirred as the deadbolts retracted.

Noah followed me down the metal staircase and into Unseen operations.

If North Korea had an interior designer, he'd definitely worked on this place. The room was sparse and utilitarian, with three desks on one side covered in computer screens that were hooked up to a very sleek looking server unit. Four metal chairs sat next to a fold-out plastic table, and a map of the city was taped to the back wall. Two work lights on stands illuminated the room, hooked up to a solar powered battery station that ran this whole system. Staying off-grid was critical for the Unseen. There could be zero evidence that anyone was here.

A storeroom door opened, and she stepped out.

"Ari."

I swallowed. Rachel was across the room from me, I could still see the scars on her arms.

"Hi," I ventured.

Noah stepped back a little. He knew I needed to handle this alone.

"Are you here to complete your induction?" She was all business. There was nothing personal in her voice at all. It was like she didn't know me.

I took a step towards her. "Rachel, I'm sorry about—"

She waved me off. "No need. We're in a war, after all. Are you here to complete your induction?"

This was worse than shouting. Worse than screaming. I wanted her to snap and yell at me and blame me for everything, but she didn't. She just stared and waited.

I took a breath to try my apology again, but Noah moved forward, saving me from the awful silence.

"We need to find out everything we can about the guy who owns Elements Gallery. He's been kidnapping street kids and taking them to the gallery. He puts out a weird resonance, like nothing I've heard before. I need to use the secure server. We didn't look him up on our phones, in case it set off any flags with the Kindred."

Rachel frowned, and nodded. "You guys have been busy. It's all yours."

Noah sat down at the computer desk and opened up a search console.

Rachel stood off to one side, close enough to see the screen but still distant from me.

A face popped up on the search window, a photograph from a few years ago. Wild blonde hair, blue eyes, thin face. He was younger, then, but it was definitely the gallery man.

"Thomas Wheeler," said Noah. "Says here he started the gallery four years ago. He's an art dealer and glitterati type who knows everyone who's anyone." He flicked through some photos. "Wow, he really does know everyone. Look, here he is with the mayor, and the Coleton senate rep, and that girl Tammy from that reality show with all the Botox."

"If he's that well connected, he's definitely Kindred," said Rachel. "What about the kids?"

"He runs a charity," Noah said. "Several, actually. One of them, Streetlyfe, helps feed the homeless. There's the connection."

I shook my head, furious. "So, he uses the charity to find them, then kidnaps them?"

"They didn't seem upset about it," said Noah. "They seemed grateful. Like he was their father."

"I don't care. We need to stop him."

"I'm not saying it's right," Noah whirled around in his seat. "Just weird. There's more going on here than we can see."

Rachel cleared her throat. "At this stage," she said, "we can't investigate this any further."

"He kidnapped a baby!" I turned on her. "He's a psychopath!"

"That may be true, and while it's sad, a priority mission has come through that we need to complete first."

"Trust me, Rachel, this is important. I know it is."

She stopped for a moment, and took a breath, eyes on fire. "Last time you used your intuition, a lot of bad things happened."

Noah stood. "Rachel, that's not fair. You can't—"

"Last time you went with your gut, *this* was the result." She pulled up her shirt, revealing an awful pattern of scars that wrapped around her entire body.

I shook my head, eyes burning with tears. "I'm sorry, Rachel. I didn't know. I thought you were—"

"You thought. Exactly. You made a decision without all the facts, and a lot of people died. The Kindred might have thought you were special, but the Unseen? We don't buy into all that prophecy crap. That's why we left. If you're going to survive here, you'll have to learn your place. And right now you're nothing special, just a dumb girl who nearly killed the lot of us."

My face was hot, and I went to speak, but nothing came out.

Rachel turned on one foot and stormed out of the room, slamming the door behind her. My hands shook, and I felt sick for a moment.

Noah put his arm around me. "It's not true," he said. "You didn't know."

"I didn't, but that's no excuse," I whispered. "I was so focussed on getting my family back, I acted without all the facts. I'm not doing that again. If Rachel says we leave this Wheeler guy alone, we leave him." I slumped down and the computer chair creaked.

The photo of Wheeler stared at me from the display. I studied him carefully, memorising his face. It wasn't one I would forget in a hurry, but if I ever saw him again, I wouldn't hesitate to kill him. His eyes... there was something about his eyes. Like there was no life behind them, just a mask. He was a living shell covering a dead soul.

I shuddered. It wasn't the feeling I'd had in the basement. Back then I'd been uncomfortable, scared, but then that resonance, that beautiful, inspiring, wonderful tone… Looking at him, being with him… it would make everything alright. I smiled thinking back on that moment. How calm I'd felt. Unburdened.

Free.

"Noah? Is that you?" A voice came from behind me, someone entering through the door Rachel had exited. I turned to see a short boy who looked like he'd walked out of a band photoshoot. His hands were thrust into the pockets of his torn jeans, and he wore a black shirt emblazoned with a white crucifix. His dark hair was shoulder-length and framed a face that would have fit on every punk singer I'd ever seen. Despite this, he grinned broadly, walked over to Noah, and slammed him in a bear hug.

Noah smiled. "Hud! I had no idea you were here!"

"Hud?" I asked. "You were on the phone that time, back at Ettney. You sent in backup and saved our lives."

He shrugged. "Wish I could have been more help. You must be Ari."

I nodded.

"I thought you were in the country with Bek," Noah said.

"I was," Hud replied, and the spark went out of his eyes. "No change with her, but something bad is happening to me, and it has to do with this city."

Frowning, I turned to Noah, who shook his head and looked back at Hud.

Hud's face went dark. "There's something terrible coming to Coleton. And I think I've already seen it."

SEVEN

The door behind Hud opened, and Rachel came back in. She sat down quietly on one of the metal chairs. I thought it best to ignore her for the time being.

"Something bad is coming?" I asked.

Hud shrugged. "Yeah. I'm sorry, I don't know much more than that."

"That's a weak reason to leave Bek behind," Noah said.

"Trust me, I wouldn't have left her unless I was sure."

"Hi, sorry," I interjected. "New girl here. Who's Bek?"

Hud sighed and sat on the computer chair in front of the giant screens. They framed him as he talked.

"Last year, the night Noah found me, I was camping in the Ettney National Park with my girlfriend Bek and best friend Daniel." He faltered for a moment. "A Shadow killed Dan. We found him washed up in a swimming hole. A lot of scary crap happened, and long-story-short the Shadow grabbed Bek, but I stopped it before it could finish feeding."

"You were the missing campers? I saw that on the news. But how did you stop the Shadow?" To take down a Shadow was impressive.

"That Shadow was more primal somehow, not like some of the others I've heard about. I killed a bunch of Kindred, mostly by accident, and it got distracted and fed on them instead. Once I got Bek to safety, Noah got in touch with us. Bek's been unconscious ever since. She's not in a coma, exactly… At least that's what the medics say. Her brain function is running high, like she's lucid dreaming. She won't wake up, though."

"I'm sorry," I offered.

He stared past me, like he was seeing someone else. "It's okay. At least she's alive. Dan wasn't so lucky."

There was a long silence.

Rachel stood. "Hud's been helping us on the intelligence-gathering front. Somehow it seems he's connected to the Shadows."

I took a step back. "Connected?"

"I can sense them," Hud said, "At least, I get flashes of what they're thinking. Nothing clear or concrete. More of a feeling than anything else."

"And you feel they're coming here?"

"It started a few nights ago. I was sleeping in the safehouse where they're taking care of Bek, and I saw Coleton, almost like I was flying over it. I could see the whole city. I was inside one of the Shadows, I think, and when I looked around there were more of us—*them*— scattered in the sky above the city. Every night, I've seen the same thing. They're gathering for something. It's like they're up there watching the city, waiting."

"Hang on," I turned to face Rachel. "This is the reason we can't go after Wheeler? Because Hud had a nightmare? No offence, Hud."

"It's not as simple as that, Ari." Rachel snapped.

Hud looked hurt, but I wasn't going to take this lying down. "Well, then how about you tell me? I'm sorry for what happened to you, Rachel, I really am. What they did to you was horrible, and I wake up every night picturing it and hearing you scream... But if you two," my gesture included Noah, "had been honest with me from the beginning, none of that awful stuff would have happened. Skye wouldn't have to leave every light in the house on to sleep at night, and Mum..." my voice cracked, and I left the words unfinished.

Hud glanced between the three of us, frowning.

Rachel glowered at me, and Noah placed his hand on my shoulder. My face was hot, and I blinked back angry tears.

"So, this is awkward," said Hud, trying to break the tension. It didn't work.

"I was about to give you a full briefing, Ari." Rachel said. Rage bubbled in her throat, barely under control. She marched over to the computer screens, and Hud stood to let her sit down. "This isn't Ettney. We aren't the Kindred. It would help us all if you'd remember that."

Rachel bashed the keyboard, bringing up a map of the city.

"One of our contacts inside customs was asked to clear out the docks last night. He stayed behind, hidden, and saw a few shady looking guys bringing huge crates on shore. It could be nothing, or it could be connected to whatever Hud says is coming. Tomorrow night, there's another delivery coming in. You three are going to head down and check it out."

"What about you?" Noah asked.

Rachel paused, and the fight drained out of her voice. "I'm not cleared for field duty yet. That's why I'm stuck here passing on messages like a glorified reception girl."

She stood and cleared her throat, regaining her attitude. "Study the map, look for decent vantage points, and then go home and get some rest. It's going to be a late one tomorrow night."

Hud looked at his watch. "Tonight, really. It's way past midnight."

Rachel ignored him and left the room.

We spent an hour or so studying satellite images of the docks. Nothing fancy, just the ones we could find online. When we thought we had a plan, it was time to head home.

"You know," Hud said, "This will be my first official mission."

"Are you really up for it?" Noah asked.

Hud grinned. "Sure. I mean, what could go wrong?"

Noah shook his head. "There's a reason they're sending three teens out on a mission like this. There aren't many old Unseen. We don't live long enough to *get* old."

"Wow, that's a downer."

"Sorry. I just want to make sure you know what you're getting into."

Hud nodded. "I'll be fine. If I can survive a psychotic park ranger and a troop of Kindred, I'm pretty sure I can survive anything."

Noah smiled, although his eyes didn't, and he turned to me. "There's a few bikes in storage, want to take one home?"

"Sure. We can use them to get to the docks tomorrow night. At least they're quiet."

"Already back in soldier mode, hey?"

"You know me," I grinned. "Always a fighter."

Hud looked at me, then Noah, then back at me. "You guys are cute together."

"We're not together," I said quickly. "We're just, uh, we're—"

"It's all good," Hud laughed. "No judgement here. Took me five years to ask Bek out." He sighed. "Although, I don't suggest waiting that long. We only really had a few hours together before..." He stared off into the distance again, like he was seeing that night.

I knew the feeling. Awful moments came back in flashes, sometimes when I least expected it. We'd all had our own horrors to deal with.

"We should go," Noah said. "See you tomorrow, Hud."

Upstairs, on the ground floor of the warehouse, was a locked roller door with a motorcycle and four bikes behind it. Noah and I took a bike each. Neither of us had a clue how to ride a motorbike, and anyway it would have been far too loud for the following night.

We walked our bikes out to the road. Behind the industrial estate was an old tramway that had been turned into a bike path. It ran through bushland right around the city and came out near dad's apartment in Eastbrook. The night was clear now, and the stars bright enough for us to keep our headlamps off.

I looked up for a moment as we rode, the trees flicking past and framing the sky between them. Hud had said he saw Shadows up there, watching, hovering above the city. For a second, I thought I saw a few stars disappear. I blinked, and they returned.

My legs burned, I was so tired. The night had been long, and my eyes felt heavy. I led the way for a while, but Noah rode up beside me and kept pace. He struggled a bit; his lung capacity was smaller since the Kindred had burned him from the inside out, so he panted as he talked.

"Hey, so you were pretty quick to jump in there when Hud said we were together."

"I didn't want him to get the wrong idea," I replied.

We were coming up on a huge stone tunnel that cut through an overpass. It was left over from the old tramway day, and was as high as it was wide. Orange lights kept it lit at night, but that mostly just made it easier for kids to paint the walls. Graffiti spread right up each side, almost to the apex of the tunnel. It was cool artistic stuff like cartoon characters and skater graphics, rather than the usual boring black tags.

Noah hadn't said anything for a while, but I could tell he wanted to.

I skidded my bike to a stop and got off, letting it fall to the ground. He did too.

"What?" I said. "I know you want to say something." My voice echoed in the tunnel.

He looked around for a moment, making sure we were alone, then spoke quietly. "I know you're not ready for anything yet, that you don't want to commit. I get that. We've all been through hell, and things are still pretty messed up, for you more than anyone." He took my hand. "But sometimes you act like we're together, and sometimes you don't. If we're not that's fine, but I'm getting mixed signals, and I don't know how I'm supposed to act."

"Is this about Josh?" I asked. "Because I already told you that's not a thing."

It was true, too. Since everything that happened, whatever I had with Josh was gone, if it was ever there to begin with. I'd used him, back at Ettney. Used him to feel safe, like a drug that helped me forget. But since then, so much had changed. Especially me. I was different now, not the scared girl I was. At least, not as much. I was a soldier, and Josh just wasn't a part of this world. We didn't connect like we used to. Noah, though; he was in the same boat as me. We'd changed together, trained together. That bonded us like nothing else would. Still, I wasn't ready for a relationship. Not a proper one. If nothing else, sometimes I was terrified Noah would see me for who I really was. A girl with a terrible darkness inside, just waiting to come out. And his face in my vision at the Chapel, when he saw what I was turning into… Every time I looked at him, I couldn't get that moment out of my head.

Noah hadn't answered, so I filled the silence. "I can't do this right now. Not the way you want. When all this is over, this war, I'll be ready. I promise."

"*If* this war is ever over," he said, shrugging. Hefting his bike back upright, he got back on and pedalled off down the tunnel, leaving me to race to catch up.

Everything was different after Ettney.

Even him.

EIGHT

I got to the apartment just before dawn and flopped into bed, leaving the bike chained up on the ground floor so I wouldn't have to explain it to Dad.

When I woke, it felt like the early morning, but it was actually past three in the afternoon. The clouds outside had made everything dark.

"Ari, you're awake!" Skye said, and I jumped. She was standing in the doorway in her school uniform.

"Skye, sorry. I was supposed to walk you home."

"It's okay," she said, "You worked so late last night, I thought I'd come home by myself."

I thought back to the creeps in the car I'd burned the night before. "Still, you should have called. I don't want you walking around the streets by yourself. It's dangerous."

Skye nodded sadly. She looked older, suddenly. Wiser. Like I'd missed her growing up over the past few months.

I waved her over to me. "Come here."

She wandered over to the edge of the bed, and I grabbed her and pulled her in, tickling her like crazy. She laughed, and screamed, and told me to stop, and then once she had recovered, she poked me in the nose until I tickled her again. I'd lost her for a while after Mum died, but I felt like I was finally getting her back. She liked living at Dad's, too. He was more engaged than Mum, spending time with her and hanging out. He wasn't sure what to do with me, though. It was like he'd forgotten how to talk to me, probably because I was older.

Dad had trained as a lawyer in Coleton before he met Mum, but after they got married he'd moved out to Ettney to be with her. He spent his time there working for the regional Council, mostly in project management. After he and Mum split, he got back into law in the city. That meant he worked long hours and wasn't home a lot. In some ways, life with him was pretty similar to life with Mum, except with a higher income—and minus an alcohol addiction.

"Dad's coming home early today," said Skye. "He called me while I was walking home."

"That's great. You didn't tell him I forgot to pick you up, did you?"

"Nah, I covered for you."

"You're the best."

Skye grinned. "I know." She flounced off the bed and across the room. "Also, Josh is here."

I sat up and swore.

Skye's mouth dropped open. "Language!"

"Sorry," I said, "but why didn't you tell me?"

"He said he didn't want to wake you."

My mouth felt like dirt, and my hair was a beehive, plus I was still wearing my clothes from the night before, which stank with sweat from the bike ride back.

"Tell him I'll be out in a minute." One of the benefits of Dad's income was a pretty sweet apartment, which thankfully included my own bathroom. I jumped in the shower, washed as fast as I could, and put on my comfy dark blue jeans and a plain black shirt. Not that I had too many other options. I was still building up my wardrobe after the fire, and thanks to my laziness I didn't have many clean clothes left either.

Josh was sitting on the lounge when I came out. I ran over and hugged him. He pulled away, slowly.

"What are you doing here?" I asked.

"Sorry for the surprise. I was down here for a follow-up appointment and thought I'd drop by. Skye let me in." He held up the stump of his right index finger, the one Hackman had chopped off because of me. "On the bright side, it's healing well."

"I've missed you."

"You too. Caitlyn wanted to come, but she had to work."

I sat down next to Josh. "I haven't seen her in so long. It's like we're not even friends any more. I wanted to go visit, but I just don't think I can go back to Ettney."

Josh nodded. "I get what you mean. It's a different place now. I'm counting down the days until school ends and I can get out of there for good. Caitlyn still talks about you, though, and misses you."

"I miss her too, but nothing is the same."

"I understand. I mean, you've had it way worse than me, but even having old Stumpy here has taken some adjusting." He wiggled the stump of his finger.

"You've given it a name?" I groaned.

"Makes it kinda cute, don't you think? Watch this." He raised his voice like he was calling a dog. "Here, Stumpy. Here Stumpy!" He wiggled the stump, and then made it come leaping over to his other hand. "Good boy," he grinned, patting it. In the corner of the room, Stewie our pug lifted his head from his bed, then put it back down when he realised he wasn't being called. He'd been a bit down since we'd moved into the apartment.

I laughed at Josh and shook my head. "You're an idiot."

"Attitude is everything. That, and naming your appendages."

I raised one eyebrow. "Appendages? You mean you've given *other* things names?"

"Yeah, that's not the only Stumpy I've got."

Chuckling, I watched Josh's face turn red.

"Oh wow. I meant my left big toe, you know, how it's all tiny."

I laughed harder, and he went even redder. "Yeah, alright. I left myself open on that one."

Taking a deep breath, I calmed myself down. "It's okay," I replied. "You've said worse."

"Oh, gosh. I have, haven't I?"

"Remember that time you complimented Mrs Baker on her enormous melons?" I smiled.

"Oh, no, don't bring that up. For the last time, we were making watermelon smoothies in Cooking, and she had brought in some super massive melons from her garden. They were just so big and juicy, I had to say something!"

I burst into laughter again. "Josh, when you reach the bottom, stop digging!"

Skye wandered in from her room. "What are you guys laughing about?"

I looked at Josh, who was trying to hold back another wave of laughter. Instead of holding mine in, I snorted by accident, and we both lost it again. Skye joined us, despite having no idea why we were actually laughing.

The front door clicked, and Dad entered the loungeroom.

When I was younger, I always thought Dad would make a great British Lord, if he spoke with the accent and wore a top hat or something. His greying-black hair was always perfectly slicked back, and he had a face that, while thin, was never haggard. He looked tired today, though, as if he was carrying the city on his back.

"Hi, girls."

Skye ran to greet him. "Daddy!"

He picked her up and squeezed her tight. "Hey, princess."

I wasn't quite up to the hugging stage yet. Not after what had happened before my parents' split. Things got violent. Never towards me, but Mum copped a lot. The first time he tried to hug me after Mum died, when he put his hands on my shoulders, I couldn't stop seeing them hitting Mum. Those hands that were trying to comfort me had caused so much pain. It made me sick.

He'd been trying, though, especially with Skye. She didn't remember that stuff, and I didn't want to tell her, didn't want to destroy her relationship with the only parent we now had. He'd never done anything to us girls, and he told me he'd been seeing a psychologist the past few years, to help him deal with his issues. Apparently, a lot of it traced back to things he'd gone through when *he* was little. So, at least he was trying. But no, I wasn't up to hugging. Not just yet.

Dad glanced at Josh and me. "Josh, nice to see you."

"You too, sir."

"Sir? That makes me feel about a hundred years old."

"If the shoe fits, sir." Josh grinned, and Dad chuckled and put Skye down. Josh knew about what had happened, about our family's past, so he didn't have a lot of respect for Dad. In Josh's own weird way, that came out as jokey insults.

"I'm home early today, girls," said Dad. "I'll be out late tonight though, after dinner. Work thing."

"No!" said Skye.

"It'll be after you've gone to bed, princess. How about you go watch the TV in your room for a minute while we work out the details." Skye grunted, and wandered off down the hall. Dad turned to me. "Ari, are you okay to watch Skye?"

"Uh, not exactly. I'm working."

He frowned. "Again? You're pulling too many hours at that pizza place."

"You're one to talk about work hours."

Dad stopped and sighed. "You're right. Sorry. Is there any way you can take the night off?"

Unseen missions weren't exactly negotiable, but I couldn't leave Skye alone either. "What about Josh?" I turned to him. "If you're free, that is."

"Well, it's Friday, so I don't actually have to be back for a few days. I could swing it with my folks," Josh said.

Dad thought for a moment. "Look, Josh. You're a good guy for offering, but I'm just not comfortable having you look after Skye alone."

"What?" I said, frowning.

"It's just, I'm not comfortable with it. Skye's a young girl, and Josh is almost an adult male."

"Almost an adult or almost a male?" Josh joked, but his red face showed how awkward he felt.

"I'm sorry, it's just not okay." Dad crossed his arms.

"Are you kidding? Dad, that's ridiculous," I said. "Josh would never... he's the best guy I know."

"It's okay, Ari," Josh said. "I should get home." He stood to leave.

"No, you don't need to leave," said Dad. "You're more than welcome to stay as long as Ari is here."

"It's really fine, I'm more than happy to—"

My fists clenched. "Dad, you've made this really awful. Besides, if you were worried about anything you should be more worried about Josh and *I* being alone together!"

Dad stopped, frozen.

Josh's left eyebrow went up.

I swallowed. "I'm not saying that. I mean, it's not as if…we're not…"

There was a long pause. Finally, Dad spoke slowly. "Ari, you're a different case. You're seventeen now. You're almost a woman. And I know that at your age, teens are exploring each other, and—"

"Stop!" I buried my face in a lounge cushion. "Please, do *not* finish that sentence." I willed the couch to swallow me whole and save me from this horrifying conversation that I would never be able to erase from my brain.

I snuck a look at Josh, and he was trying desperately not to laugh.

Burying my face even more into the lounge, I shook my head. "Just go, Dad. Please, before you make this more awkward."

There was silence for a while, except for a squeaking sound. I looked up, and Dad had gone off to his room. The squeaking sound was Josh, who was having trouble containing his laughter. His eyes streamed tears, and his mouth was pressed firmly closed. "Excuse me for a minute," he forced through compressed lips, and he strode out the front door of the apartment, closing it quietly behind him. Outside in the hall, he couldn't contain himself anymore, and belly laughs exploded down the hallway.

I shook my head. I'd survived explosions, supernatural attacks, and the destruction of the Ettney complex, but that conversation with Dad had nearly killed me.

Plus, I had a problem. Josh couldn't look after Skye, not alone, and I knew no-one but the Unseen in this city. With a mission coming up, there was only one person I could call for help.

NINE

When I opened the door, Rachel didn't look thrilled. She'd brought two suitcases, and she passed me one as she walked inside. It was so heavy the handle slipped out of my grip, and the case thunked onto our grey carpet.

"Be careful with that," snapped Rachel. "It's the gear I need to run the mission tonight." I apologised, but she ignored me. "Where can I set up?"

"My room has a desk," I answered. "That's probably the best place."

The toilet flushed, and Josh wandered out of the bathroom.

"You washed your hands, right?" I asked.

He wandered back in again.

"Josh is still here?" Rachel asked.

"Yeah, he's staying around for the weekend, just in case something happens. He can cover for me with Dad."

"Seems like a good guy," she said. Her voice was softer than before.

"He is, yeah."

Rachel and I lugged the suitcases into my room. Skye was in bed, and normally slept like a hibernating bear.

She'd been waking up less and less lately, and the nightmares seemed to be fading. If she had one, though, they normally woke her after two in the morning, and I'd be back way before then. I had to be; Dad would be home sometime after midnight, knowing his usual work schedule. That left four hours to get down to the docks and back. Should be enough time.

Josh came into my bedroom, pointedly drying his hands on his pants. "Better?" he asked.

I nodded. "Help me with this suitcase."

Rachel frowned. "I'm not sure if Josh is the right person to do that."

"Hey," Josh said, "I handled the Kindred back in Ettney. I mean, I can't shoot brain fireballs but—"

"Flares," Rachel interrupted.

"Right, flares. I can't do that. But I'm good with computer stuff, at least that's what my teacher told me after I accidentally took down the school network."

"That doesn't fill me with confidence, but I suppose you're as much a part of this as any of us," said Rachel.

"It'll be fine, trust me." He hoisted the suitcase onto the desk, and something inside clunked as the case hit the wooden surface.

Rachel glared at him.

We opened the suitcases and unpacked the gear. There was a small satellite dish, a portable server, and some radio communications gear. They all patched into a chunky laptop.

Rachel sat at my desk. "This will allow me to monitor the mission from here. This links back via satellite to the secure server and gear in the warehouse, so nothing can be traced back to this apartment."

"What's the mission, anyway?" Josh asked.

"Noah, Hud and I are checking out some weird stuff at the docks."

Rachel coughed loudly.

"It's okay, Rach. Josh has kept our secret this long. It's his secret too, really."

She grunted and loaded up the laptop.

Josh sat on my bed, and the springs creaked. "Secret missions at the docks? That's all very double-oh-seven." He put on a deep Scottish accent. "I shuppose that makesh me Mish Moneypenny."

I stared at him. "What?"

"Only the most famous secret agent of all time. Licence to kill? Goldfinger? No?"

I shook my head.

"Ari, your complete ignorance of pop culture references is breathtaking."

Rachel snorted but kept looking at the laptop. "Okay, we're good to go," she said. "I can monitor you guys from here." She took out an earpiece from the laptop bag, plus a smooth black case the size of my phone. "These are our comms units. They have an inbuilt microphone that switches on when you talk. They're not exclusive, so you can all talk and receive at the same time, although for the sake of my sanity please try not to. The black thing is a GPS transmitter, so I can monitor your movements." She pointed to the laptop screen, which showed a map with dots and coordinates. One was our address, and the other two were moving fast along the train line near Green Point. "Looks like the boys are on the subway. The transmitters are powerful enough to penetrate the tunnels."

Josh whistled. "Where do you guys get tech like this?"

"We have a few rich backers," Rachel explained. "Mostly former Kindred who amassed wealth through weapons production and private security. They managed to take most of their assets with them when they defected."

"Wow," he replied.

"Don't be too impressed," Rachel added. "Keep in mind the Kindred are even better resourced. There's more of them, and they have more friends in higher places." She turned to me. "With that in mind, Ari, you need to be prepared for anything. This is just a small reconnaissance mission, but you know by now that recon can very quickly go south."

I nodded, and she handed me a small backpack with some extra gear.

"Stay safe," she said, and I went to the loungeroom to put on my black shoes. I was wearing entirely black, tonight, to remain as hidden as I could. Josh came out too and sat next to me on the lounge.

"Hey, so, before you go out..."

I stopped tying my left shoelace and looked up at him. "Yes?"

"I haven't had a chance yet, with everything. I haven't asked you where we are. Where you are. With us."

My heart sank. This was a conversation I had to have, and now I couldn't put it off any longer.

"Josh, I—"

"I guess I just need to know either way. I feel like you're different, ever since Ettney, and I know that you're not ready for a relationship, but I just have to know if you'll ever be. If I have a chance with you. 'Cause if I don't, I can stop waiting. The waiting is the worst part."

I took his hand, and it was warm and familiar. "Honestly? I'm not sure what happened in the Complex. I was scared and alone, and I needed someone."

"And that someone was me."

I paused and took a deep breath. "Right. Thing is, whatever we had back there, I don't feel it any more. I've tried, honestly, I have. But I've changed, and so have you, and the world is just so different now. I love you, I really do, with all my heart. But not in the way I did. I don't think that's going to come back, either. I'm sorry."

His eyes shone with unshed tears, and I wanted so much to love him, and kiss him, and hold him, and for those things to really mean something, but I couldn't give him that. I was awful. I'd used him back at the Complex. I'd kissed him and been loved by him, and it had been my only comfort. But now I only thought of him as a friend. A wonderful, strong, caring, kind friend. But while I wasn't ready for anything with Noah just yet, I wouldn't ever be with Josh. I knew that now.

Josh stood, quietly, and nodded. "Thank you for being honest with me," he murmured, and walked off to the bathroom, closing the door behind him.

I finished lacing my shoe, wiped my eyes, and stepped out into the frozen night.

TEN

I met Noah and Hud at City Station. They both had bikes from the Unseen warehouse, and the three of us rode to the docks together. The city was quiet, save for a few office workers still heading home after a long day. Skyscraper windows formed checkerboards of light as we cycled down King Street. Just about every city and town in Australia has a King Street. It's this weird colonial throwback to when we still cared what the British thought of us. Coleton's King Street was one of the busiest roads in the city during the day, but it was quiet this time of night.

Homeless types were scattered here too, huddled under awnings in sleeping bags and blankets. There were a handful of shelters in the city run by well-meaning people, but they were overwhelmed by the need and had trouble making even a dent in the problem. Mostly, Coleton just didn't care about these lonely figures. They were easier to ignore.

We kept silent as we rode. To talk properly would have required volume, and we couldn't afford any Kindred overhearing our conversation.

57

Getting to the docks required a zig-zag off King Street through a series of alleys at the back of Chinatown. Normally, I loved walking through Chinatown. Beautifully sculpted red dragon gates marked the entrance to the food quarter, and the air was filled with noise and incredible smells. It was one of the few parts of the city centre that was still alive, partly because Coleton had a sizeable Chinese population, and partly because the prices were really, really good. A few weeks before, I'd spent hours here just wandering around, watching the people and looking at the lobsters crawling around in their tanks out the front of each restaurant. Chinese New Year was months away, but I was looking forward to coming down here for the celebrations. In the movies, it seems like every night in Chinatown is Chinese New Year, but normally it was a pretty chill place.

Tonight, we skirted around Chinatown, using the access roads behind restaurants and shops, weaving past dumpsters and layers of cardboard left out for collection. Posters crumbled off stained walls, and occasionally one of the dumpsters made me hold my breath—likely filled with expired seafood.

We came to the edge of Chinatown, ready to cross over Pier Road and ultimately wind up at the docks. Traffic was heavier here, and I pressed the button on the pedestrian crossing at a busy intersection. As we waited, I looked up again into the dark sky. There was too much light pollution here to see the stars. Either that, or the sky was filled with Shadows, blocking out the heavens and swirling around like clouds.

I shuddered. That wasn't a helpful train of thought. The light was taking ages to change, so I looked back down the street to distract myself.

Murmuring came from an alley behind me, and I turned to see where it was coming from. A group of kids, probably street kids, were gathering around the back door of a store. They were busily swapping things between their hands. One of them came out of the back door with an armful of food. I looked closer. The back door lay in splinters on the ground. It was as if...

"Noah?" I whispered. He looked my way. "I'm pretty sure those kids vaped that door."

He frowned and squinted their direction. "Maybe. I ran into a few before Ettney, remember? They're probably Unseen or Kindred orphans, using their abilities just to survive."

"I remember. We talked about helping them."

A few of the kids behind us broke into a scuffle, fighting over the largest pack of bread rolls.

"We should head over, see if we can help," I said.

"No!" came Rachel's voice over the radio earpiece. *"Our priority right now is the docks. You can track them down later."*

"She's right," said Noah. "If Hud's seen correctly, and the worst is coming, helping them now won't matter if the whole city goes down."

"It's bad, trust me," said Hud. "Whatever's happening here, the Shadows expect a bloodbath. I can feel it. They're hungry."

"It'll only take a minute. I just want to talk to them." I said.

"I said no!" snapped Rachel.

"Fine," I frowned. "But I don't like this."

I looked back at the alley. One of the kids had stopped handing out food and was walking slowly towards me. Bright eyes, dark skin, black hair hidden under her hoodie.

"That's her," I said to Noah. "That's the girl."

"The one who tried to kill you?"

"Definitely. These kids are connected to Wheeler, for sure."

"You need to get to the docks right now," Rachel interrupted.

I took out my earpiece. "We're not going to have another chance like this," I said to Noah. "I need to talk to her."

Noah paused, then nodded. "Go. I'll cover you."

Hud nodded too.

I stepped slowly towards the girl with my hands raised to my shoulders, palms open to show I meant no harm. She was still halfway down the street but marched towards me with intent. She barked instructions to the gang of kids, and they stopped their squabbling and formed a line behind her like a rear guard. They didn't come any closer, but it felt like a standoff. There were so many eyes on us, it would be impossible to tune, so our powers were both disarmed for now.

She stopped several steps away, and I stopped too.

"Hi," I offered. She didn't respond. She was young, like I'd thought, but her eyes showed seething anger rather than the innocence of youth.

"So, you want to tell me why you keep trying to kill me?" I asked, smiling.

"You don't know, Ari?" she growled.

"I really don't. But how do you know my name?" Dumb mistake. I shouldn't have admitted who I was. If the girl was Kindred, they now knew for sure I was in Coleton.

"I know everything about you," she said. "I know exactly who you are. I know exactly what you've done."

What I'd done? What was she talking about? I'd done a lot of things.

"I'm sorry, I don't understand," I replied, trying to keep my voice calm. "Can I at least know your name?"

"That's fair," she said. "I'd like you to know my name before you die, so you can know who took you down." The girl took a step forward again, until she was only an arm's length away. "Eden," she said. "My name is Eden."

Her right fist darted forward, thrusting a knife at my stomach.

Somehow, I managed to twist away from it, leaving only a knife-sized slit in my jacket. I jumped back, poised with my hands out in a defensive stance. That had been close. Way too close. And now she had a knife out, and I had only my bare hands. I jumped back again as she slashed at me with the knife, and tried to tune into the blade, but the interference was too great from the crowd of kids watching.

"You don't want to do this," I said.

"Yes, I do." She lunged at my throat, and I raised my right hand. The knife glanced off my arm, cutting into my skin. I yelled, blood dripping onto the ground.

Eden grinned and raised the blade again.

I stepped back, hands raised.

There was a crack, and she dropped to the ground, convulsing.

Noah grabbed my hand. "Time to go."

"Good idea," I agreed, thankful for the tasers Rachel had put in each of our packs.

The other kids ran for us, but we were taller and faster. They threw the food they were carrying. A tin of something hit my leg, and I swore.

"Get moving," shouted Hud. "These kids are crazy!"

He held our bikes upright for us, ready to go, and we jumped on and pedalled furiously across the road, ducking through the traffic. The kids stopped at the edge of the road, unwilling to risk dodging the cars that now sped through the green light.

My arm hurt like crazy, but the wound didn't feel too deep. Still, blood ran down my wrist onto the handlebars and dripped onto the road. I'd need bandages to stop the bleeding.

We came to a stop in a park just on the edge of the docklands, and Noah opened his pack to get supplies to wrap my arm. I took off my jacket so he could reach the wound easily, but' I only had a black singlet underneath. It had felt hot in the apartment, but now I was regretting my decision to ditch my long-sleeved shirt. I was freezing.

The park was empty, and here the night was still. There was no sign of the kids, but I had the feeling I'd be seeing Eden again, and sooner rather than later. While Noah bandaged my arm, I tried to latch on to what I could have done to make her vendetta so personal. I was responsible for a lot of deaths, anyone of which could have been her relative or loved one. It was honestly a wonder more kids weren't trying to kill me.

Once my arm was all patched up, I put the earpiece back.

"- your damn comm in, Ari! Noah! Make her put it in! Hud! Get her to -"

"It's in, Rachel. I've got it back in," I said.

"Thank goodness," said Hud. "She's been yelling like that for like ten minutes."

Noah put his earpiece back in, too. I hadn't even seen him take it out.

"The shipment is due to the docks in the next few minutes. Stop wasting time and get to your positions, now!"

I was a bit unsteady from adrenaline, but I'd be okay.

Hopping back on our bikes, we rode out across the park, and up to the back entrance of the docks.

Mission time.

ELEVEN

On paper there were three entrances to the docklands, but only one was quiet enough to give us decent cover. The docks operated at all hours of the day and night, taking shipments from across the world. At Coleton's peak, there'd been a queue of fifty ships waiting off the coast for their turn to come in and unload. There were only a few tonight.

The entrance we wanted was under a highway on-ramp. Huge concrete columns arced overhead, leading up to the steel reinforced road that hissed with traffic. The tall, spiked barricade that circled the docks was impossible to climb safely, and we didn't want to use any tools or our abilities. The mission was an in-and-out without being detected; the Kindred could never know we were here. Fortunately, there was a gap in the fence, possibly from a vehicle colliding with it. Rachel's source said that normally security patrolled the spot every half-hour or so, but tonight there weren't any patrols at all. They'd been bribed to leave by whoever was bringing in tonight's shipment.

Squeezing through the fence, I joined the boys, who were hiding behind a porta-loo. From the smell, it hadn't been emptied in a while.

"How's the arm?" asked Noah.

"Throbbing, but it's nothing I can't handle. The bleeding has mostly stopped."

"Good." Rachel said over the comm. *"From where you are, you'll need to turn right and head around the edge of the docklands to find a vantage point into berth three. That's where our contact said the shipment's coming in. Noah, you're on point."*

I nodded, then realised Rachel couldn't actually see me. "Got it. Hey, shouldn't we be using codenames?"

"This tech is running through the most secure radio communications scrambler on the planet, but sure. Use your codenames."

"Codenames?" asked Hud.

"I guess they didn't give you one," said Noah. "Our phones have numbers stored under our codenames, in case the data is compromised."

"Cool. Very cloak-and-dagger. What's yours?"

"Phoenix," said Noah.

"Sweet. 'Cause you died and stuff. I mean, sorry about that though. Rachel?"

"Just call me Basecamp for now."

"I'm Firewatch," I said.

"Cool. So, what are we going to call me?"

"Weren't you into video games?" Noah asked. "What was your screen name?"

Hud laughed. "Yeah, I don't think you want to call me that. I made it when I was like twelve and thought it was hilarious."

"What was it?" Noah smiled.

"Seriously, you're not calling me that."

"But what was it?" I grinned.

Hud sighed. "Fine. It was MyGiantButt."

Noah and I both laughed. So did Rachel over the comm. *"What?"*

"Shut up. I thought it was funny. Anytime I beat someone in multiplayer, the game would say, "You were killed by MyGiantButt."

I laughed again. "That's actually pretty good. I don't think it's a great callsign though. I might burst out laughing in the middle of the mission."

"How old did you say you were when you came up with that?"

"Twelve," said Hud. "Wasn't my best work."

"What about Twelvie?" Rachel chuckled.

"No." Hud shook his head. "No way. That is not going to be my callsign."

"I like it," said Noah. "Twelvie it is."

"You guys suck," laughed Hud. "But, uh, all this talk of butts…"

I raised one eyebrow. "Yes?"

He looked sheepish. "While we're next to the porta-loo, I kind of have to go."

"Seriously, man?" said Noah.

"It was long trip here, and I'm nervous. And you know when you get nervous, and it makes you need to do a —"

"Just go!" I interrupted. "But be quick, we're way too exposed here."

Hud ducked around the front of the porta-loo, closing the door behind him. There was a pause, then some unusual sounds coming through my earpiece.

"Hey, Hud?" said Rachel.

"Yes?" came his voice from inside the toilet.

"Turn your microphone off, please. Or your call sign will be Two. As in Number."

"Oh. Right. Sorry."

I snickered, and Noah joined in.

"Hey everyone," came a new voice over my earpiece. *"Josh here."*

"Josh? What are you doing on the line?" I asked.

"This stuff is so cool, I just wanted to try it out. Rachel—uh, Basecamp—let me say hi."

I smirked. "She did, did she? She must think you're pretty special to—"

"Alright, that's enough," Rachel butted in. *"Do we have an ETA on Twelvie?"*

Hud's mic clicked on. *"Uh, I'm working on it."*

I chuckled again. Hud was a dork, but I liked him. Switching my mic off, I motioned for Noah to do the same.

"I talked to Josh," I said once he had flicked his switch to *mute*.

Noah raised his eyebrows. "And?"

"I told him that I wasn't in that place any more. That I don't think of him as more than a friend."

"Wow. How did he take it?"

I rested against the wall behind me, until I realised it was the porta-loo. I stood upright, grimacing. "Not great, but better than I'd hoped."

Noah put his hand on my shoulder. "You did the right thing."

"I know," I sighed.

"Plus, it sounds like he might have a fan in Rachel."

I smiled. "Yeah. That'd be sweet. I don't know if he could handle her, though."

"You two know I can still hear you, right?" said Rachel. *"Twelvie left his microphone on, and your voices are coming through the wall."*

Noah and I stared at one another, cringing.

"Wow, this tech is seriously good!" came Hud's voice from inside the porta-loo. The door opened, and he stepped out. "Figured I shouldn't flush. Might be too noisy. Is there any hand sanitiser in our packs? These things don't have a sink."

Noah shook his head.

"Gross," said Hud. "Don't touch my hands, okay?"

"Wouldn't dream of it," I grinned. "Let's go."

The docks were massive. We were at the very southern end, and it was a long way to berth three. The berths were where ships moored, and huge cranes could load and unload shipping containers with cargo inside. The docks were full of these containers, stacked five or even ten high in rows around the entire yard. This meant a lot of cover, which was good. But we also had to check carefully around the end of each row before crossing to the next, which would slow us down.

We stayed quiet as we walked. Security was light, but we couldn't afford to blow our cover.

Coming close to berth three, we stopped.

"No need to get any closer," said Noah. "We should be able to see everything from here."

"There's got to be a better viewing point," I said, looking around. Just behind us, nested between the giant stacks of shipping containers, was a huge crane used for loading and unloading trucks. It sat on a raised platform, with a ladder as access. I pointed to it.

"I don't think the driver box is high enough," said Hud. "But one of us could shimmy out the window and up the crane arm. It looks climbable."

"That'd be crazy," said Noah. "It's at least five storeys above ground."

"I'll do it," I said.

"Your arm is cut up," Noah pointed out. "I'll go."

He had a point. My arm was still hurting. "Okay," I nodded. "Be careful"

Noah stretched his arms, ready for the climb. "Rachel put the surveillance equipment in my pack. I'll take up the camera and laser mic, and one of you two can check the monitor. There's no way I want to take the whole relay kit up there. Whoever's left can stand guard."

"I'll keep watch," said Hud. "Ari's seen enough action tonight."

"Fine." I said. "I can set up in the driver's cab of the crane. Hud, stay at the base of the platform. If anyone's coming, radio up to us."

Noah climbed the ladder first, and I followed. The ladder was surrounded by a cylindrical cage that made it feel a little more secure, but a big. sign at the bottom demanded the driver wear a harness before ascending. No harnesses here. We'd just have to hold on tight.

Climbing a five-storey ladder was tough, but at least I didn't have to get out on the crane arm like Noah. I had to take a break halfway up, especially because my arm was hurting. A red blotch had bloomed on the bandage; it was bleeding again.

Noah climbed into the cab, and I followed, panting.

"That was higher than it looked," he said, wheezing. "And my lungs aren't what they used to be." He chuckled. "I sound about eighty years old saying that."

The boom arm stretched out in front of the cabin, shifting slightly in the wind. "You going to be okay out there?" I asked.

"Yeah," he nodded. "Just give me a sec."

From this far up, I could see almost the entire docklands. The place stretched forever, rows upon rows of shipping containers lined up in stacks that formed a kind of maze. Floating on the dark horizon were isolated lights; huge ships waiting their turn to come into port. Despite the line-up, no cargo ships were docked at present. The Kindred had kept the place clear for whatever they were bringing in. I couldn't see the edge of the water from here, so it wasn't clear if any smaller boats had already arrived. Behind me, the city scattered orange light into the salty air, misted from the ocean like a fog machine. With the dark skyscrapers and shuttered buildings, Coleton was like a hulking shipwreck, a cargo carrier left to rot on shore.

Above, still, I could see no stars. The Shadows were out there. I could feel it.

TWELVE

While Noah caught his breath, he showed me how to use the monitoring gear. It was pretty simple, so it didn't take long.

"Okay," he said. "I'm going out there. Wish me luck."

Shoving the telescopic camera and microphone back in his pack, Noah swung out the window and onto the surrounding crane platform. It was thin, so he pressed close to the cab to work his way around the front. The metal cross beams that made up the crane arm were close enough that they formed a ladder, and Noah began his treacherous climb.

"Wow. This is high," he said over the intercom.

"It's just like when we climbed that tree into the Ettney complex," I said, trying to reassure him.

"You fell off that, remember?"

"Right. Sorry."

"You guys went through a lot together, hey," said Hud from somewhere far below.

"Yeah." I replied. "It was pretty intense."

"It's nice being out here with you guys," said Hud again, *"I mean, this is terrifying, and it makes me want to poop again*

just watching *Phoenix up there, but it's nice to be a part of it. That morning in Ettney, when you guys called, I felt so helpless that I couldn't assist. Especially seeing as I owe Phoenix my life. Bek will too, if she ever gets better."*

"She will," said Noah. *"I think I'm high enough now. I can just see an open space near berth three. Looks like there's movement. I'll get out the gear. Firewatch, you ready?"*

"I'll switch the monitor on now."

The screen lit up when I opened the case. On it was a direct feed from Noah's camera, which was whirling around as he took it out of the bag. It made me dizzy, so I worked on plugging in the headphones. They rumbled as Noah set up the mic, and then settled. He had headphones on too, so he knew where to point the gear to get the best sound. The camera zoomed in.

"Wow, this really gets us close to the action," I said.

"Twelvie, I can see you're too close to the base of the crane," Rachel warned. She'd been so quiet I'd forgotten she was still listening. *"You won't get enough notice if someone's coming. Can you head around to the right and find a better vantage point?"*

"Sure."

The camera was steadied now, and even though berth three was right across the docklands, we had a great view of the loading zone. There were at least a dozen men carrying gear off a barge. They looked like dock workers. To the right, though, were more men.

"Kindred. At least six," confirmed Noah.

He panned the camera to get a better look, and zoomed in. They wore the masked robes of Kindred, so none of their faces were visible. The dock workers kept shooting nervous looks at them, like they didn't know who they were or what was going on. They were clearly just doing a job they'd been bribed for.

The open space was already filled with black, steel reinforced containers. Whatever they were bringing in looked military. The dock workers brought the last of the boxes off the boat, a huge one on wheels that they struggled to push up the ramp. One of the Kindred stepped forward to inspect the shipment.

"A box is missing," he said, voice sounding like an echo as it came through Noah's laser mic.

The lead dock worker scratched his head. "This is everything they had at the pickup point."

"I don't believe you," the hooded man's voice rose. "You're trying to damage us. You're Unseen, aren't you?"

"I haven't *seen* anything, if that's what you're talking about. We're paid for discretion, I understand that."

"Liar. Traitor. You don't just betray your sponsors, you betray our entire agenda. You betray *me.*"

"Mate, seriously, I don't even know who you are, and I honestly don't want to." The worker took a step back, and so did his colleagues. "Your masks are creepy as hell. All we want is our payment and we'll be on our way. You can take up the issue with your supplier."

The Kindred speaker stepped forward, and his hand whipped around, knife glinting off the dockland lights. The worker tried to scream but, with his throat cut, he could only gurgle, and cough, and clutch at his neck. He fell to his knees, and his killer kicked him to the ground.

The other workers ran, but six more Kindred stepped out of the darkness behind them, brandishing blades.

"We have to do something," I said.

"What could we possibly do? We're completely outnumbered," said Noah.

"He's right," said Rachel. *"Stand down and gather information. That's more important right now."*

I shook my head but stayed put. I was brave, but I wasn't stupid.

"What's going on up there, guys?" said Hud. *"I'm blind down here."*

The lead Kindred removed his mask to reveal a thin face, blue eyes, and blonde, wispy hair.

Noah swore. *"Is that…"*

My eyes widened. "Yep. It's Wheeler. Guess he's connected to this after all."

"Alright, don't gloat," said Rachel. *"Keep on him."*

Wheeler stepped right next to the lead dockman on the ground. "Unseen scum," he said, and brought his boot down on the man's head. There was a crunch, and the man stopped moving. I felt sick.

"Are they our people?" said Noah.

"No," Rachel replied. *"No reports of anyone in that crew being one of us."*

"That doesn't mean they deserve to die," I said.

"There's nothing we can do to help them."

"I'm going to try and get closer," said Hud. *"Maybe I can create a distraction."*

"Don't you dare!" Rachel yelled. *"Stay put, Twelvie. Back up your team. That's an order."*

"Sorry, but I don't take orders well," said Hud. There was a click. Hud had turned off his mic. Far below, I saw him take out his earpiece.

"Firewatch, get down there and stop him!" Rachel screamed. *"He's going to compromise you all."*

"Alright," I said. "Phoenix, you're on your own."

Noah gave me a thumbs up from out on the crane gantry, and I began the climb down. Looking below, I saw

Hud run through the shipping containers and towards the Kindred berth.

Screams rang out from across the docks. The Kindred were slaughtering the workers like sheep. I descended as fast as I could manage, but the cut on my arm slowed me down. There was no chance I'd make it in time to stop whatever Hud was planning.

More screams.

I reached the bottom of the ladder and sprinted to the edge of the containers. There were eight rows of containers between the crane and the docks, but they were staggered, meaning I had no direct line of sight to the water. The screams had stopped, which meant either Hud's distraction had worked or everyone was dead.

Four rows in, I turned left. Up against a red container wall was Hud. He looked injured.

I ran to him. "Hud! Are you hurt?"

He shook his head. "No," he gasped. "Panic attack." He heaved for a moment, like he was going to be sick. "Give me a minute."

"We don't have a minute. We're too close to the Kindred."

Hud looked at me, face sweating. "Not helping the panic."

"Sorry. What can I do?"

"Nothing. You go. I'll sort myself out."

"No way am I leaving you like this."

Hud stopped shaking and his face cleared. "That's weird," he said. "I feel fine suddenly."

"Great, let's go." I grabbed his arm ready to run.

"No, it shouldn't be over that fast. Why do I feel so good?" Hud looked behind me, and his eyes widened.

I turned around.

At the end of the row, stood Wheeler.

He'd found us.

THIRTEEN

Wheeler held a huge knife in his left hand. It was stained red, and his dark robe was sprayed with even darker spots.

"Ari," he hissed, eyes wild. "I knew you'd find me."

I turned to run, but the way was blocked by three Kindred. We were trapped, and unarmed. My backpack was in the crane, and Hud wasn't wearing his.

"I've been searching. I knew you'd come to Coleton. It was only a matter of time before our lives entwined."

He spoke with the same intensity as Hackman, although Hackman had been more controlled. Wheeler felt untamed and unpredictable.

"Keep him talking," said Noah, *"I'm coming."*

"You've been looking for me?" I asked, taking a step towards Wheeler.

"Of course," he smiled. "We all have. I've felt you. I knew you were close, in the park last night. That's why I took the girl and led you to my gallery. I had to know for sure it was you."

"You knew I was close?"

"Of course. Your resonance—I'd heard of it from my brothers and sisters in Ettney, but I had to feel it for myself."

I smiled. Why was I smiling? Forcing my face into a frown, I tried to look scary. "In that case, you know what I'm capable of. I took down the Ettney complex, and I'll take you down too. You and your psychotic children."

Wheeler chuckled quietly. "Yes, Eden mentioned she'd found you. I did ask her to leave you alone for now, but you know how children are. Why, your sister has the same impudent defiance from what I've heard."

Clenching my fists, I stepped towards him again. "Leave my sister out of this."

"Why?" he said. "She's a part of this, as we all are. This whole city is key to the Agenda, although it doesn't know that just yet."

I had to fish for more. For some reason, Wheeler seemed to like me.

"The Agenda?" I asked. "How does Coleton fit into all this?"

He smiled, and for some reason I did too. I wanted to run to him. Hold him. Be safe with him. He would look after me. If he was with me, everything would be fine. Next to me, Hud took a step forward. He wore the same smile. We would both be okay if we just—

Wheeler fell, writhing.

"No!" I screamed. Why was I so upset?

Noah stepped out from behind the container holding his taser. He couldn't disconnect the wires from Wheeler, so he threw the unit down and yelled at us both. "Run, you idiots!"

With Wheeler down, I now felt no desire to stay with him. I grabbed Hud's hand and we ran for it.

My legs burned as we sprinted past rows of shipping containers. The Kindred behind us shouted, finally snapped out of their stupor.

"You need to move fast," Rachel barked. *"Get out of there."*

A flare burst behind me, illuminating the night and reflecting off the container walls. Someone had me targeted.

"Should we split up?" I asked, eyes darting round for a way to lose our pursuers.

"No way!" panted Hud. "Haven't you ever seen horror movies?"

"Don't need to," I shouted back. "I've lived one!"

"Guys?" said Rachel. *"Shut up and run."*

I'd lost sight of Noah. So much for sticking together. I zig-zagged left, towards the water. They wouldn't expect us to move away from our only exit.

Another flare lit the night, and Hud swore.

I turned but kept running.

Hud staggered for a moment, hit on the back. He gritted his teeth and powered through the pain. "Freaking hell, those things hurt."

A dark figure barrelled into me from the right, and I screamed and kicked it in the knees.

Hey!" Noah gasped. "It's me! This way!"

Hud and I turned to follow Noah. He ran to the right, back towards the city and away from the ocean. Ahead, a shipping container door sat half open.

"In here," he said. "We're outnumbered. Best to stay put and wait it out."

I ran inside and Hud followed. Noah pulled the door closed.

It was completely dark in the container, and the air was musty and old.

Shouts came from outside, and footsteps ran past. I held my breath as they came close, but after a moment, the Kindred kept going, off into the night.

"Sorry, guys," whispered Hud. "I thought I'd be okay, but the panic attack got the better of me. Haven't had one for a while, so it caught me by surprise."

"What the hell was that?" said Rachel over the intercom. *"Twelvie, you idiot! You nearly got yourselves killed!"*

I rounded on Hud, too. "That was incredibly stupid."

"I'm sorry, I just—the panic attacks started after my mum died. I thought I'd been managing it."

Hud looked so sad that my anger deflated. "Sorry, I didn't know."

"It's okay," he said. "I know I'm not the only one with dead parents around here." Hud saw my face. "Sorry, that was insensitive."

"Never mind," I said.

But he was right. Noah, Hud, Rachel and I—all our stories grew from tragedy. We'd all lost someone. Our parents, especially. It was weird, almost as if it were part of some master plan to shape our lives and have us all end up here. Maybe Wheeler was right. Maybe it had just been a matter of time before I crossed his path.

"Rachel, were you able to get anything from the video feed?" I asked.

"Just boxes. Lots of boxes. No labels. Nothing to give us any idea what's inside."

I shook my head. "So, we're still at square one."

"It's quiet out there now," said Noah. "Maybe we could sneak back out and take a look."

"No chance," I said. "They're on high alert. No way we'd get close enough before we got caught. And there's something about Wheeler."

Hud fidgeted with his collar. "You felt it too?"

Nodding, I sat down on the floor of the shipping container. My arm was throbbing, and I had to rest.

"It was weird, hey," said Hud. "My panic attack went away the moment he turned up. Like instantly. That never happens."

"I kept smiling at him," I said. "And when Phoenix tasered him, I was so upset, like he meant something to me."

Noah frowned. "It must be connected to his resonance and that weird tone he gives out."

Rachel chimed in over the com. *"I've been doing some more research on Wheeler. He's built incredible influence in the city, like Phoenix found before. But I can't see how. He's not particularly special or gifted. His gallery was laughed at for its bizarre, creepy work when it opened. But somehow, he's worked his way into the power circle, and everyone loves him."*

"Gotta be the resonance he gives out," I said. "When he was with us, it was like I never wanted him to leave. It was like a drug."

Hud put on a husky voice, "Hey bro, gimme two hits of creepy blonde guy. Make it quick."

I laughed, in spite of myself.

"Guys, keep it quiet. They're still out there somewhere," Noah snapped.

We both fell silent.

The shipping container creaked as it cooled in the night air. A seagull squawked, circling overhead. On the horizon, a foghorn cut through the night.

Hud looked at the roof of the container. "The Shadows are up there," he whispered. "I can feel them. It's like they're keeping watch."

I stared at the roof, too, half expecting a smoky tendril to reach through and grab me, feed on me, and leave me a dead husk like I'd seen back at Ettney.

The patch on my stomach burned cold. It always burned when something awful was near. I put my hand to it. Noah took a step toward me, eyebrows furrowed.

The container door screamed as it flew open.

Wheeler stood at the entrance, flanked by his crew.

"Found you," he grinned, and I dropped, writhing from the taser embedded in my thigh.

FOURTEEN

My whole body ached, but at least the convulsions had stopped. Cable-ties cut into my wrists, holding me in a chair. I'd tried to fight back when they strapped me in, but my muscles wouldn't obey. I was in the same shipping container we had hidden in, but Hud and Noah had been taken somewhere else. In front of me, two huge masked Kindred stood guard, staring straight at me, so I couldn't use my abilities. I was going nowhere.

Out in the night, someone yelled. Hopefully, it wasn't one of the boys.

My mouth was dry, and I had to work up enough saliva to talk. "Please, don't hurt me." I threw a tremor into my voice, to make them think I was just a scared little girl. Maybe they'd let their guard down. I didn't have to force my hands to shake, though. They were doing that on their own.

"I'm really scared. That Wheeler guy is mean."

The masked figure on the left snorted. "You can stop that," she said. "We know exactly who you are and what you're capable of. My brother died at Ettney. The only reason I'm not killing you is because Wheeler told us not to."

I dropped the innocence from my voice. "Dare you."

"Don't try that, either. I'm not an idiot. If I move my gaze, you're probably strong enough to override my friend's interference." She indicated to the other figure, who hadn't said a thing. He could have been a mannequin, for all I knew.

I tried to tune to the ties on my wrist, but there was too much interference from the two of them.

Time to try something else. From what I'd learned, many of the lower level Kindred didn't realise they were the bad guys.

"You two know you're on the wrong side of this, don't you? The Kindred, everything you stand for, everything you've done. It's evil."

They both chuckled, and she spoke again. "I know exactly what we are. I'm no low-level scrub, and even if I was, the juniors believe too much in our cause to turn on the word of a traitor. What you fail to understand is the beauty of our mission. The rebirth of humanity in *their* image."

"The Shadows?"

She nodded beneath her mask.

"Why would anyone want to be like them?"

Her voice echoed around the shipping container. "You will see, in time. I can feel it. You have the mark. You carry the seed."

My heart thumped. The black stain on my stomach, put there by the Shadow in my room. "How do you know that?"

"Like calls to like, Ari."

"I'm nothing like you."

She didn't answer. The black holes in her mask stared me down.

A scream rang out again. That was definitely one of the boys.

I looked dead into the eye-holes in the woman's mask. "What are you doing to them?"

"Motivating them," she said. "Don't worry. It'll be your turn soon."

"I'm not worried," I said, but that was a lie.

The door behind the two Kindred clanked, then screeched as it opened. Wheeler entered the container. "Out," he ordered.

"She's strong," the woman protested. "She might override your—"

"Enough," he snapped. "Get out, now."

The masked Kindred left, and Wheeler stepped slowly towards me.

"The boys weren't particularly forthcoming about the location of Unseen operations in this city. I was hoping you would be a bit more useful."

I stared him down and said nothing.

"Alright then," he smiled, "let's start from the beginning. Our first introduction was a little combative." Wheeler walked behind me, and I tried to tune in to the cable tie on my left wrist, but his strange pulsing interference made it impossible. He brought a metal folding chair around from behind me and placed it on the floor a foot away. Turning the chair backwards, he straddled it facing me and leaned on the back-rest with both arms.

"My name is Thomas Wheeler, although I'm sure you know that already."

My heart fluttered a little, and I smiled in spite of myself. He was charming, in a strange way. I felt like I was meeting somebody famous, and considering Wheeler's position in the city, I sort of was.

He saw my smile. "See, we don't have to be so antagonistic. Whether you know it or not, we're working towards the same goal. We all want the world to be better."

"Not in the way you want it. Not like the Shadows."

He sat up a little. "They know more about humanity than we know about ourselves. They have watched us for millennia. They know our truth. They *are* our truth."

"That is some serious philosophical crap," I spat. "I know truth, and the Shadows aren't it. They're awful, and evil, and they shouldn't exist in our world."

"Isn't honesty the greatest truth?" said Wheeler, leaning into the back-rest. His eyes glowed with passion, like I'd woken a fire within him. "Isn't acting truthfully simply a matter of removing the barriers to our desires, of pursuing the parts of ourselves we keep buried? The art in my gallery —"

"Is awful," I finished. "It's violent and crude and disgusting."

"It's truth," said Wheeler. "The truth about ourselves. When we stop fighting the darkness inside us, when we set it free, that is when we are truly ourselves. That is when we are truly *human*."

I shook my head, but my heart thumped in my chest. His words were beautiful, in a way. They were so passionate and dynamic and authentic. No wonder he was so popular in Coleton. He was magnetic.

"Surely, there's a part of you that wants to be set free. Surely, there's a desire in you that you've left unfulfilled, that you've pushed deep down inside, unknown even to yourself. Wouldn't it feel wonderful to let it out? To stop lying to yourself? To just. Be. Real."

"Noah," I blurted out, and my face burned. Why had I said that? Was it something to do with Wheeler's resonance?

Wheeler smiled and stood up, walking around to my left. "There you are, my darling. You've been honest with yourself and with me." He leaned close to my ear, and I could feel his breath as he hissed. "What about him?"

I almost couldn't hear him, my heart was pumping so loud. "I want him. I want all of him. I've been lying to myself, trying to stay distant because I feel so guilty about his dad, but I want him. I want to kiss him, and hold him, and—"

"Wonderful," Wheeler exclaimed, standing upright and clapping his hands. "Truth is freedom!"

He knocked on the door and whispered to the woman outside.

My mouth was open in a huge grin. I felt amazing. I could do anything. I could be anything. I was finally free to do whatever I wanted with whoever I wanted. Wheeler walked over to me and cut the cable ties from my wrists. I didn't fight him, though. I didn't want to. He'd freed me, and I owed him everything.

The door creaked open, and the woman dragged Noah inside.

"Out," said Wheeler again, and she left.

Noah's ear was bloodied, and his cheek was red like he'd been punched.

"Noah!" I laughed. "He's brought you here. I'm so glad you're here."

"Ari?" Noah frowned. "What's wrong with you? Why are you smiling?"

Wheeler turned to me. "Noah here was surprisingly resistant to my inspiration, but I think you can show him the way."

Noah's hands were tied, but he staggered to his feet. "Ari? What has he done to you?"

I smiled. "Truth is freedom."

With both hands, I pushed Noah up against the container wall. He was so warm, and he was everything I wanted. I pressed myself into his chest and kissed him, hard, like I wanted to be part of him, like I wanted to absorb every piece of him into me. I grabbed at his hair and his shirt, and I didn't care who was watching.

"Ari, what the—" Noah said, although his voice was muffled by my mouth.

"Shut up and enjoy this." I pulled his shirt over his head, but it got stuck, bunched up on his cable-tied hands. Laughing, I ran my hands over his chest, tracing his scars and ignoring the worried look in his eyes.

Then the floor lifted, and twisted, and we flew, tumbling, into the air.

FIFTEEN

My head throbbed, but Noah had taken most of the impact. I pulled myself off him and stood. The whole container was on its side, and the door lay flat like a ramp into the night. Wheeler staggered to his feet, but he was bleeding from his forehead, and he lost his balance, falling forward onto the floor. He was probably knocked unconscious, because whatever spell he'd had over me was broken.

"Get up!" I said to Noah. "Now's our chance!"

Noah was still lying flat and groaned at me.

I grabbed his tied hands and pulled him upright.

He blinked, dizzy, and then steeled himself. "We need to kill him. Now."

I tried to use my abilities, but Wheeler began to stir and moan. Even semi-conscious, his interference was too strong. He really was powerful.

I had no weapons. If I wanted Wheeler dead, I'd have to either beat him to death, or choke him. I took a step towards his body. Could I really kill a man in cold blood with my bare hands? If I did, surely the darkness in me would win.

Wheeler sat up, eyes wild.

"Time to go," I said, and pulled Noah out of the shipping container. The container had tipped entirely to the right and crushed both of the Kindred watchers underneath it. Their masks had fallen off, and they stared at me from the gap under the container, faces soaked in blood. One of them blinked slowly, and I felt sick.

Noah and I lifted the container door off the ground and pushed it shut, sliding the latch in place. Now that Wheeler was behind the door, his interference was gone.

"Look away," I told Noah, tuning in to the handle on the front of the container, heating it until it glowed and melted over the rest of the door.

Wheeler swore from inside, a muffled curse, then started banging on the door, demanding to be let out.

"Hey!" came a shout from my left. "This way!"

Josh waved from the ladder of the crane control booth. He was climbing down to meet us. My eyes followed the crane arm to where it had smacked into a huge stack of shipping containers, knocking them onto ours and tipping it over.

Noah and I ran to the ladder base as Josh jumped down.

"I've got an exit," he said. "But we need to move, now. More Kindred are coming from the direction you entered. At least, that's what Basecamp tells me." He tapped the comm on his ear. Neither Noah or I had ours anymore.

Josh ran for the end of the docklands, opposite to the way we'd come in. We ran through five rows of containers. Noah was wheezing and had to stop for a moment. "Wait a minute guys. I'm wiped, and my head's spinning from the fall."

I stopped and Josh did too.

"Sorry about that," Josh said. "It was the only way I could think of to stop them. I don't have super powers like you guys."

"Nice work," I panted.

Josh grinned. "It was easy," he said. "Well, actually I almost stuffed it. Once I started the crane, I only had a few seconds before they worked out what I was doing."

"You know how to drive a crane?" I asked.

"No. But the controls have labels. And I'm awesome at that arcade game with the claw."

I smirked, and then frowned. "We need to get Hud."

Josh shook his head. "When I got here, he was being bundled into a car. The Kindred took him somewhere."

Oh no. They had Hud.

"The only way we get him back is if we make it out of here," said Josh. "So can we run now? And also," he gestured at Noah. "I don't know why you're half-naked, but can you *please* put on a shirt?"

My face burned and Noah's went bright red. His shirt was still down around his arms, stuck on his wrists which remained tied together.

"Here, let me." I said, lifting it up his arms and back over his head.

"Seriously, what was he *doing* to you guys in there?" Josh asked.

My face went supernova. "Just lead the way."

Josh set off again at a sprint. Noah and I both had trouble keeping up, after all we'd been through.

"Not that I'm ungrateful," Noah wheezed at Josh, "but why are you here? I thought Rachel would have come. You're not exactly field trained. Or even Unseen."

Josh looked at Noah over his shoulder. "She's not ready for the field, despite her complaining. Also, I didn't exactly ask permission. When I heard you guys were in trouble, I just took the comm and caught a taxi down here."

Josh kept running, but I could tell he was listening to his comm for a moment.

"Basecamp says she's gonna kill me when I get back," he grinned. "But she liked my move with the crane."

I flashed a look at Noah, who chuckled.

Josh looked at both of us. "What?"

"Nothing. Are we nearly there?" I was running out of steam and talking wasn't helping.

Josh nodded, and I stayed quiet to conserve my energy. We were heading past berth five. There were at least seven before the end of the docks. Noah ran next to me, teeth gritted. He was struggling.

There were no sounds behind us, but that didn't mean we weren't being followed.

At the end of our container row, a forklift sat empty.

"Reckon we could get a ride?" I asked Josh.

"If the keys are in it, maybe," he said.

"Good. My arm's killing me."

"And I'm pretty sure I got a concussion back there," said Noah.

We reached the yellow forklift. "Keys are in," said Josh, grinning. He jumped up, but there was only one seat. Noah and I would have to hold on to the edge. I stood up on the side and held onto the driver cage with my good arm. Noah did the same, except both his hands were still tied so he had trouble gripping properly. I wrapped my other arm around him, pulling him in toward the vehicle, trying not to think about that kiss from earlier.

Josh turned the ignition and the forklift roared to life. It was loud. Too loud. Hopefully it would be fast enough to keep ahead of the Kindred. Josh stared at the mess of levers in front of him and pulled one. The prongs at the front of the forklift started to rise, and a loud beeping rang out through the container rows. Josh swore and tried another lever. The forklift spun on the spot, and I hung on to Noah and it for dear life.

"Josh!" I cried.

"I know, I know. Gimme a sec."

"Josh, there's pedals," said Noah.

"Oh. Right. Sorry guys. Good thing I've been getting driving lessons."

He hit the accelerator and the forklift sped off. At least, it went as fast as a forklift could go. It was probably only twice our running speed at full throttle, but that was better than nothing. I took a moment to catch my breath and tighten my grip. If I fell off, I'd end up with some seriously nasty gravel rash.

Now that he had sorted out the driving, Josh explained the plan. "Rachel's watching the main entrance through a traffic camera near berth four. She says there's more Kindred on their way. There's a lot of them, too. The whole front fence is covered by cameras, so no chance of using your abilities to break it down. We have to make it to the tunnels."

The tunnels. Of course. The freight railway was shut now, as the tracks were disused, but back at Coleton's peak the shipping containers had been loaded onto freight trains that had run underneath the city on a separate line from the commuter subway.

"Won't they be closed?" I asked Josh.

"Maybe, but they shouldn't be too secure. The docks aren't exactly open to the public, and no dock worker would have any reason to go down there. Besides, I'm sure your fancy pants abilities can work things out. Rachel says there are a bunch of passageways to other parts of the city, and maybe even doors to the main subway line. If we can avoid the Kindred long enough, we can make it out through one of those."

We passed berth six. Almost to the end of the docks. The rain started in again, drizzling from clouds lit orange by the city. At least I didn't have to wonder if the Shadows were up there. I'd see them for sure against the glowing sky. We didn't have Hud and his strange connection to them now, so we were driving blind in more ways than one.

Hopefully, he was safe. I'd only just met Hud, but his willingness to run blind into danger made me like him, despite the mess it had caused. I had been the same at the beginning; making snap judgments and bad calls, but I'd learned from them, gotten smarter. Hud didn't have the battle experience we did, and so his impulsiveness was almost expected. If he toned that down, and played it smart, maybe he'd stay alive long enough for us to rescue him.

As if in response to that thought, Josh put a hand to his comm. "Basecamp says she's doing her best to track Twelvie, but it's not looking good."

A hum came from somewhere behind us. The forklift hit a bump and Noah and I were nearly thrown off again. Rain had wet the driver cage and it was getting slippery.

The hum became a roar, and I turned to find the source. Six container rows back, a huge black four-wheel-drive was hot on our tail. The headlights were blinding. No doubt it was full of Kindred. It was moving fast, and the engine revved as it sped towards us. The driver was going to mow us down.

"Josh?" I yelled over the noise.

"I know," he said. "But I can't go any faster!"

They were catching us, now only three rows behind. The driver gunned the gas, and the vehicle surged forward. We had seconds before it ran us down. I closed my eyes to focus for a moment and tried to tune to the car. Static burned through my mind. I looked closer. They had cameras strapped to the car, pointing at the vehicle to protect it from tampering. No chance I could burn the fuel tank. I tried to tune into the shipping containers, but there were too many eyes on them. Time for plan B.

The car roared again. They were almost on top of us.

"Josh?"

"Yeah?"

"Turn left, now!"

Josh spun the forklift wheel to head for the gap in the container rows. Its left wheels came off the ground, and the whole thing started to tilt towards Noah, who tapped his foot down on the ground and pushed up, making the forklift level again. The car hadn't turned. It kept going up the row. Then, its brakes squealed, and the driver threw the car into reverse. A second engine sounded close by.

"Now, turn right!" I yelled.

Josh slowed a little this time, so the forklift stayed on all four wheels through the turn. Behind us, the car roared. It was almost around the corner. Now or never.

"Hey boys? I need you to close your eyes."

Noah nodded, but Josh laughed out loud. "You're kidding, right? I'm driving!"

"Just for a second. Do it on my count!"

He shook his head. "Fine, but if we die, I'm blaming you."

"On three. One."

The car was making the turn. The headlights blared into the container row, but they wouldn't be able to see me yet.

"Two."

The second engine roared again. The other vehicle hadn't appeared, but it was close.

"Three."

Noah and Josh shut their eyes. I looked just ahead of the forklift and tuned into the bottom shipping container, raising the temperature as high and as fast as I could. Melting was too slow. I had to vape this one. The container glowed red, but it wasn't enough. I gritted my teeth and raised it higher. The metal was white hot now. Still not enough. I yelled and gave it one final burst of energy. The metal vanished, exploding in a cloud of atoms.

"Open your eyes and floor it!"

Josh did. The four-wheel-drive was in our row now, its headlights bearing down on our position. Behind, the second car had joined the chase. If I'd mistimed this, we were dead.

Having lost its base, the container row started to topple as we passed. Container crashed down on container, and the whole row wobbled.

The car behind us hit the brakes just as a shipping container crushed through its roof. No-one inside that would have survived.

The second vehicle hit reverse and disappeared behind the row of containers as they fell like the world's biggest game of dominoes.

Josh whooped, and Noah grinned at me. "Nice work," he smiled.

I frowned. "It's not over yet. There's one more car, and they won't fall for that move again."

"We're almost at the tunnels," said Josh.

I looked ahead of us and saw two giant wooden doors that formed the entrance to the train tunnels. They were surrounded by solid concrete retaining walls. This part of

Coleton was hilly, and the tunnels had been carved right into the rock. There was no way I could vaporise our way through that much dirt, so the only way out of here was the tunnel entrance.

The remaining car revved its engine somewhere behind us. We had to break the doors down before it got here.

"Noah, I'm wiped; can you do this one?"

"Sure," he said. "Close your eyes."

We did, and when I opened them a second later, the tunnel doors were a mess of holes and burning wood.

"Sorry, didn't get the resonance high enough."

"There's still space to get through," I said.

The forklift slowed down.

"Josh, what are you doing?"

"I can't get the forklift in there; the tracks are in the way. We're going to have to leave it and go on foot."

He pulled up in front of the burning tunnel doors, and we jumped off. There was just enough space to squeeze through into the tunnel, although the air inside was filled with inky smoke from the fire.

The Kindred car stopped outside, headlights cutting through the smoke and filling the space with scattered light beams. Car doors slammed.

"Here we go," Noah said, and we set off at a jog into the pitch-black tunnel.

"They're not following us," said Josh. I turned back, and in the receding distance, torches added to the headlight beams, sweeping through the holes in the tunnel doors. He was right, they weren't coming in. I slowed to a stop.

"Why aren't they chasing us?" I asked quietly.

"Maybe we're trapped, and they know it," said Noah.

"I don't think that's it," said Josh. "Look at them; they're not even crossing the threshold. It's like they're afraid."

"Of us?" whispered Noah.

"I doubt it," I replied in a hushed voice. "What could the Kindred possibly be afraid of down here?"

"Regardless, I'll take the win." Noah shrugged and kept moving down the tunnel.

I followed, and Josh did too, trying to whistle to lighten the mood.

I shushed him. I knew better than he the things that lurk in the dark.

THE CITY UNSEEN

SIXTEEN

These tunnels were much larger than the main subway tracks. Two sets of rails ran down each side, with a huge space in between. There was a slight bend in the tunnel, and soon we were completely out of sight of the Kindred at the entrance.

Josh pulled a small LED torch from his pocket and switched it on. It wasn't much, but at least gave us some light to work with, bouncing around the tunnels and covering us in a faint blue glow.

Noah faced away for a moment, and there was a burning smell in the air. He turned back around with his hands free, smoke rising from the melted rope on the ground behind him. "Good thinking, Josh. What else you got in there?" asked Noah.

Josh rifled through his pockets. "Uh, a protein bar, three tampons, and a snake bite kit. On reflection, I should have let Rachel help me pack. Speaking of Rachel, you there, Rach?" Josh said into his comm. "She's not answering." He checked his phone. "No signal."

"The tunnel must be blocking the transmission," I said. "And our GPS trackers were taken."

"See, this is why spies have them implanted," said Josh. "Much harder to take out."

"And much bloodier when they are," said Noah grimly. "Either way, we're on our own down here. Hopefully the tracks are easy to navigate. I can't imagine a freight line being complicated."

"At least, if we get lost down here, we've got the protein bar to keep us going." I smiled, trying to calm myself. My heart was still thumping from the chase, and my entire body was on high alert. I was totally wired.

"Your hand is shaking," said Noah.

I held it in front of my face, but it wouldn't keep still. "Still coming down from our rally car impersonation."

"I've gotta say," said Noah. "I think that might be the world's first forklift pursuit." He patted Josh on the back. "Well done, by the way."

Josh shifted uncomfortably. "Thanks." When Noah glanced away, Josh rolled his eyes. He wasn't okay with Noah, despite pretending things were fine back at Dad's apartment.

Trapped in a tunnel with a guy I just dumped, and one I just made out with. Awesome.

What on earth had happened to me back there with Wheeler? It was more than just his words, something inside me had felt so free when he'd said all those things. It was like I'd lost control, lost my ability to think on a rational level. It had to be connected to his resonance somehow. That strange, pulsing note had done something to me. And that was obviously what kept the kids so calm, what made them follow him.

Honestly, I missed that feeling, the feeling that nothing else mattered, that I could do anything with anyone. A little part of me wanted to return, to head back to Wheeler and ask him to make me feel free again. It was addictive.

I caught Noah looking at me and my face burned. He dropped back for a second, just a little out of Josh's earshot. I matched him. Josh didn't notice and kept walking, his torchlight not reaching back to us.

Noah took my hand, walking beside me. "What happened back there, in the container?" His voice was quiet and tender and did nothing to slow my heartbeat. "Just before you kissed me, and, you know, tried to take my clothes off..."

This was way too embarrassing. "Sorry about that."

"No, don't be," Noah stammered. "Although it was a little weird with Wheeler standing there. And do you remember? You said, 'truth is freedom.' What did you mean?"

"I don't know. Wheeler was talking about honesty and freedom. He said that when we act on our deepest impulses, that's when we're free. He asked me what I wanted, what I really desired..." I couldn't finish the sentence.

"And then he brought me to you," Noah said slowly.

My mouth wouldn't move. I couldn't bring myself to say it.

Noah stopped walking, and I did too. He brought his hand up to touch my cheek. "You too."

Before I could stop myself, I was kissing him again— quietly, this time, not the crazed animal woman I'd been in the container. But this was somehow more beautiful, more special, like we were the only two people in the world. I forgot about everything for a moment, caught up in Noah's lips, his eyes, his hands...

There was a cough, and I pulled away.

Josh had stopped walking and shone the torch back at us. "So, we escaping the crazed apocalyptic cult, or what?"

I dropped my hand from Noah's. "Sorry, we were just—"

Josh turned away and kept walking. "It's okay. You guys were just held hostage. Don't have to apologise to me. Seize the day, carpe diem, and all that stuff." His voice cracked a little at the end.

I was a fricking idiot. The worst person in the history of people. He'd just run down here and saved both our lives, without any kind of powers, and I was making out with the guy I'd dumped him for, quite literally behind his back. I could use Wheeler as an excuse, but deep down I knew it wasn't true. I was just being selfish.

"I hope Hud's okay," said Noah as we marched on. None of us responded. There was nothing any of us could say to make that situation better. Hopefully Rachel was tracking him right now. We'd rescue him as soon as we made it out of the underground.

It was getting hot. Hotter than expected, and not just because my face still burned. The air was still, and humid, like it had been trapped down here for decades. It smelled wet, and old, and occasionally of death. Animals had likely wandered in here over the years and died.

The stench grew as we walked, growing until it became as thick as the humidity, like the air itself was death. It was waiting for us, curling around us like a snake, suffocating, squeezing. I was crushed under its weight.

Josh stopped ahead. "Oh, yuck. Guys, cover your noses. This is disgusting."

He pointed the torch back our way, at the ground, so we could see where we walked. Rat bones lay everywhere, spread across the tunnel like a nest. I gagged and pulled my shirt up to cover my mouth and nose.

Noah and I caught up to Josh, and he swung the torch back to the front to show us what he'd found.

No.

Not this.

Not again.

A pile of animals, dead and dried out like they'd baked too long in the sun. Rats, dogs, cats, birds, anything that had wandered too close to a tunnel vent, or maybe a stormwater drain. They'd been captured and eaten, just like the Shadow's hunting ground in the mountains. The corpses had been stacked together forming a mound of decay, like a tribute. Or an altar.

"They're here," I whispered. "They're in the tunnels."

"Is this what I think it is?" asked Josh, terror in his voice. "In the complex, just after you stopped our execution, I saw what that *thing* did to a human body. These bodies look the same."

Noah nodded slowly. "We're in a Shadow hunting ground. I've never seen them outside of the mountains before. Nobody has, not even the Kindred. They've been out of the cities for centuries. But this means the Shadows have been lurking under the city, feeding, waiting. Hud was right. They're here, and that is completely unheard of in all the Kindred's written history."

We could either move forward or back. Back lay the Kindred, and forward lay the Shadows. There was no way out. I shivered. "Let's keep our mouths shut and our eyes open. I don't want to come up against a Shadow down here. There's literally nowhere we can hide."

There was a rasping, throaty growl from farther up the tunnel.

Josh pointed the torch ahead, and two red eyes stared back.

SEVENTEEN

The thing was crouched on two legs over the body of a cat. The dead tabby had been desiccated by the Shadow already, but this creature was ripping pieces out and shoving them in its mouth, eating the leftover parts. It looked up at us again, and growled, a husky, guttural sound that set my teeth on edge. It was hairy, with long strands drooping from its head and face. The body was covered in a sort of dark red fur. It bared its teeth, which gleamed white.

"What *is* that thing?" Noah whispered.

"It looks almost human, but furry, like a really hairy man." Josh replied, backing carefully away but keeping the torch trained on it. The thing hadn't made a move for us, but it might. It picked the entire cat up and took a bite out of its side, before growling at us again, standing upright, and sprinting away, further into the tunnel. Josh kept his torch pointed firmly ahead of us, but it was gone. Deep in the darkness, it growled again, but further off this time.

"What the actual freaking hell," said Noah.

"You've never seen this before?" I asked. As our resident ex-Kindred, if Noah didn't know, no-one would.

"Never. It wasn't a Shadow, and I haven't read of anything like this in Kindred records."

Josh shook his head slowly. "A new creep to add to the freak-show. Great."

I took a step into the darkness, approaching the corpse pile. "Hopefully it was the only one. Maybe it's got nothing to do with the Kindred. Maybe it's one of the mole people or something."

"The what-now?" asked Josh.

My voice echoed off the tunnel, despite my attempt to keep it quiet. "The mole people. You know, that urban legend about the people who live in the subway? They've adapted to the low-light conditions and spend their lives down here. At least that's the story. I can't believe you've never heard of them."

"Yeah, no," Josh said. "That sounds ridiculous. Although, six months ago I would have said scary shadow creatures and secret mind-powers were ridiculous too."

Noah glanced around the cavernous roof. "I don't think it was a mole person. It barely looked human at all."

"Either way," I tried to sound brave, "we need to get moving. If we move fast, hopefully we can reach an exit before we meet that thing again. Or a Shadow. We're still in its hunting ground, remember?"

"You're right," Noah said. "Let's go."

Josh sighed, but nodded, and set off down the tunnel again, albeit a lot slower. He stayed close to us now, not getting too far ahead.

We walked for almost an hour. Josh's phone said it was nearly midnight. If Dad came home from work and found me gone and Rachel there with the surveillance equipment... Well, hopefully she'd work something out, otherwise I was dead. Of course, if we ran into a Shadow down here, I was dead anyway. One problem at a time.

The worst part was, if I died down here, Skye would never know what happened to me. Even though she was bonding with Dad now, she still needed me. If nothing else, I alone knew what she'd really been through. She was tough, that girl, keeping the secret. I'd have cracked a long time ago if I was her age.

In the hours after Mum died, she'd been so quiet, so strong. She had probably been in shock, but after the Unseen rescued us we sat together in the rear of the semi-trailer and cried for hours. Thinking back, I wasn't just crying because of mum and everything we'd been through. I was crying because of what Skye had lost. Her childhood. Her innocence. She'd been hurting from when Dad left, but that was different than understanding just how broken the world really was. Just how dark it could be. Kids see the world the way it should be, full of life and joy and purity, but life and brokenness get in the way and steal the magic. Everyone grows up when they see the world for what it really is. For some, that coming of age happens far too early.

I understood why parents sheltered their children. When I was fourteen, we used to laugh because one of the girls in our school year wasn't allowed to watch movies with violence or swearing. But now, in a way, I envied her and her innocence. What I wouldn't give to forget some of the things I'd seen, go back in time and forget about the creature in my room, and the way Skye's voice sounded when the Shadow talked through her. In a way, she still carried that Shadow with her. Not literally, but in her mind, her heart. There was always a shadow with her now.

I absently reached for the cold spot on my stomach. It was always with me, too. A constant reminder of what I could become, what I'd seen myself turn into.

The worst part was, a little part of me wanted to let it out, to let go and let the darkest parts of myself take hold.

Truth is freedom.

Josh stopped for a moment, and I almost ran into him.

I began to apologise. "Sorry, I was just—"

He held his hand up to signal silence.

Noah froze too.

Moving slowly, Josh pointed forwards, but kept the torch low.

A snuffling sound came from the black void ahead. There was something there.

Slowly, Josh raised the torch until it met the creature. It was hunched over something, eating once again, although what it ate was difficult to discern.

"Guys," I said, "look at its feet."

Josh tilted the torch down a bit more. It was wearing white joggers. Noah swore.

My palms were damp. "It's human. That's not red fur, it's clothing. Old, ripped clothing. And I think its red from…"

"Blood," finished Josh.

It growled again, and leaped up from its meal, standing fully upright. It was definitely human, but not quite right, like it had been underground too long. It ran for us, screeching, and we stumbled back in the darkness.

Josh tripped over the track sleepers and the torch hit the ground, lighting up the tracks but leaving the tunnel dark.

The thing smacked into me, hair dragging across my face, hands grasping, scraping, scratching. Its nails were long, and the fingers were deeply calloused. It smelled of sweat and death, and I choked from the stench more than its hands, which closed around my throat. For a moment, it raised its head, baring its teeth, and I saw its eyes glowing in the torchlight. There was no iris in each eye, just black pupils in white space. Whatever this thing was, the humanity had been drained from it a long time ago.

The creature thrust its mouth towards me, teeth aiming for my neck.

I raised my bandaged arm and it bit down on the cloth. Pain shot through me, and I screamed. I tried to tune to the creature, but the boys' eyes must have been on us, and I got nothing but static. The creature still had my arm in its teeth, so I brought my other hand up to its face, jamming my finger in its left eye.

It screeched, let go of my arm, then went limp and fell on top of me, smoke curling from its head.

I shoved its body off and lay still for a moment, panting.

Noah stood over us with a piece of rail track. One end glowed red hot, and he'd taken his shirt off to wrap it around the other end like an oven mitt.

"Sorry," he said. "Took a while to melt the track and get this bit out. Plus, the metal's still really hot."

So are you, I thought, taking in the view. I swallowed and looked back up at his eyes.

"I'm going to hold on to this," he said, brandishing the sleeper. "It could be useful." Noah held out his hand, and I grabbed it with my left arm. My right one had started to bleed through the bandages again.

"Are you okay?" Noah nodded at my wound.

"I'll be fine." It was throbbing, but I could handle it.

Josh pulled himself upright on the other track, and picked up the torch, shining it my way. "My shoe got stuck in the sleepers. Sorry, Ari." He turned to Noah. "Dude, are you allergic to shirts or something?"

"Leave him alone," I snapped at Josh. "He just saved my life."

Josh looked hurt, but I didn't care right now. I didn't have time for his jealousy.

Noah kicked the body of the thing that had attacked me. "It's definitely human," he said. "But twisted. Like it's missing something. On the bright side, it's not breathing."

Blood pooled from an open space where its skull should have been.

"That was one heck of a swing," I said to Noah.

I should have felt awful that we'd killed someone, even a deranged monster. I didn't, though. I felt nothing but relief. That scared me.

Noah picked up Josh's torch and bent down to inspect the body. Now that it was closer, the details were more apparent. Under all the hair he was probably twenty, twenty-five at most. His shirt was torn to shreds, and the blood on him had caked it into strips. None of the blood seemed to be his own though; he was unharmed, aside from the giant hole Noah had made in his head.

Using the metal railway bar, Noah rolled the body over, so it was facing down. "Guys, look at this," he said. Noah lifted the torn strips of shirt with the metal bar. My mouth dropped open. The man's back was covered in burn marks, old scar tissue in patches.

"I know these marks. These are flare marks," he said.

"Really?" said Josh. "He could have been in a fire or something. How can you tell they're flares?"

Noah turned around to show us his back. It was covered in the same radial marks, scorch lines coming from a central point. "Got these that night in the Boulders," he said.

I grimaced. That would have hurt.

Noah turned to face us again. "My point is this guy has seen some action. Look," he pointed, "some of these are red. These are newer. No way he's a civilian either; if the Kindred try to take someone out, they finish the job straight away. This guy has seen battle. Several, actually. That means he's either Unseen, or Kindred. Hopefully Kindred."

"What on earth made him this way?" I said.

Noah stepped back from the body. "Don't know, but I'd prefer not to find out."

There was another growl from behind us in the tunnel.

And a second.

And a third.

Noah turned and shone the torch the way we'd come. Eight red eyes stared back. There were four more creatures down here with us.

EIGHTEEN

The four creatures glared at us. Their hands dripped red, as if they'd just finished digging through a body.

The largest one snarled. He had bushy, dark hair and an open gash on his cheek. It looked like he was wearing the tattered remains of a business suit. He took one step forward, then two, advancing on us.

Noah held up his track piece, and the big one jumped back a touch.

"We're outnumbered," Noah said, "but only by one. They're not sure they can take us. Let's try to scare them off. Make heaps of noise and look threatening."

I roared, holding my arms above my head, trying to look as big as possible.

Josh yelled too, raising his fists and staring straight at the biggest one.

But, instead of moving away, all three began screeching at us and swinging their arms menacingly.

"They don't seem scared," said Josh.

And he was right. They bared their teeth, saliva dripping from their lips.

"Yeah, we're screwed," Josh murmured.

"New plan," whispered Noah. "On the count of three, run."

The creatures charged.

"Three! Run!" yelled Noah.

I turned and sprinted deeper into the tunnel, side-by-side with the boys. We were so far underground, there was a real danger of us getting lost if we didn't pay attention to the turns. A fork branched ahead, and we took the right one. The creatures weren't as fast as they looked, and we beat them around the corner, meaning they wouldn't see us for a few seconds. On the left was a small side tunnel, a dead-end siding with debris scattered through it. A single abandoned coal carriage sat on the tracks.

"Up there," said Noah. "When you get in, torch off."

Josh clambered up the ladder, and I followed him in, dropping down into the carriage. My feet kicked up coal dust, which threatened to send me into a coughing fit, but I held it in, switching off my torch and scurrying up the back next to Josh.

Noah dropped in too, wheezing from the run and the dust in the air.

"Quiet!" hissed Josh, and Noah muffled his breathing with his sleeve.

The tunnel was totally black without our torches on, but my ears caught every sound. I heard the gravel scattering as the creatures ran past, their howls as they realised we'd escaped, the screeching fight that ensued between them, probably over whose fault it was they'd lost us—if they were even capable of that kind of thought.

Several minutes passed, and there was only silence.

"What are those things?" I whispered to the others when I felt safe enough to do so.

"I don't know." Noah squeezed my hand, and I became aware that I was holding both their hands. Noah and Josh were pressed up on either side of me in the back of the train carriage. The irony was absurd.

"They're definitely human. The girl was wearing a dress," Josh said.

"One was a girl?" I asked.

"Yeah," Josh sighed, "although she was pretty hairy. Not that I'm judging," he said with a hint of a smile in his voice.

"They were all really hairy," Noah pointed out. "Strangely so."

"Plus, they eat dead things," I said, feeling sick. "From the look in their eyes, maybe live things too."

"I got the vibe that we were on the menu," Noah added. "That first one bit you."

"Yeah," I said, rubbing my arm. "Although, I don't think it was out of hunger. More like…" I shuddered. "Desire."

"That's creepy," Josh said quietly. "What do you make of their eyes?"

"It's like their pupils are dilated way more than is possible. Their whole irises were gone."

Josh spoke slowly. "I was thinking about that. You know how some creatures are nocturnal, right? They have really big pupils to help them see in the dark. Their other senses are heightened, too."

"Yes?" Noah said.

The realisation dawned on me, and my heart beat faster.

"Well," said Josh, measuring each word. "It's just with pupils like that, those things can definitely see in the dark."

A warm puff of air blew against my cheek.

No.

Oh no.

Josh fumbled for the torch in the dark and switched it on.

A bushy face sat inches from my own, grinning, black eyes staring into mine. The other three were on either side. Two in front of Noah, the girl in front of Josh.

The bushy one pounced, pinning my arms to the carriage wall, his spit spraying across my face.

I kneed him in the stomach, but it had no effect.

Noah swore as the two other males held him down, stopping him from using his weapon.

The girl clawed at Josh, ripping at his shirt, cutting gashes across his chest.

He punched her across the face, but she laughed hysterically, bending down and licking his cheek instead.

All three of us were trapped. If we didn't break free, we were all dead. The bushy one lowered his face to mine, beard scratching against my lips.

"Mine," he hissed.

"No chance, buddy," I spat back. "Boys, close your eyes. Now."

I knew they did, because the static I'd been feeling disappeared. No-one was looking at the roof. I tuned into it, raising the resonance to breaking point. An ear-splitting crack ripped through the tunnel, and chunks of rock fell from the ceiling. One hit the girl on Josh, and she fell to the floor, limp. Josh dove on the bushy man, shoving him off me and slamming him unconscious on a metal brace. The two others looked at us, knowing they were outnumbered, and shrieked, leaping from Noah and clambering out of the carriage, sprinting down the tunnel to who knows where.

Noah staggered to his feet. "Thanks," he said to me. "And thanks Josh."

"Don't thank me yet," Josh replied, rubbing his chest and wincing. "We're not exactly home free."

"Josh, you're bleeding badly," I said, surveying the jagged wounds on his chest.

He put on a British accent. "Only a flesh wound," he said pompously, smiling more with relief than humour.

"We need to get moving," Noah said. "They might be back." He bent down and grabbed the torch, holding it in his left hand with the steel bar in his right.

Climbing out of the carriage, we dropped to the gravel and moved slowly to the end of the siding.

"We came from the right," I offered, and turned that way. Cautiously, we walked to the intersection, which branched in four directions.

"I thought this was only a fork," Noah said. "We must have missed the other turn when we ran. Which way did we come from?"

I shook my head. "I have no idea."

"Great," said Noah. "Well, how long can this tunnel be anyway?"

"Rachel said the tunnels run right across the city," said Josh. "So, pretty long."

"Let's just pick one," I said. "We can backtrack later if we need to. So, left, or right?"

Noah shone the torch to the left tunnel. "Left looks familiar."

"What about the right?"

He moved the light to the right-hand tunnel, revealing ten of the creatures staring at us, led by the two males from before.

"Let's not take the right," Josh squeaked out.

"Left it is!" Noah yelled.

We sprinted down the left tunnel, pursued by the snarling pack. They were faster now, perhaps buoyed by their numbers.

"There's no way we can outrun them," I yelled.

"Up ahead, that door," panted Noah.

A metal access door hung open a few steps ahead. Josh reached it first, kicking it fully open. Noah and I dove inside, and Josh slammed it shut behind us, sliding a huge metal bolt across to lock it. The creatures slammed into it from the other side, but it would hold for now. They scratched at the door, their screams passing through the steel as they vented their anger.

I turned, and saw Josh and Noah staring ahead into the darkness.

The spot on my stomach burned cold. This place was evil, and we had no way out.

NINETEEN

"This chamber is massive," said Josh, and his voice echoed through the space. Noah pointed the torch towards the roof, but the light didn't reach it. He whistled slowly. "That's got to be at least six storeys high. What is this place?"

A light flickered in the distance, and I stared for a moment until I worked out it was Noah's torch reflecting off water.

"I can't see a way out," I said. "Guys, close your eyes for a minute. I want to try something."

They did, and I focussed on a space in the air near the roof. If I could flare, I could light up the area for a moment, get a good look at the space and find a quick way out.

The world went still as I tuned into the resonant frequency of the air. I hadn't done this since that night in the Chapel, and even then, it hadn't been on purpose.

The air in here was still and old. Nothing had come through here for a long time. The frequency rang for a moment, and I raised it rapidly to hit the burn point. The air sparked, then went dark. I was tired, which wasn't helping.

Tuning into the air once more, I raised the frequency again. This time, a small flare built in the middle of the space. It wasn't bright, but the flickering light was more than enough for me to make things out.

The light warmed the rough-hewn rock roof and bounced around the edges. We were in a cavern at least as big as a football field. It had been cut somehow, shaped from the rock and supported by huge brick pillars that ran in rows across the space. To my right, a sign read "City Exchange." At one point, this place must have been designated as a new subway interchange but was never completed. The floor was covered in water that shimmered orange from the flare-light. So much open space, so deep underground, had flooded from years of rain from the city streets above. At the opposite end from us was another train tunnel. Hopefully, it led somewhere useful.

I lost focus, and the flare disappeared.

The boys opened their eyes, and I explained what I'd seen.

"Want me to try as well?" Noah offered.

"No point using up your energy too. That flare smashed me, and we need at least one of us feeling fresh if we encounter any more of those *things*." I took a step forward, and my shoe sunk into the water. "If we follow the line of brick pillars to my left, it'll lead us straight to the tunnel mouth and we can get out of here."

I took another step, and the water rose to my ankles. The boys followed.

Josh grimaced as his feet hit the water. "Far out. This is cold. I wonder how deep it gets in the middle."

"If it gets too deep, we can swim across," said Noah. "The torch is waterproof, so we can always use it underwater if we need to."

"Swimming underground in a creepy lake. Sounds good." Josh groaned.

"You can always go back and make friends with the angry blood creatures," I snapped. Two more steps and the water was up to my knees. It sloshed against my legs as I walked and made movement difficult. Noah's torch lit up the lake in front of us, and I could just see the bottom of the cavern through the water. It was surprisingly clear, although my feet were stirring up debris around me and making the bottom cloudy.

Now that we were closer to the brick pillars, I could tell they were really old. The bricks were rough at the edges like they were handmade. This was probably an ambitious project for its day, a bunch of politicians and engineers getting together and planning for the future growth of the city. It was sad, thinking that their dream had never been realised; just turned into a rotting underground water-table that was home to corpse-eating madmen. I stopped and looked around. Hopefully there weren't any of those things in here with us.

The boys stopped too, water splashing in ripples around them.

"Everything okay?" whispered Noah.

"Yeah," I shrugged, "just a bit paranoid."

"Aren't we all," Josh said, and started trudging through the water again.

I felt awful dragging him into all this. If I'd never been involved in the Kindred conspiracy, Josh would be back at home, living a normal life, with all his fingers still intact. Instead, he was stuck down here in this cave with me, and he didn't even have powers to defend himself. Was it his feelings for me that had driven him to save us at the dockyards? It was my fault he was here, and I'd broken his heart only hours ago.

Josh caught me looking at him, and I shifted my eyes towards the edges of the cavern. I couldn't see where water met the wall. Turning in a slow circle, I couldn't make out the way we'd come, either. The boys and I were likely in the middle of the space now, but there was no way to know for sure as the little circle of light from our torch didn't reach beyond the next brick column. We could have been drifting in the ocean for all I knew, except that the freezing waterline barely reached my waist.

Movement was slow, now. Wading through the water was hard going, like I was moving through honey.

"I think we're about halfway," said Noah.

"Yeah," said Josh. "Oh man, I just realised we're going to be wandering for ages in wet pants. Chafing is going to be an issue."

"We were just chased by a pack of murderous man-creatures," I pointed out, "but sure, chafing is our biggest problem."

Josh laughed at himself. "Good point." He looked back for a moment and stopped dead in the water.

"What?" I asked.

"Did you hear that?" His eyes darted around.

I frowned. "No."

"I could have sworn there was—there!" Josh pointed behind us.

Noah shone the torch that way.

And I saw it—a sliver of movement, a dark shape under the water.

I grabbed Josh's arm. "Run. Now."

Running was even harder than walking, and water splashed around the three of us like the wake behind a boat. Noah pointed the torch back once more, and I turned my head to follow it. Another flash of black under the surface. There was something in the lake with us, and it was fast. It speared left and right through the water, zigzagging rather than coming at us directly. Then, it stopped, and rose from the surface like a black hole. No water dripped from it, but the shape stood still, swirling tendrils sucking up the light from Noah's torch. I stopped running as fear took hold.

A Shadow. It was here, and it was hunting us.

Noah swore. "Get out of the water! Get to the tunnel now!"

I didn't bother looking back, not any more. None of us did. The torch flickered across the surface of the water as we ran, illuminating the bottom of the lake in bursts. The Shadow circled us, appearing and disappearing, like it was toying with us, or rounding us up, shifting through the water like a shark. I could see the edge of the lake now, the tunnel entrance and possible freedom, but the Shadow was here already. There was no way we would make it to the edge before it killed us. It surrounded us, swirling and spiralling, like it was playing with us, building the anticipation before it fed.

"We're not going to make it," yelled Noah between breaths. "It's too fast!"

"Can't you flare it or something?" shouted Josh from two steps ahead. "Burn the damn thing!"

"They feed on flare energy," Noah panted. "There's nothing I can do."

I was making a low moaning sound, and I couldn't stop. I dropped down into the water to see if swimming was faster. It wasn't, and my face was closer to the water. Closer to the dark flashes spinning around us.

I stood back up and ran. We were almost to the edge. If we could just make it out of the water maybe we'd have a shot at survival. The water grew shallower, and my legs picked up speed. It was at my knees, then my ankles, and I ran up onto dry ground, lake water sloshing from my shoes. Noah was next to me, and I turned to make sure Josh had made it. I stopped running.

Josh stood behind us in the lake, water up to his waist in the deeper section. He'd stopped.

"Josh! What are you doing? Run!"

He shook his head. "We can't outrun this. I'm going to slow it down. Remember the Apex? They can't resist a feed. I can buy you guys a few seconds. Now run!"

Noah shone the torch at Josh. The darkness spiralled around him, a black tornado in the water. He raised his hand to block out the torch glare, squinting at me. He was only twenty feet away, but it might as well have been a chasm between us.

"Josh—" my voice cracked. "Don't do this."

"Don't waste this, you idiot!" he yelled. His hands were shaking. "Run, Ari."

He paused and took a deep breath. "I love you."

Josh's eyes went wide, and he was sucked, screaming, under the water.

TWENTY

I froze, watching the ripples grow from the place Josh had been. My legs tensed to run back into the water, but Noah grabbed my hand.

"We need to go."

"But, Josh."

"I'm sorry, he's dead, Ari. He's only bought us a couple of seconds. Don't waste it."

Shaking Noah's arm off, I glared at him. "I'm not leaving." The ripples kept circling out in the water, spreading until they reached the shore. Noah shone the torch directly at the spot Josh had disappeared, but there was no movement. Nothing.

A dark tendril reached out from the centre of the ripples. The Shadow was almost finished feeding.

"Ari..." Noah's voice was tense.

I blinked back tears. "I know. I know."

With no way to stop the Shadow, our only way out was to run. I turned and followed Noah into the tunnel. Running was hard now, not just because I was exhausted but because I was in shock. My hands were cold and sweaty, and I wanted to lie down and stop running, to let the Shadow take me, let this whole awful war be over.

But still I ran.

In the dark, behind us, screeches and splashes echoed through the tunnel, the screams of the creatures who had broken down the door and were coming across the underground lake. I was shaking now, not only from the loss but from what they could do to me, to us. Just ahead, emerging from the dark, were graffiti-stained walls lit by our torchlight, walls that had remained hidden for decades under the city. Some things should remain undiscovered. If I'd never found out about this war, Josh would still be alive. I let out a sob, trying to focus on the gravel crushing under my feet.

And ran on.

Maybe the Shadow would consume the creatures first, maybe it would stop and take them, give us more time to escape. Ahead was another pile of animal bodies. These were deeper in the rail network, but they'd been ripped apart, pieces scattered across the tunnel. The creatures had gotten to them and torn them to shreds, like they'd do to us if they caught us. Maybe they'd done that to Josh's body in the lake.

I realised I was swearing, the same word over and over again forcing its way out through tear-choked breaths.

Next to me, Noah carried the torch in one hand, and his metal bar in the other. His face was set, emotionless. Determined. I hated him for that. I hated him for surviving, for making me leave, for not saving Josh, for not falling apart like I was. It should have been him instead of Josh. He'd chosen to be part of this war, to bring me into it, to fight this stupid fight. He should be dead, not Josh. Not my friend, who'd saved us twice tonight even though he'd never wanted any of this in his life.

We reached an intersection and the gravel was interrupted by a train line. We were back into the newer section of the tracks, the industrial path that was closed but at least closer to civilisation.

I hated myself, too. I hated myself for surviving, for being alive when so many others had died. I hated that Josh had found me worth dying for. I'd never asked for that. I'd never wanted it.

Behind me in the dark, a scream. An awful, guttural scream. Noah spun the torch around and caught the two eyes of a creature glowing red in the torchlight. It was the female and she stopped for a moment, snarling through bloodied teeth. Noah raised the metal bar and readied himself to strike. Behind her, black tendrils emerged from the darkness of the tunnel, sucking up the torchlight, wrapping around her like an octopus. She snarled again, then the Shadow lifted her in the air, and she whimpered. Her skin drew tight, lifeless, grey, and then she stopped moving. I turned to run.

"Ari, look." Noah pointed at the Shadow.

It swirled, almost like a whirlpool, spiralling slowly, a black hole feeding on itself. The tendrils lost their smoke, becoming more solid, and some of them fused together to create larger, stronger, almost snakelike limbs. A melted face pushed out from inside the largest limb, dripping black smoke which gathered in rippling pools on the floor.

"What the hell is going on?" I said.

"It's changing."

"Into what?"

Noah shook his head. "Nothing good."

We ran, but the Shadow ignored us, too busy with its abhorrent metamorphosis.

Something about its limbs, the scaly texture, it reminded me of the very first Shadow I'd encountered, the one on my bedroom roof. Not all Shadows were the same, it seemed, and this one felt stronger. My stomach was ice cold, but I ignored it. Right now I had to get out of here. Right now, we had to survive.

There were no more screams behind us, which probably meant all the creatures were dead. Only one thing chasing us now, and it seemed distracted by whatever it was changing into.

This whole night had been insane. First Eden, then Wheeler and these creatures and the Shadows. It was like the whole city had turned on me, on us, like Coleton itself wanted us dead. There were Shadows in the sky and Shadows underground. They had the place surrounded, infesting the water, the air, like a virus spread across the whole damn city.

Maybe Coleton would become the city from my vision, the city caked in blood and smoke. The place where I would change into my own worst nightmare.

We came to another intersection, and this one was lit with a sickly green signal light. We were back on the main branch line. "Here," said Noah, lifting the torch to shine on a stencilled indicator sign to our left. The word CITY was sprayed on it in white paint, with an arrow and the number three.

"City Station's not far. Just a little further. We'll be out of here in no time."

We kept jogging, staying to the left in the widest gap between the track and the tunnel wall. Every so often, there was a maintenance door cut into the edge of the tunnel, which left a little more space for us to shelter if a train came past. This early in the morning, it wasn't likely, but we could reach an access door in a hurry if one came barrelling through.

I realised I hadn't thought about Josh since we'd seen the Shadow take the creature. My stomach turned. I'd already forgotten him, and it had only been an hour, maybe less. I had to keep thinking about him, had to keep him in my memory.

The tracks rumbled. A train was coming. The nearest access door was only a few steps away. It was small, but Noah and I both managed to squeeze into the opening. Crouched inside, it was hard to breathe.

I felt sick, suddenly, and leaned over to throw up. Nothing came out, but my stomach clenched, and clenched again. Bile burned the back of my throat. My belly was empty, but my mind was determined to bring something up, as if vomiting would expel the nightmare I'd just lived through. My face dripped with sweat, and I sat, panting, wiping water from my eyes. No train came, and the rumbling faded. It must have taken a different track.

I stood, slowly. "Time to go," I said to Noah.

Noah didn't move. He was holding his legs tight, staring at a spot just above his knees. Both his hands were shaking.

"Noah," I said firmly. "Time to go."

He broke his gaze from the distance and looked slowly up at me. "Yes," he said quietly. "Sorry. I'm coming." He looked back at his knees.

"Noah!" I yelled, grabbing his arm and pulling him upright. Now that the immediate danger had passed, and the adrenaline was fading, he was starting to feel everything. I didn't hate him anymore. I wanted to hold him, so we could fall apart together. But that would have to wait.

We reached City Station a few minutes later and climbed carefully up onto the platform. A smarmy businessman in a plaid suit sat on a bench, smirking at the sight of two sweaty teenagers emerging from the subway tunnel. He probably thought we were up to something dirty. Let him. I didn't care anymore. I didn't care about anything.

Staggering slowly up the subway stairs, we made it to the station entrance. The city was dead quiet, and the sun was just beginning to wash purple light into the street. With Noah at my side, I turned and began the slow trudge to Dad's apartment.

Three blocks down a big black van pulled up beside us. My brain flooded with adrenaline again. The Kindred had found us. I readied myself to fight.

The window rolled down.

"Get in!" said Rachel. "No trace of Hud, but I saw you two on the subway camera. I've been checking all of them for hours since Josh didn't take a GPS. Hopefully the Kindred didn't see you on the cameras too."

She paused.

"Where *is* Josh?"

I didn't answer and climbed slowly into the back seat of the van.

TWENTY-ONE

Bleary-eyed, I woke to Skye prodding me awake. I rolled over to face the wall.

"Ari, you've been asleep the whole day."

"What time is it?" I grunted through my parched throat.

"Afternoon. I just got home from school. Dad took me. He said you had to work an overnight shift or something."

I sat up. "Did he say anything else?"

"Only that your friend Rachel seemed nice. He met her last night when he came home; she said you asked her to look after me."

The night came hazily back. The chase, the running, Josh... And me creeping quietly back inside first thing in the morning, as the sun blared onto the apartment wall.

I sat slowly up, and Skye gasped. "Ari, you're bleeding!"

My bedsheet was coated in blood from my arm, and my shirt was crusted and red, not only from my own wound but from the creature who'd attacked me in the tunnel. I ran my hand over the bandages and winced. It hurt, but the bleeding had stopped for now.

"I'm okay. It's mostly—it's not mine."

Skye wouldn't come close to me, and I didn't blame her. I looked awful. She frowned. "You were on a mission, weren't you?"

I nodded.

"What happened?"

I had to tell her. Not everything, not about the creatures or Wheeler or any of the awful details. She had enough nightmares as it was. But I had to tell her.

"Skye, you need to know something."

She raised one eyebrow.

"Thing is, I got into a bit of trouble last night."

"No kidding."

"Skye, please," I snapped. "Josh came down to help us, and he rescued me, and Noah. Twice, actually."

"Is he okay?"

I couldn't meet her eyes. "No. He's—"

"He's what?"

"He died saving me."

Josh had always been the big brother Skye had never had. Her mouth quivered, and she ran to her room, sobbing. This was her second loss in six months. Our second loss.

I had no energy to follow her.

My mind was empty. So was my heart. Nothing mattered now, not anymore. This was worse than when Noah had died, well, when I thought he had. I'd known Josh for so long. We'd survived Ettney together, and he was the only person I could talk to who was outside of all this. He knew of it, but he wasn't *part* of it, not really. At least, until last night.

I shut my eyes and saw him disappear again, mouth open in a scream. I couldn't hear the scream in my head, so the memory played silently in my mind. Over, and over, and over. Maybe I could have saved him. Maybe, if I'd been strong enough, or brave enough.

But I wasn't, and now he was dead. I wasn't a soldier, not really. No, Ari Carpenter was a helpless little girl playing with forces bigger than she could possibly understand.

There was a knock at the door. From my room, I heard Skye run to the door. "Josh?"

My heart jumped for a moment.

The door creaked open. "Oh," she said. "It's you." Her feet slapped on the hallway tiles as she walked sadly back to her room.

"Can I come in?" said Noah from outside my door. I grunted yes, and he sat next to me on the bed.

"Ari, I—"

"Don't." I shifted away from him. I didn't want to be near him right now. It reminded me of everything I'd done. Of the guilt. I'd broken Josh's heart, and then he'd died for me. Maybe if I hadn't pushed him away, he'd still be alive. Maybe if I'd felt differently, lied even. Looking at Noah, I felt nothing but shame.

"Ari, please, let me talk to you."

I couldn't look at him, staring instead at a spot on the carpet, urine-stained by Stewie when he was adjusting to being an inside dog.

"I wanted to say sorry that I fell apart last night," Noah said. "It all just got to me. I couldn't pull it together, and I should have." He reached out and put his hand on mine. "And I'm sorry about Josh."

I glared at him. "No, you're not." Snatching my hand away, I shifted further away from Noah, out of arm's reach.

"What do you mean?"

"I mean you're not sorry! You wanted me to hurt him. You forced me to tell him how I felt, and now he's dead and he died knowing I didn't love him. I can never take that back. I can't take back the look in his eyes out there on the couch. I can't take back the pain in his voice. I can't take back—"

My voice crumbled, and I sat in silence. Noah did too, until his phone buzzed. He checked it, and then put it back in his pocket. He pulled out a different phone and handed it to me.

"New phones from Rachel. She figured ours were gone last night when Wheeler grabbed us. She dropped them off this morning. Anyway, she says Elements Gallery has been empty since yesterday, but she has a lead that might take us to Wheeler, and maybe even to where they're holding Hud. At the least, it might tell us more about what Wheeler is planning."

I flopped back onto my bed, feeling the cool of the sheets wrap around my arms. "Fine, you go."

Noah stood. "She wants both of us."

"Screw Rachel."

"You don't mean that."

"I've never meant anything more. I'm done with this. With all of this. I'm done with this war, and the death, and the fear, and running for my life, and losing the people I care about. I'm out. You go fight, but I'm officially finished. I quit."

"Ari—"

"Get out!" I screamed, throwing my pillow at Noah. I swore at him, and ranted, and screamed again, and eventually he left.

I stayed on my bed until the afternoon sun disappeared behind the cityscape, fading all the colours into a purply-grey. Lights started to flick on around the city, making patterns on my roof from the streets down below. My window was open, and through it drifted snatches of car horns, people laughing, yelling, and music from the café on the ground floor of our building. Everything was still so normal. The whole city was carrying on like Josh hadn't died last night. They didn't care. Of course they didn't. Ettney would care more. Josh's parents would, although the Unseen would create a cover story to keep things quiet. His parents would never know the truth. They'd never know he died a hero.

I sat up, and suddenly felt the cold air drifting through the window. Wrapping my doona around my shoulders, I shuffled to the glass door that led from my bedroom out onto the balcony.

On impulse, I opened it and stepped out. From our apartment on the tenth floor I could see all the way to the skyscrapers that made up the city centre. Our suburb was mostly apartment blocks and small office buildings, but it was still buzzing this time of night. Out there, in the glowing criss-crossed streets, Dad would be making his way home from work. Unless he was working late, in which case he was in the second-biggest skyscraper, a huge black monolith covered in glass, checkered with windows lit up by whoever was still inside.

The sky was a clear, deep purple that faded slightly at the horizon. There were no dark Shadows to mark it. No inky shapes swimming though the dusk.

Maybe Hud was wrong. Hud—who was out there somewhere at the mercy of Wheeler. I had a pang of guilt. He was missing, and here I was sitting the whole thing out.

Nope. Not my problem. I'd probably do more harm than good anyway. The Unseen could handle it. Hopefully, Hud would be alright.

There was a cough from behind me, and I twisted around.

"You going back out there?" Skye asked. She had a blanket wrapped around her too, a garish pink thing with unicorns all over it.

I shook my head. "No. I'm done fighting this war. I quit."

She frowned. "You're not going to pay them back? Hurt whoever hurt Josh?"

I turned to face the skyline. "I'm finished. I can't do it anymore. I can't fight anymore. I'm tired."

"I'm tired too, Ari." She moved up next to me on the balcony. "I'm tired of having nightmares. I'm tired of people dying."

Skye shivered a bit in the evening air. I put my arm around her and drew her close.

She sighed. "The bad guys don't get tired though, do they?"

"I don't know. Why?"

"Because they won't stop. They love doing bad things. I think maybe we're tired because we're the good guys. The good guys are supposed to get tired 'cause it's easier to do the wrong thing than the right thing. So, if we're tired, it's 'cause we're on the right side."

Down below, across the road in the bar, someone laughed hysterically and a glass smashed. They were starting early tonight. It was tempting, that life. To forget about the war, about good and evil and making a difference and instead just party and dance and drink the world away. But Skye was right. Checking out wasn't the answer. That would make me part of the problem, and if I just stood by and let the Shadows win, I might as well be on their side.

"If I'm not against them, I'm for them," I said quietly into the night.

"What?" said Skye.

"Just something I heard once. You're right, though. Good guys are supposed to get tired. The easy thing and the right thing are almost never the same."

Skye smiled.

"Also, when did you get so wise?"

Shrugging, she wandered back inside. I followed her and picked up the new phone Rachel had given me. There were eighteen missed calls and twelve voicemails, but they'd just be Rachel trying to get me to come back. Thankfully she'd programmed her and Noah's new numbers in already. I opened a new message and sent it off.

I'm in and I'm coming. Where do we meet?

TWENTY-TWO

Dad got home late, so it was past ten before I was able to sneak out. I met Rachel at the Unseen bunker. Noah was already there putting new backpacks together to replace the gear we'd lost the night before. I was wide awake. I'd become practically nocturnal with all these late-night missions. As I arrived, Rachel was sitting at the computer desk, typing frantically. She turned to me.

"Last night was a disaster in more ways than one, but we might have gotten a lead."

Noah nudged her.

"Sorry about Josh, too," Rachel said. She tried to sound tough, but she did seem sad. She'd liked him, after all.

I swallowed and motioned for her to continue.

"Noah fully briefed me on last night. It got me thinking. They have to be connected—Wheeler, and the human-creatures you encountered. That can't be a coincidence. Thing is, I've never heard of anything like that before. I reached out to our network, and nobody knows what they are. The Unseen heads are so concerned that they're sending a team to Coleton as backup. They're flying in from Korea, so they'll be here tomorrow. In the meantime, we have our orders."

"We're rescuing Hud?" I asked.

"Not exactly. We don't have any idea where they've taken him. Our best chance at getting him back is finding out what Wheeler's up to."

Rachel turned and brought up a screen with data points and numbers.

"The intelligence team started working on our problem and came up with something weird. In the last eight months, there's been a steady increase of violent crime in Coleton. Violence where there was no prior history to speak of, random men and women lashing out at the people around them like they've totally lost control. More than once, there's been *eating* involved."

I sat down on the roller chair next to her. "I'm sorry, what?"

"Eating. As in people have been eaten. By other people."

I felt sick. "Why hasn't this been on the news?"

"That's why it's probably Kindred related. Nothing they love more than a good cover-up. Remember, they have key players in the police, media, even Government House. It doesn't take much to get the truth shut down."

Noah stepped in. "The things we ran into last night were crazy. Really messed up. But one of them tried to bite you, remember?"

Shuddering, I swung slowly back and forth in my chair. "I can still smell its breath."

"That's why I think there's a connection between the crime spike and your tunnel zombies."

I shook my head. "They're not zombies." I laughed quietly. "There's a sentence I never thought I'd say. But they're smart. Even though their eyes were freaky as hell, there was intelligence behind them. It's like they're human, but—you know—crazy, deformed, cannibal humans."

Noah shrugged. "The Kindred have really outdone themselves this time."

"Is there anyone else who can help us?" I asked. "Any other Unseen cells in the city who can fight?"

Rachel sighed and shook her head. "I'm not supposed to tell you this, but we're the only cell left active in Coleton. Up until a few weeks ago, there were six, but members have been going missing one at a time. I haven't been able to raise anybody on comms for the last few days."

"If someone's targeting Unseen, I think we had the right to know," Noah growled.

"Take it up with management," Rachel snapped, "But the fact is we're on our own here until backup arrives from Korea. I tried to get a closer team in, but the powers-that-be don't think our situation is urgent, and don't want to risk exposing active teams. Nearly everyone's on mission right now. The Kindred are ramping up their activity across the world." She turned back to the computer screen, "So until backup arrives, here are our orders. We need to find a body."

"As in, a dead one?"

"Yep. I don't think heading back into those tunnels is an option, so we're going to get the next best thing." Rachel tapped a few keys and brought up a schematic of the city morgue.

"You have got to be kidding me," said Noah.

I turned to Rachel. "We're going to break into the morgue?"

She nodded. "One of the strangest things about the crime wave is that exactly zero perpetrators survived their arrest. The police had orders to shoot on sight, and some are probably still being held in the morgue. If we can get our hands on one, we might be able to find the connection between Wheeler and the creatures. Or even better, work out what he's planning."

"Great," I sighed. "Let's go rob the morgue."

Rachel took the van from its hidden storage garage next to the warehouse and drove it around front. Despite not being field-ready yet, she'd pushed for clearance to head out on the mission with us. We needed as much experience on the team as we could get; last night had proved that.

Noah and I sat in the back, and Rachel drove. The seatbelt was broken on the passenger side, and we couldn't afford to get pulled over by the cops, especially considering some of them were Kindred.

Rachel spoke like the Kindred were everywhere. Like they could be anyone. They'd certainly stepped up their activity. Unseen cells from London, New York, Madrid, Moscow, Beijing; every major city on the planet reported aggressive Kindred recruitment in their districts. They were growing by the day. By now, they numbered in the tens of thousands. Pretty soon it would be hundreds of thousands.

Did we have any shot at winning this? I didn't know how many Unseen were out there; operational information was kept compartmentalised, for obvious reasons, but from what I'd picked up it couldn't be more than a few thousand around the world. They were mostly young, like us. There weren't a lot of old Unseen, as Noah had said. At least we seemed to have a few key players, important people who backed our operation.

My mind wandered throughout the drive into the city. Traffic was light this close to midnight, so the trip didn't take long. Every time my mind went to Josh, I swallowed, and clenched my fists, and thought about something else.

I would have played a game on our new phones to distract myself, but I'd probably get carsick. Regardless, the phones were locked down. When I'd first arrived at Coleton, they'd destroyed my old phone and given me a new, secure one. Wheeler had that one, now, but it didn't matter. The phones were set to wipe all data every hour, aside from key numbers programmed under our code names. We'd need new code names, now, because if Wheeler cracked the phones, it wouldn't be hard to figure out who we were.

Rachel pulled up four blocks from the city morgue. We were right near Century Park, but on the north side, opposite to the spot where I'd melted that jerk's car.

This side of the park was close to Downtown. From here, multi-coloured tents were visible sprawled out under the bridge. The woman whose baby Wheeler had taken was probably under there somewhere, worried sick to death. It was awful. If only I'd taken Wheeler out that first night, none of this would have happened. She'd have her baby, Hud would be safe with us, and Josh would still be alive. My inaction had thrown us into all this mess.

"Coming?" said Rachel from outside the van's sliding door. I pulled my mind back to the present moment and got out.

My breath fogged in the night air, illuminated by the red traffic light at the end of the street. It was almost like I was breathing fire. Then, it switched green, even though the street was empty. I turned backwards and tuned into the black road behind us. Not to change anything, but just to hear the city. Feel it breathe. Even the quietest places are brimming with sound if you know how to listen. A part of me secretly hoped I'd hear Josh somehow, tune into him, his resonance. But he was lying dead in a lake somewhere under my feet, so I didn't.

The city pulsed with its own sounds, though. A touch of static for a moment, and then it went away. Noah or Rachel had probably glanced my way and realised what I was doing. The road hummed, an earthy, warm hum from the rocks and gravel held by oily tar. Lamp posts shimmered with a clear metallic buzz. The newsagent at the end of the street was a cacophony of sounds, glass and paper and plastic. The whole city was alive. But underneath it all, something else. A single, clear, pulsing note. Wheeler's sound. I glanced around the street. No static meant no-one was around. But Wheeler's note was still there, churning and bleeding through the city's veins. He had infected the city with his sound. The more I listened, the more I heard it under everything. The whole place buzzed with his note. The city was sick, and Wheeler was the cause.

I turned to tell Noah and Rachel, but they were already far down the street. When I caught up to them, I told them what I'd heard, and they both tried to tune into it for themselves.

"I can't hear it," said Rachel.

"Me neither," Noah added. "That doesn't mean it's not there, though. Maybe you're just more tuned to it from the time he spent interrogating you. I hardly saw him back at the docks, but you were with him for a while. It's possible you're more connected to it."

Or he's infected me, too.

139

Rachel kept walking, and I followed. The City Morgue was right next to the police station, which meant we had to be super careful and go around the back into the access alley they used as parking. There were no security cameras there, just several places on the wall with bare bolts and wires sticking out. Someone had removed the cameras, which was helpful for us, but concerning as well.

The back door was solid steel and locked with a security panel, hand scanner, and padlocks

"You want to melt the locks, or should I?" Rachel said.

"What about security alarms?" I asked.

Rachel swung her pack around to her front and rifled through it. "You know our mysterious paramilitary benefactor?" She pulled out a small oval device the same size as our phones and pressed it to the security panel. After a few seconds, the panel beeped and turned green. "It's nice to have friends in high places," she smirked. "So, door melting. Any takers?"

Noah and I were drained from the night before, so we were happy to let Rachel do it. She melted the locks in a few seconds and pushed the door silently open.

Inside, everything was black.

Outside, Wheeler's note still rang bleeding through the city streets.

TWENTY-THREE

Rachel and I closed our eyes, and Noah tried to tune.

"No static," he said. "No security cameras in here, either"

"That confirms our intel," said Rachel.

The three of us switched on our torches and the hall lit up. The corridor was long and straight, doors branching off into rooms that glowed dimly now that my eyes were adjusting to the dark. Stepping forward, my shoes stuck slightly to the yellowing linoleum floor. It was cracked in places, running blackish-brown lines across the hallway, and lifting off around the edges. A mechanical hum echoed off the white walls. On my right, a stain ran down the plaster from the roof, probably caused by a water leak. The whole building needed a major renovation. Although, I thought grimly, the occupants probably didn't mind too much either way.

My thoughts went to Josh again, but I steered it back to our mission. We had to know what Wheeler was planning.

"The cold chambers are two doors down on the right," said Rachel. She was whispering, even though no-one was around. What we were doing wasn't just illegal, it felt sacrilegious; trespassing on the dead before they were even properly buried.

The door was locked with a key-card reader, which Rachel overrode with the oval code-breaker. She pushed it open slowly in case of backup alarms, but none went off. A rush of cold air hit me, carrying a musky, pungent scent mixed with antiseptic. This room was enormous; at least a hundred tiny doors lined the walls like a bank's safety deposit room. Each door was square, and I'd seen enough cop shows to know what was in there. The hum I'd heard before made sense now; it was the noise of the fridges that held the dead, keeping them cold to stop them decomposing. Still, nothing could stop time altogether, and the stench in my nose was of death and bodily fluids. In the middle of the room was a stainless-steel table with raised edges, sitting on a giant metal platform. Above, a machine hung from the roof. It looked like a giant claw and was probably used for moving the heavier bodies. A glowing exit sign lit the room from above our heads, and on a melamine desk in the back corner, a computer sat logged in, cursor blinking.

Rachel moved straight for it, bringing up the storage records. "There's a body in number 43 that was connected to one of the violent crimes."

"Let's try it, then," said Noah.

Noah and I walked to the door marked 43 and, taking a breath first, swung it open. A rush of stale, rotting air blew out, and we gagged. I lifted the collar of my shirt up over my nose, and Noah did the same. Rachel came and stood next to me.

Grey feet faced us from inside the chamber. Three sets of them, pointing all different directions.

"Uh, guys, we've hit the jackpot," I said grimly.

"Either that body grew a bunch of bonus legs, or there's more than one person stored in there," Noah frowned.

"There's only one listed on the manifest. Let's find out," Rachel said, and slid the tray out.

The corpses were stacked on top of each other, shoved in like sardines, and as Rachel slid them out, one toppled and fell towards me.

I put my hands out to steady it without thinking, and cold, slimy skin met my palms. "Guys, help!"

Rachel and Noah came around to my side of the tray and tried to roll the body back onto the stack. It was too unstable to balance back onto the tray, though, so Rachel pushed the stainless-steel autopsy table over to us, and we lowered the body onto it. The two bodies left on the tray were mostly stable. My hands felt gross, but now was not the time to worry about that.

Once everything was steady, we took a step back and examined the bodies.

They were all naked, as were probably all the people in here. There was a male on the autopsy table—the one that had fallen out—leaving another male and a female on the fridge tray. All three were grey and gross, with big Y shaped stitches on their chests from their autopsies. The man on the table looked thirty, maybe. The one on the tray was twenty at most. And the female was about my age. I felt a pang of sadness rush through me, and a sudden need to know their names, their stories. But I couldn't. I shouldn't know their names. I couldn't think about them as human. That was too awful. Instead, I thought about them as statues, like the plastic cutaway torsos we used in science class.

"What now?" I asked.

"I'll check out the autopsy reports," said Rachel. "You examine the bodies more closely, see if there's anything that might be connected to Wheeler. Noah, check the other fridges. See if there are more stacked up like this."

"Sure, you take the desk job," grumbled Noah. "Leave me to play corpse bingo."

He moved to the drawers near the door, covered his mouth and nose again, and started opening them.

I looked more closely at the body on the table. The torso had a bullet hole above his heart. His head was shaved, and stitches ran in a ring around his skull just above his ears. They'd looked inside his head. Two eyes stared at the ceiling, milky and grey. I forced myself to look closer at them. The pupils were dilated almost completely.

Just like the creature in the tunnel.

Mouth twisted into a grimace, I walked over to the other two. The female had three bullet holes and the Y cut, plus the same ring of stitches around her head. The other male was the same. Their eyes were closed, but I had to know. I reached out my hand, shaking, and pulled open the male's eyelids.

Black irises, now milky with death, same as the body on the table and the creatures in the tunnel. Whatever had happened to those things had happened to these people, too, although the creatures were much worse. These bodies didn't quite have the same inhuman quality as the things in the tunnel, but I couldn't put my finger on exactly why.

The girl's eyes were closed, too, and I walked around the table to look closer. I had the overwhelming urge to cover her with a sheet, give her some privacy in this awful, frozen room. Her dignity had been stripped away along with her life and, judging by the creatures in the tunnel, perhaps some of her humanity as well. She was just a shell, now, but a shell I felt I should protect. My stomach turned, suddenly, as I became fully conscious of how awful this all was. Bodies stuffed together like sardines, stripped and cut and examined and studied. It was a human abattoir. A place to butcher the dead. Head spinning, I sat for a moment on the floor, leaning against one of the drawer doors for support.

"You okay?" called Noah from across the room.

I nodded and took a deep breath before returning to my feet. I had to see her eyes. From this side of the table she looked almost calm, although her lips were blue-grey, and her skin was pallid. Each cheek was just starting to draw back, to furrow slightly into her bones. She'd been here for a while. Her eyes were drawn, too, sinking in their sockets. I reached my hand to her eyelids.

"I'm really sorry," I said, and pulled them open.

Her irises, too, were black, pupils dilated beyond possibility. Strangely, her eyes weren't milky with decay. They almost looked alive. I looked at the huge Y cut into her chest, leftover from the autopsy that had weighed heart and lungs and liver. There was no way she was alive, and yet…

Her chest moved. Only slightly, but I was sure of it. The Y expanded, opening her wound a fraction, causing the incisions to tear from slits to canyons. I didn't move. Couldn't. I checked her face. A tiny burst of fog escaped her lips. Her blackened eyes turned to me.

TWENTY-FOUR

I backed away, knocking over an equipment stand, scattering scissors and scalpels to the floor.

Rachel swore. "Ari, be careful!"

"The girl, she—" My voice cut off. Her eyes were closed again, and her wound no longer moved. Whatever I'd seen, it had either been in my head, or it was over now. Either way, there was no point telling the others.

"I tripped," I finished, picking up the stuff I'd knocked over.

This was the second time I'd seen a body move. The first was in the Chapel, where the body had become me— my eyes, my face. This time had been different, but I felt like I was supposed to know something, like she was trying to communicate.

My heart was still thumping, but hers remained still. If I could only reach out to her, turn back time perhaps, and let her know I cared, that there was at least one person in this world who was sorry for what had happened to her.

Maybe the only way to make things better was to kill Wheeler and everyone involved in this, to make them pay for what had happened to this girl, and to Josh, and for whatever they were doing to Hud somewhere out there.

"Hey guys, come check this out," murmured Noah from the middle of the room.

Tearing my eyes from the girl, I stepped over to see what he was looking at. My mouth dropped open. Noah had opened all the doors, and each compartment was stuffed full of bodies. Almost every single one had at least three bodies in it, sometimes four if the corpses were small enough.

"That's not normal, is it?" he asked.

Rachel shook her head and stepped towards him, taking in each compartment. She took a deep breath and gagged. "Some of them have been in here a while," she coughed. "The computer records have huge numbers coming in over the last few months, but only lists sixteen bodies that are supposed to be in here. The rest should have been buried. They *were* buried, on paper. It looks like the families had funerals and everything."

I covered my nose from the smell now pouring out of each of the compartments. "Someone's been hiding bodies in here, keeping them in storage," I said, stating the obvious. "They've been affected by the same thing as the creatures in the tunnel. All the bodies I looked at had those strange, black eyes."

"Maybe they're keeping them for research," Rachel said, "Tracking whatever's happened to them." She walked back to the computer and tabbed to an open file. "Look at this," she said. "It's the official autopsy report. The brain was affected in each of the bodies who died during arrest. The notes say the amygdalae, specifically, but *how* they've been affected is redacted."

She brought up a search window and typed in "amygdalae". Multiple results came up, and she opened the first one.

Noah moved to Rachel and looked over her shoulder, reading aloud from the entry. "The amygdalae are responsible for emotional processing. There are two amygdala, one on each side of the brain. Together, they moderate and produce fear, anxiety, joy, sadness, anger; a whole range of emotions. They are also involved in fight or flight stimulus, which is our automatic response to either attack or run away when confronted with dangerous situations. Anger and violent behaviour were reported in monkeys who experienced damage to their amygdalae..." he trailed off, and looked over his shoulder. "Wait a minute."

Noah walked to one of the drawers, a big one that looked more like a chest freezer. "I opened this before but didn't think it was important." He picked out blue latex gloves from a box on the wall and slipped them on. "This is gonna be gross, but..."

Reaching into the freezer chest, he pulled out a metal tray with something white and fleshy on it.

"Is that..." Rachel took a step towards Noah. "Is that a brain?"

"Unfortunately, yes," he said. "Human, I think. Taken from one of the subjects during the autopsy. It's got a cut down the middle. I didn't take a closer look before because it was disgusting."

I walked closer to him and the tray, and he placed it on the aluminium table next to the male body we'd saved from falling. The brain was frozen, so it wasn't squelchy or bleeding, but it was still one of the grossest things I'd ever seen, its snakelike rivers running across the top. The *sulci*, I suddenly remembered from science.

Grimacing, Noah placed a hand on each side of the brain and pulled it apart. It had been sliced perfectly down the centre during the autopsy.

"I don't think it's supposed to look like that," Rachel said slowly.

Cross-sectioned into the brain were two huge, dark sacs that took up at least half of the surface. Black streaks reached out from them into the rest of the brain, running through the tissue like veins.

"Are those the amygdalae?" I said.

Noah nodded. "Yeah, that spot in the brain is where they're supposed to be, according to the wiki entry at least."

"What happened to them?" I said.

"I don't know," he frowned, "but whatever it is, it's messed up, and almost definitely responsible for those creatures in the tunnels."

Suddenly the bright overhead lights switched on. We were not alone.

Footsteps sounded from the corridor outside. They must have switched on the lights from the entrance. There were at least two people coming. Maybe more. We had no way out, except the way they were coming.

"I'll freeze the lock and stall them," snapped Rachel. "You two get that brain and the bodies put away then find a place to hide."

Noah closed all the doors and threw the brain into the freezer chest. I pushed the tray back into the fridge, hiding the male and female I'd inspected. There was still a body on the table, but I had no idea what to do with it. The footsteps reached the front door, and the door handle rattled.

"Door's stuck," said a muffled man's voice from outside.

Rachel gave us a thumbs up. She'd made the lock sticky, buying us time. Not much time, though.

"Here," she whispered and grabbed the body on the table. Noah helped her put him into the freezer, and they closed the lid quietly.

"Our packs," I said frantically, pointing to our bags which were on the floor in the middle of the room. Noah picked them up and threw them into the freezer too.

The door lock rattled more.

"Bloody hell," said another male voice. "The maintenance on this place is shocking."

"There are two empty drawers at the back of the room," Noah hissed. "Only option."

We ran to them, and Noah pulled open the door to the first compartment.

"Dammit," he said, "Got it wrong. It's occupied."

Two grey feet stuck out at the end, belonging to the body inside.

"Doesn't matter," said Rachel. "I'll take this one."

"Really?" Noah said.

The door lock rattled again.

"No time. Get in!" she said, and crawled feet first into the compartment, trying to avoid contact with the body inside. Noah slid it closed for her.

Then, Noah and I got into the second, empty compartment. He was bigger than me, so he slid in first, putting his feet towards the back of the fridge.

The voice outside the door swore, and the lock rattled again.

I slid in next to Noah, lying on my side, and pulling the door closed from inside. But I left it open a fraction, terrified that we'd get locked in and never get out.

There was a thump, and the entrance slammed open. We'd left no trace of our presence, save a few misplaced items. Hopefully they wouldn't notice and search the room.

"Finally," muttered the voice. I couldn't see anything, but he sounded old. "Need to get maintenance onto that. If they ever bother getting around to it."

The tray inside the fridge was cold and stuck to my skin. I was lying on my left side, facing Noah, and my arm was going numb.

"Which stiff did they want us to look at?" asked a younger voice.

"Seventeen. John somebody. He's in the bottom drawer, two from the left."

Far away from us. Good.

There was a click, then some grunting and heaving, and the slap of flesh on metal.

The older voice spoke again. "See, here. Excess hair growth. That suggests more than just amygdalae corruption. It's spread to other parts of the brain. Pituitary gland or thyroid, probably."

"Wheeler will be pleased."

"Wheeler? The art guy?"

"He's been working on this for a long time. Now the effects are certain, we can proceed to stage two."

"Wait. I thought this was a virus." The old man sounded genuinely shocked. "They said we were keeping this quiet to avoid panicking the public."

The younger man laughed. "That's adorable. You've gotta be a special kind of dumb to buy that crap."

There was a thump, and a struggle, then a horrible, gagging noise, like someone choking. Then, nothing.

"It's me," the younger voice said. "We're ready. Tell Wheeler stage two can proceed." A pause. "The final demonstration is tonight? Excellent. The gallery entrance will likely be watched by Unseen vermin, so use the backup instead. The Unseen aren't a threat, but we can't afford distractions." Another pause. "He's dead, obviously. I'm going to put him in storage. It will buy us a few days before anyone finds the body. Not that we'll need days. By this time tomorrow, this city will burn." His phone beeped as he hung up.

The entrance door opened again, then closed with a click. There was silence.

Neither of us dared to move. Noah was pressed up against me, body heat radiating through my skin. The compartment was so tight we had to alternate our breathing. I could feel his heart beating in his chest, thumping against my ribcage, pulsing through my body. His breath was warm on my cheek. This didn't feel romantic, though. His eyes were dark, and so were mine.

The voice had said tomorrow. By this time tomorrow, the city would burn. We didn't have long to stop whatever Wheeler had planned. If we could get to this demonstration, maybe we could stop it.

The vision I'd had in the Chapel had shown a city in chaos. Maybe it was Coleton. Maybe, tomorrow, Noah would be lying in a pool of his own blood as the city died around us.

I clenched my jaw.

No way.

While I still had breath, I'd fight that future.

TWENTY-FIVE

Minutes passed before any of us dared to move. There was a click from the compartment next to ours, and the rustling of clothes. Our compartment door opened, and Noah and I looked up at Rachel, standing over us with her hands on her hips.

"How was your seven minutes in heaven?" she smirked.

Noah grinned back. "Better than yours, I bet." He pointed to her shirt, which had some dark lines on it in the shape of a Y. "There's bits on you."

"Dammit," she frowned. "It stinks too."

"I've got a spare shirt in my pack," I offered, before crawling out. I kneed Noah in the crotch by accident, and he groaned.

"Well," said Rachel. "You two *did* have a good time in there."

Noah tried to respond, but couldn't, whimpering instead.

Sorry, I mouthed.

"I'll be out when I'm ready," he grunted, waving me away. I walked to the freezer chest to remove my pack, sidestepping a fresh puddle of blood on the floor that likely belonged to the older man. It was careless of the killer, not cleaning up after himself. Perhaps it didn't matter and whatever he had planned was already in motion.

I found the spare shirt in my pack and threw it to Rachel, who took her dirty one off and put it in one of the fridges. Her chest was covered in scars and melted burn marks. I swallowed.

Rachel caught me staring at the damage and frowned, turning around to put on the black shirt I'd given her. Her back was scarred too, full of lines and splotches from her torture in the Kindred complex. No wonder she was sharp with me. The things they'd done to her...

She put the shirt on, then gave Noah a hand crawling out of the compartment.

"Grab your things," she said. "We're going to the gallery. That's our way in to whatever Wheeler's planning."

The corridor was quiet, and we left the morgue without incident. The gallery was about ten minutes away by car, but Rachel took an alternate route to make sure we weren't being followed. While she drove, we made plans for our next move.

"The man said the gallery was an entrance," Rachel said. "An entrance to what, though?"

Noah pulled out his phone and started typing. A minute later, he looked up. "Got it. Look at this."

He turned his phone to me. There were a bunch of crisscrossing lines on it. "This," he pointed to the red one, "is the closed rail line. The one we were on last night."

"Where did you find that?" Rachel called from the front.

"A website called the Coleton Rail Enthusiast Club. They mapped the tunnels years ago, probably before they got so dangerous."

"Look," I said. "That huge red space. That must be the old station that never got built. The lake where Josh..."

Noah nodded sadly. "Yes, it's all connected. But watch this." He pulled up a map of the city and swiped between the two. "This pin here is Elements Gallery," he swiped left, "And this is the old rail line."

"It runs right underneath the gallery," I said.

"Exactly."

"The entrance must be in the basement somewhere," said Rachel.

Noah leaned forward between the front seats to talk to her. "Last time we were there, it was full of kids, plus that crazy girl who attacked Ari."

"If they think we're watching the gallery, it'll probably be empty," I said. "Although I have no desire to run into Eden again." As if on cue, my arm twinged from the knife wound.

"He's probably fixed the front window I vaped," said Noah, "but we could use the loading dock."

"We should keep an eye out for traps," I warned.

"You're right," said Rachel. "Thinking like a soldier. That's good."

I wasn't sure just how good it *was*, but I smiled anyway. A compliment from Rachel was rare.

Rachel pulled the van into an alleyway two blocks away from the gallery, and we sat still for a while to make sure we hadn't been followed.

"I think we're good," she said and unclicked her seatbelt before getting out.

Noah and I followed, slinging our backpacks over our shoulders and sliding the van door open. The door closed with a metallic thunk that echoed down the dark alley we were parked in.

There was a clatter next to me, and I jumped back as a mottled cat ran from behind a bin. It reminded me of the tabby the creature had been eating in the tunnel, and I shuddered.

Elements Gallery was halfway down the second back street, and we stopped at the alley entrance to check for an ambush.

"I'll do it," I said, so Noah and Rachel closed their eyes while I tried to tune. The tones were clear, no static at all, although Wheeler's pulsing tone still ran beneath it all.

"No static, no-one's watching," I said. "Let's move."

"We should still go slowly in case of traps," Rachel said in a whisper. "A tripwire would be hard to pick up with our abilities, so keep an eye out."

Two doors from the loading dock, Noah stopped.

"Look," he whispered, pointing to the ground a few steps away. In the moonlight, a wire glistened just above the ground.

"You were right," I said to Rachel, tracing the tripwire with my eyes to a piece of black metal stuck to the wall.

"Claymore mine," she replied. "Nasty stuff. It's pointing straight at us. Hit that tripwire, and we're ripped to shreds."

"Can we vape it?" I asked.

"Not a good idea. If it's Kindred modified, who knows what safeguards they've built into the system. Best just leave it alone and step carefully over."

Rachel took the lead, slowly lifting each foot over the wire.

"Rachel, wait!" The asphalt road had been disturbed in a long trench just after the tripwire, right where Rachel was.

A beeping sounded from beneath the road. She was standing on a mine.

"Close your eyes, both of you," I yelled.

"There's no time," said Rachel.

"Shut up and do it!" I snapped.

They did, and I tuned into the road, lowering the temperature of the asphalt and the mine beneath. I had to get it low enough to freeze the detonator. Hopefully there wasn't a failsafe built in to prevent it.

The asphalt froze solid, but the mine kept beeping.

"Run," said Rachel. "Get away, now!"

"No chance," I said. "I'm not losing someone else."

I lowered the resonance even further, and the beeping stopped.

Rachel opened her eyes. "Did you get it?"

I shook my head, forehead sweating. "I don't know."

"Only one way to find out. Both of you get back."

Noah and I moved away, hopefully out of the blast radius.

Rachel lifted one foot from the road, then dove over the tripwire towards us, skinning her elbows on the road's surface.

Nothing happened.

She stood and walked towards us. "Well done, I think we're—"

The road lifted behind her, thrusting chunks of rock into the air. A jet of flame blasted through the surface and triggered the tripwire, which set off the claymore mine, throwing Rachel to the ground. Debris and fire slammed across the alleyway, and the sound hit me in the chest. I staggered backwards.

"Rachel!" I yelled, but I couldn't hear my voice. There was nothing but ringing in my ears. Rachel lay on the road, and I ran to see her.

She slowly rolled over.

"Are you okay?" I yelled. I still couldn't hear anything.

Rachel moved her mouth, but I had no idea what she was saying. I shook my head, and she gave me a thumbs up instead.

Noah joined me next to Rachel, and we grabbed her hands and pulled her upright. None of us could hear each other talk. Staggering back to the van, we jumped inside to catch our breath and let our ears recover.

Finally, the ringing subsided enough to hold a conversation.

"Nice dive," said Noah, although he was still yelling to compensate for our hearing loss.

"Thanks." Rachel turned to me. "And thanks, Ari. If you hadn't bought time by freezing the mine…"

"Don't mention it," I said. "I'm just glad you're okay."

"Reckon anyone heard it?" Noah said.

Rachel sat up, rubbing her sore elbows. "Kindred are likely on their way. If we're going to go, we need to go now. Hopefully there's no more traps."

"I think all the buildings are connected," I said. "The loading dock had a door leading into the next space. If we use those, we might be safer."

"Good plan," she said. "Who knows what else they've got waiting for us on the street."

We got back out of the van and stopped three doors from the gallery dock. The lock on the rolling door was easy to melt, and we made it inside without incident. I snuck one more look at the giant hole in the road before we went in, flames still flickering from inside. The Kindred had some serious weapons at their disposal, and we had tasers.

How on earth were we supposed to win this?

TWENTY-SIX

It was easy to enter the gallery now that we'd come through the side entrance. We moved slowly, but we encountered no more traps. Strangely, we heard no sirens in response to our explosive moment outside. Either the cops were busy elsewhere, or the Kindred had told them not to come. Neither was a good sign.

The gallery was dark, but just the way we'd left it— covered in weird, disturbing art. The piece to my right was of Marie Antoinette's execution, but everyone was wearing black masks. From a certain angle, they looked a bit like Kindred hoods. The title simply read "Justice".

When I'd come through two nights ago, I'd been too distracted by the mirror to notice anything else, but now looking around I saw the sculptures. Twisted, contorted figures. Half human, half something else entirely. One huge statue was carved from black marble, human from the waist up, but instead of legs, dark tendrils curled to the floor. They reminded me of the Shadows.

The figure next to it looked like Wheeler, but huge and naked and holding a sceptre. He certainly thought much of himself, putting a statue like that in his own gallery.

The closer I looked, the more I saw the Kindred influence behind each piece. Shadows lurking in the background, corruption and decay and death celebrated and revered like it was spiritual. Wheeler's gallery was designed to encourage the worst parts of ourselves. The *true* parts, as he would say. His art was made to corrupt, to defile the human spirit and everything that makes us good. My art teacher used to say that art was morally neutral, that it meant nothing but what we brought to it. Looking at this art now, there was no way that could be true. This was messed up. This whole gallery was a reflection of Wheeler's polluted mind.

Noah and Rachel had already left the corridor, but I stayed staring at the art, trying to work out what Wheeler was planning. If this was his true vision of humanity, if this was his paradise, he had a plan to make it happen somehow.

A plan that involved the black stuff growing in the creature's brains.

"Ari?" called Noah from near the front of the gallery.

"Coming," I called back.

But I was drawn to the mirror once more. The one asking *Which One of You is Real?*

The mirror me was out of sync again, movements a fraction slower than mine. My stomach burned cold. I lifted my shirt for a moment to check out the dark spot in the mirror, the one left by the Shadow in my room. It still hadn't grown since Ettney, which was reassuring, but why was it burning now? I pulled my shirt back down over my stomach.

The me in the mirror didn't. Instead, she lifted the shirt over her head, taking it off entirely. But instead of my body underneath, there was nothing. Darkness. Shadow.

She was turning into one of them. I looked down at my torso, and nothing had changed. No darkness, no Shadow.

Mirror me undressed completely, but there was no body underneath her clothes, just a pulsing mess of tendrils and smoke, the fire burning black I'd seen in the Apex, in the mountains, and in my room. A smile crept across her face, and she opened her mouth to talk. She spoke silently at me, but I couldn't make it out. My palms were damp.

She reached out a slithering hand, as if she was reaching from beyond the mirror space, as if she wanted me to join her. And I wanted to. I wanted so badly to dive into that world with her, to let go and stop fighting and become the monster I saw in the glass. My hand moved on its own, reaching out, rising to the Shadow-me calling from the world inside.

"Ari!" Noah said, putting one hand on my shoulder. I jumped and looked at him, and when I turned my head back, the Shadow-me was gone. It was a regular mirror once more, and Noah stood, staring.

"You okay?" he said. We've been calling for ages. We need help in the basement."

"Sorry," I stuttered. "I was just—never mind."

"Let's go," he said, taking my hand in his.

I turned back to the mirror as I left, a little piece of me still longing to break through and join that world.

Maybe Wheeler was right. The darkest part of me sought freedom.

So many people and places had reached out to me. The Chapel, the mirror, the girl in the morgue, and Hackman. He was so convinced I'd become the Shadow creature, that I carried the Seed, whatever that was. That I'd bring about the Final Day. My mind returned to the moment he'd burned, consumed by the bushfire I started, his face melting in the heat, his eyes sure of victory even in his death, his call to Noah to look after me, to keep me safe.

Maybe I shouldn't be around Noah. After all, if Hackman wanted it, it must connect to his plan somehow. Noah could be my undoing and, by extension, the undoing of the world.

I dropped Noah's hand and let him walk ahead, stepping down the storeroom staircase and into the basement where we'd found Wheeler. Rachel was already there and had made sure it was safe.

This was the first time I'd gotten a good look at the room; I'd barely glanced at it the other night. It was larger than I remembered, and rimmed with beds that were covered in food scraps, clothes, and junk. It stank of sweat and rotting fruit. Wheeler's kids had made a serious mess.

I stopped for a moment, counting the beds. "He must have had twenty or thirty kids down here. That's a small army."

Rachel surveyed the mess. "I still don't understand how he kept them from leaving. There's almost no security. The door doesn't even have a lock."

"It's his resonance," I said. "The tone that comes from him. It's comforting somehow. Makes you feel safe. Like he's the only safe place in the world. All the burdens just disappear for a while. It's freeing."

Noah and Rachel frowned at the longing in my voice.

"Don't worry, I'm over it," I lied. Truth was, I wanted to be back there. To feel free again. To press against Noah and kiss him without prophecies and death and carnage hanging in the balance.

Noah coughed and leaned up against the concrete wall. "He's taken them somewhere, or they're out scavenging like we saw the other night. Whatever he's planning for them, it can't be good."

"Speaking of plans, we need to find this entrance to the tunnels," said Rachel. "It's got to be here somewhere."

"Behind you," said Noah. "There's a line in the wall."

A thin crack ran from floor to ceiling at the back of the room. Rachel pushed it, and the crack widened. The wall was actually two doors, leading into an even larger room. The space was dark, made darker by heavy black curtains that ran along the walls. Bright spotlights illuminated artefacts atop perspex plinths. The room was enormous. There must have been at least a hundred items in here.

"What on earth..." Rachel trailed off as she took in the artefacts on display.

Noah took three steps inside, then stopped. "Look at this stuff. It's even more messed up than the art."

Each plinth had labels explaining the artefact on top. Straight ahead, an automatic rifle took the primary spot. I stepped closer and read the text on its plaque. *Rwandan Genocide. First Shot. 1994.*

"Check out this one," said Noah, gesturing to a rusted nail sitting on another plinth. "It says *Crucifixion Nail, First Century.*"

Rachel called from another box. "This one reads *Slave Manacles, 1785.*"

The room was a tribute to artefacts from the worst moments of human history. A history of violence, death, and hatred. No, it wasn't just a history or a tribute. It was a shrine.

I walked slowly down the aisles, reading the inscriptions. *Gas Chamber Canister, 1942. Gallipoli Bullet, 1915. Agent Orange Samples, Vietnam, 1973. Child Soldier Uniform, Democratic Republic of Congo, 2013.*

I couldn't read any more. This room was evil. Looking at Noah and Rachel's faces, they felt the same.

"Wheeler wants to add Coleton to this list," I said quietly. "Whatever he's planning, it's on the scale of the things in this room. He wants to add to the history. He wants a new artefact."

"Up at the end," said Rachel. "Look."

At the other side of the room, two huge doors loomed, locked by an electric mechanism. Walking closer, the patterns on them became clear. They were the same carvings as the doors to the South Wing of the Ettney Complex. The doors to the altar. To the Shadows' nest.

"That's our way in," said Noah.

I swallowed. It felt like we were walking into the darkest place on earth.

Maybe we were.

TWENTY-SEVEN

Getting through the door was simple. Melting the locks only took a second. I pushed the left one open, met by a rush of damp air that smelled of rats and death. Instead of another huge temple like the South Wing, there were stairs leading down to the old rail line.

"Guys," I said. "I was thinking. We probably need better weapons."

Noah nodded. "I don't think those creatures can tune, but their strength is unbelievable. I doubt a taser would take them down."

"You're both right," said Rachel. "Give me a second."

She turned and disappeared back through the doors into Wheeler's death shrine. We stood, breathing quietly in the darkness, until she returned.

"These will do," she said. "Just don't ask me their history, okay?"

Rachel handed me a huge machete that was at least as long as my arm. Noah got a club with spikes in the end, and she strapped an ancient looking sword around her waist in a sheath.

I hated to think about the history of these weapons, but right now we didn't have a choice. Weapons weren't always bad. Sometimes they could be used for good. At least, that's what I told myself. No guns, though. If we ran into any Kindred down here, guns would be a disaster, exploding in our pockets before we got off a shot. These hand-to-hand weapons wouldn't be that useful against the Kindred, but at least they wouldn't blow up in our faces.

Rachel swung her pack off her shoulder. "I stocked our bags with night-vision goggles. Put them on. That way, we can see without flagging our position."

Smart move. I rummaged around in my backpack and pulled out the goggles. They were big, but as soon as I slipped them on the whole room lit up. I could see like it was daytime, although with limited tunnel vision. Appropriate, considering I was literally in a tunnel.

"Ready?" Rachel said.

"Ready," Noah and I replied.

As we descended, the staircase widened out into the tunnel, which was empty, save for the old freight line and some markings etched into the wall.

"The First Language," said Noah. *"Glorea dorcha, umlaie quantus."*

"Glory to the darkness. Bow in respect." Rachel whispered.

"You've been studying," Noah approved.

"Know thine enemy," Rachel said, running her fingers across a carved arrow that pointed to the right. "This way."

A whisper slithered across the edges of my mind. A voice I couldn't quite make out. It rasped, and sighed, and hissed, but no words made sense.

"Did anyone else hear that?" I said, turning my head and trying to locate the source.

"Hear what?" Noah said.

"Nothing."

"I didn't hear anything," Rachel said. "Let's get moving."

She led the way down the corridor, but her hand went to the sword on her hip, betraying her nerves. The machete was heavy in my hand. I hadn't realised how dense those things were. I had to be careful not to cut myself with the blade. It was really sharp.

"You know how to use that?" Noah asked, gesturing to Rachel's sword.

"I've been Unseen much longer than you," she said. "More time to train, and more time to get creative. Although I've only trained with sticks, never with an actual blade. It can't be that different, I guess."

Rachel was full of surprises.

"We'll have to spar sometime," said Noah. "I've been practicing hand-to-hand. Not weapons or anything, but I'm okay at jiu-jitsu."

I imagined Noah rolling around on the floor with Rachel, his arms on her shoulders, her legs around his waist.

"Maybe we can train together," I said, a little too quickly.

"You don't have to be jealous, Ari," said Rachel with a smirk in her voice. "Noah and I go back longer than you do, but that doesn't mean I'm interested in him. He's more like a cousin or something. Totally a-sexual."

"Thanks," Noah replied, offended. "Good to know I do nothing for you."

"As far as I'm concerned," she said, "You're like a Ken doll down there. Nothing at all going on. Just smooth plastic."

I snorted, and Noah frowned at me. He looked ridiculous with the goggles on, and I giggled again.

"Although," Rachel continued, "Ari probably has a better idea of that than I do."

My face burned red, and I stopped laughing.

"I don't—we haven't—" I stammered.

"It's not like that," Noah said to Rachel.

"Oh, were you with Josh?" she asked.

My face burned again, but for a different reason. "No!" I snapped. "And don't use his name again. He's not yours to talk about. Nobody talk about him. *You* don't get to do that."

They went silent.

My eyes shut tight for a moment, and when I opened them the lenses of my goggles were smudged. Great.

I took them off to wipe the tears from the glass, and stopped in the dark, waiting for my emotions to reset themselves, waiting for the numb feeling to kick back in like it always did. It didn't, though. I stood, crying silently in the tunnel, while the others scoped out the track ahead.

I wasn't expecting to feel that, not in the middle of a mission to stop Coleton's destruction. Of all the stupid reminders of him, Rachel's was the worst. Asking me about him — even considering what she'd been through at Ettney, she was being an insensitive cow bringing that up here, in the same tunnels he'd died in less than twenty-four hours before.

I took a deep breath, wiped my eyes, and put my goggles back on. The tunnel lit before me, but there was no sign of Noah and Rachel. They'd disappeared around the corner ahead, not even bothering to wait for me. Jerks.

The whisper came again. The slow, creeping feeling around the back of my head. I turned around, but there was no-one there. It was a voice, but it wasn't clear. Just the hint of a word, a phrase — a secret the tunnels wanted me to know.

"Guys?" I called, rushing to catch up. "Guys, where are you?"

No response.

"I can't find you, can you wait up a minute?"

Still nothing, just the whisper in my mind and a sinking feeling in my stomach.

"Noah? Rachel?"

I tried the comm unit Rachel had stuffed in our packs. Nothing but static this far underground.

Breaking into a run, I tried to catch up. The gravel scattered under my feet, sending ripples of noise echoing down the tunnel. I hadn't been stationary for that long; the others should have appeared by now, or at least stopped to wait for me. They were gone. Someone had taken them.

Something had taken them.

There was a scatter of rocks ahead, and I stopped. Rachel and Noah; they must have heard me. My goggles fogged from the run, and I took them off again, rubbing my shirt on the lens to clear the glass.

Something hit me hard in the chest, and I flew backwards into the wall, cracking my head on the stone.

The goggles fell to the ground with a crunch.

I pulled myself upright, but was thrown down again by a hand, its nails clawing into my arm.

A creature. It had to be a creature.

Before I could get up, it was on top of me, its body warm and wet from whatever it had just been eating. Its legs draped across mine, and its arms pinned me flat. My hands were empty; I must have dropped the machete when it threw me to the ground. I couldn't see anything, but I could feel the heat from its head radiating close to mine. Its breath rolled across my neck, and then into my left ear.

"Found you," it hissed, and ran its tongue from my cheek to my chin. Its breath made me gag. Unless I moved fast, something horrible was going to happen.

"Been looking. Searching. Wanting. Needing. You came to me. I have you."

My hand scrambled in the darkness, trying to make contact with the machete handle.

It ran its tongue across my other cheek, up to my right ear.

"You are mine," it rasped. "And you are so very, very good."

My breath came in panicked bursts, but I still managed to tune into the air behind the creature's head. The flare sparked for a moment, illuminating its face as the light reflected off the walls. The face was bushy and bearded, the same one that had attacked me in the train carriage. He smiled. "You have sight. That's good. You will satisfy."

The flare sparked again, and he turned to watch it, grinning darkly.

He was distracted. I ripped my hand from his and found the machete handle. He turned his eyes back to me, then they went dead as I separated his head from his body. My chest went suddenly warm, and I pushed his bleeding torso off me as the head rolled to the side of the corridor. I didn't dare look at it.

I doubled over, taking deep breaths, then threw up.

Who knew what I'd find when I tracked down Noah and Rachel.

TWENTY-EIGHT

My shirt was wet from the creature's blood. The goggles were broken, so I had to pull out a torch from my pack, which had somehow survived being crushed against the wall.

It only lit up a small circle in front of me, but it was enough to give warning of another creature-thing in the dark. Perhaps I should stop thinking of them as creatures. They weren't exactly human, but they weren't animals. From what I'd seen in the morgue, they'd once been human, at least before Wheeler got to them. I tried not to picture the headless body in the tunnel behind me. I'd had no choice, but it was still awful.

There was no sign at all of Noah and Rachel, not even a pack left behind, or footprints in the gravel. It was like they'd disappeared completely, which was a much better outcome than finding them mauled to death. If they'd been taken, there was no evidence of a struggle. Hopefully, they'd just gotten lost somewhere and we'd find each other eventually.

The blood started to dry on my shirt, making it crusty. I'd gotten used to that feeling by now, though, so it wasn't as bad as the first time it had happened, walking through the bush into the Kindred compound with Noah.

Still, that time I'd had company. Down here, I was alone.

Footsteps scuffed the gravel up ahead. Maybe Rachel and Noah had finally found the path. I started to call out, but noticed a red glow coming from around the tunnel corner. Our torches weren't red. Someone else was up there. I switched off my torch and used the red light to guide my path.

To stay quiet, I walked on the metal part of the track, balancing along it like a beam. There were a lot of people ahead. They talked quietly, murmurs turning into sentences as I drew closer to the group. The corner opened out onto a straight tunnel, and I finally saw them up ahead. They were walking away from me, and couldn't see me back in the dark, so I trailed along far behind in the tunnel.

There were at least fifteen people, wearing hooded black robes. Kindred. I was definitely heading in the right direction. If I kept following this group, I'd end up at Wheeler's demonstration. Although without Noah and Rachel, I had no idea how to stop any of this.

"This demonstration had better be good," a female voice grumbled from near the back of the pack.

"Wheeler thinks he's solved it," said a male. "At any rate, the ceremony was going to happen with or without him. At least this way we're getting two things done at once."

"Be careful of your tone," said an older female. "You're bordering on sacrilege. It is not us who determine the Agenda, or the manner through which it comes. Respect the Elders, and those we serve."

"Forgive me, Elder Melendez. I will hold my tongue."

I now recognised the Elder's voice. Lucy Melendez, the 6pm news anchor for the National Bulletin.

Coughing, another female spoke up. Her voice was familiar too, somehow. "I'm sure we've all heard Wheeler's tone running through the city," she said, "But how are we to remain unaffected? I don't enjoy being beholden to his unique charms."

The others murmured assent.

"Nothing to fear, Jacinta," said Lucy. "He's created a device that blocks the tone. We'll remain fully immune to his creation."

Jacinta. Of course. Jacinta Tarryn, the local Minister for Parliament. That's why I recognised the voice; she was on the news all the time giving press conferences. The Kindred really were well-positioned in the city.

"Yes, I'm sure we can trust Wheeler to protect us from himself," huffed Jacinta. "He's a psychopath."

"He's extreme, certainly," Lucy snapped. "But not nearly as extreme as we must be to invoke the Final Day."

If Wheeler was an extremist even by Kindred standards, we really were in serious trouble.

"None of us knew about his experiments roaming around down here," said the male who'd been told off earlier. "They're an abomination."

"They're precisely what is required in order to complete the Agenda. Are you having second thoughts? Want to run off to the Unseen like a little coward?"

"Not at all, my loyalty is complete. But there must be another way, another method of—"

"Enough!" yelled Lucy. "If you continue speaking this filth, I'll tie you up down here and leave you to Wheeler's experiments. I've seen what they do to a human body, dead or alive, and I must say they're inventive. They'll reach right down inside you and pull up your—"

"I apologise, Elder." The man's grovelling was almost funny. "I spoke out of turn. I have no doubts about our agenda or the beauty of the plan. I will do anything to see the Final Day come to pass."

Interesting. They didn't view the Final Day as a given, at least not as much as Hackman had. Where there was doubt, there was hope—for me and for the possibility of turning other Kindred to our cause. If the end wasn't certain, maybe we could change their minds about its necessity.

A hand covered my mouth and dragged me to the side.

I bit down on the fingers, drawing blood.

The person behind me swore and let go. "Ari, what the hell?"

"Hud?" I turned toward him.

"Well most of me. Some of me is now apparently in your mouth. Sorry, that sounded weird."

I resisted the urge to laugh, instead turning to hug Hud, who looked exhausted. "I'm so glad you're here. What happened?"

"I escaped. Where are the others? We're going to need them to stop Wheeler."

"They're missing," I said. "Rachel and Noah came down with me, but they disappeared."

He sighed. "Last time I saw you guys, you were trapped with Wheeler."

I told him about the night before, about how we'd run, about the car chase. I left Josh out of the story entirely, though. I couldn't tell Hud that Josh had died. I wasn't up for that story just yet.

"That's some serious spy stuff you guys pulled. Well done." He paused for a moment. "There's a back way to the ceremony chamber. If you follow me, we should get there before the Kindred group you were tracking."

He opened a metal door to my right. "This is an access tunnel built as an emergency pathway through the network. Using this, we should be able to avoid the Kindred, plus whatever the hell those creature things are."

"They're humans," I said. "At least, they used to be."

I ducked in after him, entering the access tunnel. Emergency lighting ran in rows along the tunnel walls, but none of them were switched on. Nothing down here was supposed to be in use. We had to walk single file through the narrow passage, but I felt safer in this space. If Hud was right, the creatures wouldn't be in here.

Hopefully.

As we walked, I updated Hud on our findings from the morgue.

"That's messed up," he said. "But things make a bit more sense now."

He ducked to avoid a low beam, and I did the same. "What do you mean?"

"When they took me, they threw a hood over my head, so I couldn't see where we were driving. I tried to count the turns and the seconds but couldn't do both at the same time. Wherever I was, though, it was probably twenty minutes or so from the docks. We went underground, and they removed the hood and threw me in a cage.

"There were at least a dozen cages around mine, and they were filled with those creature things, the humans, whatever you call them. They were screaming and screeching and yelling awful things. One of them had chewed his own hand off and was using it to try and hit the guard standing outside."

"That's gross," I said. "But from what I've seen of them, it doesn't surprise me."

"Yeah. Another guy came in and talked with the guard for a while. They call the creatures Zealots."

"Like fanatics?"

"I guess so. Anyway, the whole room was covered in cameras, so no chance of using my abilities to get out. They had the place locked down tight. After a few hours they took one of the Zealots, the one who'd chewed off his hand. He didn't look exactly healthy, so I guess he was the obvious choice for whatever came next.

"Aside from our cages, there was a huge red curtain on one side of the room. They took him behind that. I heard some screaming, and then he stopped. They either killed him or set him free. I'm willing to bet the former."

It was awful, but probably merciful in a sick way. Nobody should have to live the way the Zealots did.

"How did you get out?" I asked Hud.

Hud ducked to avoid a low cross-beam. "That's a story in itself. Last night, they brought in a girl. Her eyes were black, but she wasn't as hairy as the others. I think she was in the early stages of the change you saw in the morgue. Anyway, she was angry, and wild, but still aware of her surroundings. She looked straight at me, and we had an understanding. I yelled at the guard, and he looked at me long enough for the girl to bite into his neck. Straight into the artery. He went down hard. She grabbed the keys and let us all out, and we escaped into the tunnels. There were more Zealots down there, and I didn't like my chances of survival, so I ducked into the closest tunnel I could find. That was maybe ten hours ago. I've been wandering around down here ever since, trying to find my way out. I heard Kindred talking and followed the sound, and then I came across you."

"That's lucky."

"No kidding. This tunnel goes forever. I can't believe I found you when I did."

My legs were getting tired from so much walking. They were already sore from the night before, and now they were burning.

"There's so many Kindred down here. We have no chance to stop tonight unless we find Noah and Rachel."

He stopped and looked at me, face glowing in the torchlight. "If they're missing, they were probably captured. Hopefully they're holding them in those cages behind the curtain. It's not actually too far in a straight line from here to there. Surprising how fast you can move through these tunnels when you know where you're going. Although, I wish I'd found a way out by now."

I couldn't imagine Noah and Rachel allowing themselves to be captured. They would have gone down fighting, that's for sure.

We walked in silence for a while, until finally Hud stopped at a door marked "18".

"We're here," he said. "Stay low."

Cracking open the door, Hud stepped into a cavern, a huge space covered by a subterranean lake. We were in the spot where Josh died. The place that held the Shadow.

TWENTY-NINE

"No," I whispered. "No way. I'm not going in there."

"Relax, Ari. It's just a bit of water. Besides, we don't have to go into the lake. The tunnel leads off this way." Hud pointed to an opening behind me.

"There's a Shadow in the water," I said. "It's living in here. It—it took Josh."

"As in your friend Josh? What do you mean it took him? What was he even doing here?"

"He came to rescue us. The Shadow was swirling around and he let himself be taken to slow it down."

Hud stopped and looked me in the eyes. "Ari, I'm sorry. I never met him, but I can tell he meant a lot to you."

Despite the danger in staying, my eyes scanned the water, looking for any sign of Josh. Maybe he wasn't dead. Maybe he'd fought back.

Hud put his hand on my shoulder. "If he's still in there, he'll be below the water." He spoke softly, gently. "Bodies don't float for a while, days sometimes. I wish I didn't know that, but I found my best friend Dan—Never mind. The point is, my dear, I don't think you're going to see him out there."

"My dear? What are you, sixty?"

He coughed. "Sorry. My mum used to call me that when I was sad. Force of habit, I guess. You know how they say you end up like your parents."

For some reason, I wasn't sad. I'd bawled my eyes out in the tunnel when Rachel had said his name, but now I felt calm. Peaceful, almost. I'd dealt with enough death in my life to know that this was expected. My heart tended to do its own thing; being sad at all the wrong times. It had been unsettling, at first, but I was used to it now.

"We should go," I said. "But are you saying you came through here in your escape?"

Hud nodded.

"You didn't see anything then?"

"I'm sorry, no. I wasn't really concentrating on the water, but there was no Shadow here."

I sighed. "It must have moved on. Still, I'd prefer not to test that theory. Lead the way."

Hud stepped in front of me and walked into the tunnel. This one was different from the last, and it was to the left of the tunnel we'd escaped through earlier, running at almost a ninety-degree angle from our initial route. We were heading deeper into the system, and we no longer had the safety of the access tunnel. I held my fingers over the torch to baffle the light and keep us hidden.

"How did you even get around down here without a torch?" I asked.

"I've got the same abilities as you, remember? Although apparently I'm nowhere near as powerful. I found a few sticks, set them on fire. It wasn't great, but it worked well enough."

Right. I'd forgotten Hud could tune like the rest of us. Somehow, he felt like a rookie, even though he'd technically been in the war longer than I had.

We walked the rest of the way in silence. As we approached our destination, I grew tense. My heart beat faster, and my feet stepped lighter. It was as if my whole body was on high alert, conscious of every scrape of gravel against my shoes, aware of the rustling of my clothing. Everything mattered now, and everything was important. One mistake could get us killed.

Hud stopped at an intersection. To my left, red light glowed faintly out of an opening in the rock. It was big enough to crawl through, but only just.

"Here," he whispered. "That space. I found it after my escape. It leads straight in to the front part of the auditorium."

"Auditorium?"

"They call it the Apex," Hud said. "It's an important meeting room or something."

"I know the Apex. Not this one, but a different one back at Ettney."

I had a memory of stairs peeling away from the wall, men and women plummeting to their deaths, and a Shadow, draining the life out of a screaming girl.

"You alright?" Hud asked.

"What?"

"Drifted off there for a second. You going to be okay in here?"

I gritted my teeth. "I'll be fine."

Hud bent down and crawled through the opening, beckoning for me to do the same. Once inside, he stood. We were behind a rock wall, in a collapsed section of the old tunnel.

"Which way?" I whispered.

Hud motioned for me to be silent. Red light flickered off the wall a few steps ahead. He signalled for me to step forward and ducked his head around the edge of the wall. I did the same.

The Apex was incredible, and way bigger than the Apex at Ettney. From our vantage point on the second floor, this Apex was at least twice as high, and three times as long. It could have easily been a stadium — if you took away the Kindred insignia and added football banners. Burning torches rimmed the perimeter, casting rippling light up into the roof. There were no chairs in this Apex, and it was filled with people, even more than Ettney. There were thousands of masked Kindred here, filling most of the floor space, murmuring in anticipation. I shook my head. How could we ever hope to win against an enemy this size?

I pointed to a raised platform at the opposite end, which was backed by a huge red curtain. "Is that where you were held?" I whispered. "Behind there?"

"I think so. The layout looks right. If Noah and Rachel are anywhere, they'll be behind that."

The torches flickered as the side doors opened. More Kindred spilled into the Apex. I couldn't tell from such a distance, but it was probably the group I'd been following.

A man stepped onto the platform and removed his mask. Even from back here, I could tell it was Wheeler. The crowd went silent.

"My people," he began, voice echoing out into the crowd. "I have called you together to witness a truly momentous evening. But before we begin, it is only fitting that we recognise the most significant among us. No longer will they live in hiding, but from tonight, the city will know who their rulers are. Tonight, they will meet their gods. They will meet *us*."

The crowd cheered, seething with anticipation. The energy in the room was so thick I could almost touch it. I closed my eyes for a moment to tune, and Wheeler's tone washed over me. I took a deep, beautiful breath, letting the freedom into my lungs. I'd missed this feeling. Out in the city the tone was quiet, not strong enough to affect my mind. But in here, it rippled through the atmosphere, charging the air with its invitation to let go.

Hud frowned at me.

"You don't feel it?" I asked.

He shook his head.

Wheeler continued. "Step forward, Elders, Arch Elders. Step into the spotlight. Claim your inheritance."

Sixteen figures made their way on stage, removing their masks to thunderous applause. Jacinta was one of them, and Lucy another. Most of the elders I didn't recognise.

When the crowd finally died down, Wheeler raised his hands. "And finally, our guest of honour this evening. The head of our movement in this nation. The one most worthy of our respect."

There was a whisper across the crowd, and one final figure stepped onto the stage from the wings.

"Please welcome our dear, magnificent Mother."

THIRTY

My breath caught in my chest. She removed her mask. There, on stage, was the Mother. The woman calling the shots at Ettney. One of the most powerful leaders of the Kindred, and the one who'd ordered Rachel tortured. Green eyes, white-blonde hair cropped short around her head. Scar running down her neck. She was unmistakable.

"You know her?" asked Hud.

"She's an old acquaintance," I murmured.

Wheeler's tone was still soothing, but the sight of the Mother had shaken me.

"Children," she began in her warm, gravelly voice. "This family has been waiting in the wings for too long. With this moment, with our dear brother Wheeler's breakthrough, we begin not only the most significant leap forward the Agenda has ever seen, but a new era in Kindred history. Indeed, a new era in the history of the world."

The crowd applauded once again.

"And so, in this watershed moment, we shall begin the demonstration." She turned to address the wings of the stage. "Come, ancient one. Prepare yourself."

The crowd sunk to their knees. I'd seen that reverence only once before, in the execution ceremony at Ettney.

"It's coming," I warned Hud.

"What is?"

"Look." I pointed to the right of the room, where a huge set of carved doors swung open.

A Shadow entered, rippling and pulsing, entrail-like tendrils whipping through the air. This Shadow was mostly solid, same as the other one after it fed on the creatures in the tunnel. This Shadow had been feeding, and I got the feeling it was about to feed again.

The cold spot on my stomach went icy, and I put my hand to it in reflex.

"My people," Wheeler spoke over the hushed crowd. He spoke with reverence, gentleness, almost. His eyes burned with a fervour visible even from the other side of the Apex. "For a long time, our Lords have languished in the space between, living in the now and not-yet, shifting between this world and the next. But no longer. The Zealots have been birthed, and they now provide a pathway to completion. This brings hope to all of us, hope that the Final Day will soon be upon us. Hope that we can join our Lords in the time to come."

Hackman had used words like that, all the way back at the hospital. 'Now and not yet', 'the space between'. I'd thought it strange at the time, the ravings of a fanatic. Perhaps there was more to it than that. Perhaps it held a key to the nature of the Shadows themselves.

The Shadow reached the stage, rising onto the platform to take its place among the Elders, who formed a semi-circle around it. The Shadow was being patient. It was waiting for its food.

"Bring the Zealot," Wheeler commanded, and four large Kindred guards dragged a screaming Zealot on stage, one holding each of its arms and legs. Even then, they could barely control him.

The Shadow rippled with desire. It wanted the Zealot, and it wanted him badly.

The Elders shrunk back from the Zealot. It seemed not even they were fully on-board with Wheeler's plan, and from the conversation I'd heard in the tunnels, there was some dissent about the way Wheeler was conducting business. That left an opening, perhaps. One I could exploit.

"Let the ceremony begin!" Wheeler called, and the four guards stepped back, letting the Zealot drop to the floor. He tried to run, but the Shadow caught him with two tendrils, lifting him in the air to feed. The Zealot screamed, and shuddered, and stopped moving, skin dried out like I'd seen so many times before.

The Shadow swelled and flickered, tendrils pulsing and twisting. From its stomach, a face appeared, serpentine features pressing through the flesh. Tendrils retreated inside the body, and scales emerged from the smoke. It was changing, solidifying. Transforming into something new.

The crowd moved from their knees to their faces, flattening themselves on the ground as a mark of ultimate respect.

The Shadow morphed, tendrils spiralling into sinewy legs, wrapping muscle and tissue around bone, and leathery skin slithered over the top. Arms emerged too, impossibly long but growing in the same pattern of bone, muscle, and skin. The face shifted towards the top of the torso. A bone emerged from the neck, and the face slid on top, covering the neck stump and crawling around the spine. The face was distorted, but almost human, with cavities where the eyes and mouth should be. It had no eyeballs or tongue, though; they were more like holes in the skin than proper features. Several tendrils remained spinning in the air, spurting from the stomach and back of the Shadow-thing.

"Brothers and Sisters," Wheeler whispered. "Gaze upon the true nature of our Masters. Gaze upon your freedom."

The prostrate Kindred raised their heads from the floor, and a murmur of excitement ran through the room.

The Shadow looked at them, nodding slowly, taking it all in. It stretched out its arms but, a moment later, let out a skin-crawling scream. Tendrils burst from its stomach, and the skin on its legs unravelled. The body contorted, and its face blew apart in a shower of smoke. As quickly as the Shadow had solidified, it returned to its original state, smoke and snaking parts spreading out into the air.

The crowd rippled again, concerned about what was unfolding on the stage.

"Don't be afraid," said Wheeler. "The Zealots were a proof of concept, nothing more. They are useful, but only the precursor to my true method, one that provides a longer-term solution."

He motioned to the guards at the side of the stage. The Shadow waited patiently; as if it was in on the plan. It knew what was coming; the first feeding was all theatre, a show for the attendees. Wheeler was a smart performer. He knew how to work a crowd.

"Bring out the true subject."

The guards disappeared off stage.

What if they were retrieving Noah and Rachel?

"We have to do something," I said. "They're going to feed them to the Shadow."

Hud knew who I was talking about. "If we can take out Wheeler, we'll be able to bring this whole arena down. Nobody's looking at the roof. When they lie flat again, you can tune into the rocks above and destroy the entire auditorium."

"And kill everyone inside?"

"If that's what it takes. You've seen what Wheeler's planning. We have to kill them all, and we have to do it now."

"What about the city above? I don't know what's overhead in the streets. What if there's an apartment building or skyscraper up there? Everyone inside would die."

"Like I said," Hud said darkly. "If that's what it takes."

"Hud, what happened to you down here?" I frowned. I hadn't pegged him for a murderer, even with everything that was at stake.

He ignored my question. "Are you in or out?"

I shook my head. "How would you even take out Wheeler from this far away?"

Hud reached into his coat and brought out a handgun. "I grew up taking shots at feral pigs on my cousin's farm outside Jandura. I can probably hit him from here."

"It's too dangerous to use guns. The Kindred in there could melt the bullet before it hits him, then blow up the whole thing in your hand. Didn't you learn anything at training?"

"If there's a feeding they'll be facedown, and Wheeler won't be expecting it. Once I've hit him, I'll ditch the gun and you can destroy the Apex."

"What about Noah and Rachel? They'll be on stage."

Hud shrugged. "They'd want us to take the opportunity. It sucks, but this is a war. Collateral damage and all that stuff."

I couldn't believe what he was saying, but before I could respond he was taking aim at Wheeler.

"Hud, no!"

The gun blasted and my ears rang.

Hud had missed Wheeler, but he steadied his hand for another shot.

The crowd yelled, and Wheeler ducked for cover.

There was a crack on the back of my head, and the world went dark.

THIRTY-ONE

The world was blurry when I returned to it. I wasn't out for long, but when I came to, Eden stood over me, wielding a plank of wood.

"You..." I started but trailed off as the world went blank once more.

I woke again to a scraping feeling on my back. I was being dragged somewhere. My wrists were bound, and I was blindfolded.

"Hud?" I called.

There was no response.

Darkness.

"Ari?" said a voice. I was too groggy to work out who it was. My hands were tied to something behind me, but I managed to roll over and lie on my side in case I threw up. I did not feel good.

"Ari, it's me, Noah. Rachel and Hud are here too. Try and wake up."

Blinking, my eyes slowly cleared. Each of us were cable-tied to opposite corners of a metal cage. Noah was to my left, and Rachel sat across from him, diagonally opposite me. Hud was tied to my right, and he looked dazed, probably from the concussion. Rachel and Hud were gagged, but Noah had worked his free. The cage was small enough that the others were just out of reach. I tried to roll further and see behind me, but my shoulders pinched. If I moved anymore, I'd probably dislocate them.

A figure sat hunched in another cage to my right. He looked zoned out, like they'd pumped him with drugs. He was pretty hairy and was gnawing on something. The Zealot took his snack out of his mouth to inspect it for a moment. It was his foot. He was chewing through his own ankle.

I swallowed and turned away. He seemed to have no interest in us, and I didn't want to attract it. The rest of the cages were empty, probably from Hud's breakout. It was unlikely we'd be rescued that way again.

Closing my eyes, I tried to tune, but the static was too intense. It wasn't just from the others in the cage, either. A dozen security cameras lined the concrete roof, pointed in all directions. No way our abilities would work in here.

The space we were in was long, and rounded at the top, almost like a bunker. To my left, a huge red curtain blocked our view of what must have been the Apex. We were exactly where Hud had predicted; the holding cells behind the stage. He wouldn't be happy to be stuck here again.

I began to speak, but Rachel grunted at me from behind her gag. She was listening intently to the voice coming from behind the curtain. Wheeler's voice.

"My apologies for the delay, brothers and sisters. We have apprehended the Unseen filth that threatened our evening, and there is nothing more to be concerned about. Now, we continue the demonstration. You can see that the Zealots, while useful, and certainly a leap forward, are not our final solution to the problem we face. This is why I have been working on a different application of the Pulse, and one which has, to date, yielded much more powerful results."

He was going to feed us to the Shadow. Any minute now, the guards were going to burst in and drag one of us away.

"The Zealots are amusing, but they are not as purely transformed as they appear. The process of inspiration is muddy and doesn't always take well to an adult brain. Too many thoughts have already been formed. Too many memories to counteract the impulse."

Rachel frowned and shook her head slowly. She'd figured something out.

I raised one eyebrow at her, but she ignored me and kept listening.

Noah's face was dark.

"Bring out our solution," Wheeler pronounced.

There was an audible gasp from the crowd, then screaming filled with profanities and threats and hatred. The screaming of a child. A boy, perhaps no more than ten.

Wheeler was going to feed the child to the Shadow.

The screaming became muffled, as if the child had been gagged.

"If we begin the transformation earlier, if we begin when the mind is young, the result is far more functional, and far more complete. If we change a child, we create a complete, pure form of Zealot, one who offers much, much more to the Agenda."

That's why Wheeler had been collecting kids. He'd been corrupting them, somehow, transforming them, encouraging them to bring out the darkness in themselves. He was creating an army of child Zealots who were far more in control than the adult versions. Their brains were still growing and adjusted better to the changes in their amygdalae. Wheeler was clever. Sick, but clever.

"So, with that in mind, let us proceed with our final demonstration."

He paused for a moment.

"Actually, before we do, I'd like to introduce you to someone you have heard a lot about."

The crowd murmured.

"Many of you had friends in Ettney. People you cared about. People you loved."

My heart dropped. Oh no.

"Well," he continued. "Here to witness tonight's final demonstration is The Butcher of Ettney herself, Ari Carpenter!"

The red curtain drew back, and the crowd went silent. Through the bars, I could see the whole picture. The Shadow, hovering at the edge of the stage. Wheeler, pointing at me. A young boy gagged and struggling to break free of his bonds. The Mother, sneering at me. And an entire crowd, thousands upon thousands of eyes staring my way.

I expected the crowd to start yelling at me, to rush the stage and tear me apart. But they didn't. They just kept staring. That was somehow worse.

Hud, Rachel and Noah stared back. None of us knew what to make of this situation. We were like zoo animals, or maybe cows waiting to be slaughtered. Either way, this wasn't going to end well.

Wheeler walked slowly towards me, smiling, the torchlights flickering in his eyes. He stepped around the cage to my side, and grinned.

"Get away from her," Noah hissed.

"Shut up," said Wheeler, pulling out a taser and firing it at Noah's back. Noah convulsed, and knocked his head on the bars of the cage so hard he went limp. The crowd laughed, and Wheeler looked at the taser in his hand.

"Wonderful invention," said Wheeler. "I'd never used one before the other night. Thank you for sending it my way."

He was speaking quietly, so there was no way the crowd could hear, but they still kept their full attention on the stage. Wheeler had them spellbound.

Me, too.

Looking at him, I felt euphoric. I didn't even care that Noah was unconscious next to me. Nothing mattered but Wheeler, but his truth. The truth in his eyes.

He bent down to my level and whispered in my ear. "This demonstration is for you. One day you'll understand why."

I closed my eyes, a grin spreading across my face. Rachel smiled too, beneath her gag. He walked away, and I longed for him to return. His presence was a drug, and I wanted all of it.

"Now that we have our guest of honour present, let us begin."

The child was taken forward, and the Shadow slowly moved across the stage. I started to laugh. It was all so wonderfully funny.

The Shadow took the child in its smoke-limbs, and the boy screamed, and twisted, and shuddered, and I threw my head back and closed my eyes and listened to the sound and it was so awfully absurd, and it should have been horrifying, but instead it felt like flying. Rachel smiled too, and we both grinned at each other as the child screamed again, and then stopped moving, and fell to the floor, cold and grey and dead.

I closed my eyes and breathed in deep.

I was free.

THIRTY-TWO

After it finished feeding, the Shadow coalesced once more, forming limbs and body and face. The crowd was frozen, not daring to even shuffle their feet. This time, it didn't blow apart like it had the last time. It stayed solid for a minute, two minutes, maybe more. One brave soul started to applaud, and he was joined by another, and another, until the whole room was roaring with appreciation for whatever Wheeler had just done. I didn't really care, though. I was floating above it all, and nothing could touch me. I was in a cage, but my mind was free.

"As you can see, this offers a much more lasting solution to the problem," Wheeler said. "And so, with that in mind, we will accelerate this stage of the Agenda. By this time tomorrow, the city will *know* we are here."

The crowd cheered with wild, ecstatic applause that drowned out Wheeler's attempts to silence them. Eventually, they went still, and he gave them instructions.

"On the way out, you'll notice crates of dampers. They will block out the Pulse and prevent you from becoming Zealots. As beautiful as my creatures are, I appreciate you may want to stay in your present minds. Obviously, you'll need weapons to defend yourselves. They'll be available at our drop-sites within the hour. Be ready. You'll know when the plan is in motion." He chuckled. "It will be hard to miss."

The Kindred filed slowly out of the Apex under the supervision of the Elders on stage, and the Shadow, which was strangely motionless. They were normally frenzied, violent, and terrifying. Not that I would have feared it now. All my fears had been replaced with an overwhelming sense of peace.

The Mother turned to me and the others in the cage. She smiled for a moment, a caring, compassionate warmth emanating from her eyes. Perhaps she wasn't so bad after all. Perhaps she really was trying to help.

No. I shook my head, trying to break out of Wheeler's grip. My head was still floating, but I could never think of the Mother as good. If I did, I was in a really messed up place.

She sneered as she noticed the change in me, and murmured something to Wheeler, who nodded and bowed as she left.

Wheeler turned and walked over to the four of us. The Shadow moved slowly behind him, black, snakelike limbs propelling it across the floor instead of the floating I was used to. As the Shadow came closer, I got a clearer look. It was definitely similar to the one I'd seen on the roof of my bedroom six months ago, although it was in a different form. It was almost human, except for the scaly skin that rippled as it moved, and the tendrils still pulsing from its stomach like someone had ripped inside it and started pulling things out. Its face was empty of clear features, but it had the suggestion of a face, like someone pressing through a sheet. It tilted its head to look at me.

I swallowed, fear starting to emerge even through the peace Wheeler brought me. "I know you, don't I?" I asked.

The Shadow said nothing, just tilted its head slightly. Around the edges of its body was a dark haze, like a fire in reverse, sucking smoke into itself as a black halo.

I looked at the blank spaces where its eyes should be. "You were in my room."

It said nothing, but I knew it recognised me. It was the thing that had reached inside me, into my chest, into my soul, and left the black mark that festered on my stomach.

The Shadow shuddered, and its edges blurred.

"It's not working, is it?" I said. "You're turning back again. Whatever that means."

My fear was strong now, overriding the Wheeler-induced euphoria.

The Shadow bent towards my cage, putting its empty face up against the bars. This close, I could see inside the cavities in its head where the eyes and mouth should have been. They were filled with tendrils, tiny, rippling tendrils like black worms, crawling over each other, twisting and turning and shifting. Even in my current state, it was sickening. One of them reached toward me through its left eye, and I recoiled, pressing my back up against the cage. The Shadow rippled as it saw my fear. I had the feeling it was laughing.

It stood up straight again, and exited the room silently, leaving us alone with Wheeler.

Noah had woken, and he and Rachel were out of their minds. Hud sat quietly, but the other two kept laughing, grinning, falling back against the bars of the cages. I was holding it together better than that, but the tone still threatened to break my mind.

Wheeler came close to the cage, smiling. "You won't last much longer," he said. "Soon, you'll turn. Soon, you'll reveal your true nature."

"Become a Zealot?" I said.

"Perhaps," he replied. "Many of the first Zealots were captured Unseen. Since then I've expanded the program. Either way, I'm curious to see what you'll turn into."

Eden entered from behind Wheeler, smirking at the sight of us in cages. "Father," she said. "When can I have my reward?"

"When I've seen what she becomes," he smiled, placing his hand on the back of her head. "Then you can kill her."

She grinned, staring at me. "Good. She'll finally pay for what she did."

"What?" I replied. "What have I done? Why do you want to kill me?"

"You really don't know?" she asked, glaring at me.

I shook my head.

Her face twisted, losing the smile and contorting into a mask of pure hate. "You killed my parents."

I stared back at Eden, unsure how to react, or even what she was talking about. "What? I don't even know your parents."

Wheeler snickered and walked to the door. "I'll let you two catch up," he called over his shoulder, before leaving entirely.

Eden sat in front of the cage, getting close enough for me to see the marks on her arms and around her neck.

"What did he do to you?" I asked, quietly.

"Wheeler didn't do this," she replied. "He's good to me. These are from a run-in with some Zealots two nights ago. They came out worse off."

"You can certainly handle yourself," I said.

"Something you'll find out soon enough."

My mind had cleared a bit since Wheeler had left. The cameras still made it impossible to tune, but I no longer felt like I was floating above my own body.

"Eden," I said. "What happened to your parents?"

"I was eight when we moved here from Bandung, in Indonesia. I grew up there. My parents joined the Unseen before I was born. They were transferred to Australia on my birthday. They worked around Ettney, spying on Kindred communications. Until six months ago."

"The assault on the safehouses," I said.

Eden nodded. "When you exposed Rachel, the Kindred got their location."

"They were on the farm?"

"No, further out, a warehouse in the mountains." She crossed her arms.

I swallowed. "I never went there."

"Doesn't matter. It's your fault they're dead. You caused the attack. You gave them up. I hid in a cupboard and watched my parents die. I watched my dad try to protect mum, cover her, and heard her screaming as she burned from the inside out. Because of you."

I opened my mouth to speak but what could I say? She was right. It was because of me. I lived with the guilt of that every single day; I'd never known their names, but so many in the Unseen had died because of my impulsive decision to give Rachel up. I'd been trying so hard to move on, but everywhere I looked, there were reminders of the carnage I'd caused. Still, why was Eden working for the Kindred? Her parents' death was as much their fault as mine.

Eden looked so vulnerable, suddenly, talking about her loss. Maybe I could get through to her and break past Wheeler's thrall. "How did you end up in Coleton?"

"Jumped on a bus outside Ettney," she said, "and ended up on the street. I've learned a lot these last six months. How to survive. Who people really are. They're all cruel, and selfish, and take what they want. That's why they have to die. That's why *you* have to die."

She stood before I could respond and stormed out of the room.

I sat quietly in my guilt.

Rachel worked her gag free. "She's right, you know."

"What?"

"It is your fault. All of it. Everything that happened to me. Everyone who died. It's your fault." Her voice sounded strange, like she was holding back.

My fists clenched, and my heart started to race. "You know what, Rachel? I'm sick of this."

"Oh, really?"

"If you've got something to say just say it or shut up."

She pulled against the restraints, as if she wanted to break free and attack me. "Alright, I will. I hate you. I hate you for what you did to me. It's your fault I'm like this. It's your fault I'm broken. You know how I got through the torture at Ettney? Picturing your face, picturing beating you to a pulp, imagining doing to you what they were doing to me. When we escaped the Complex, I wanted to tear you apart. And I would have, too, if your mum hadn't gone and died and ruined everything."

My face burned, and my eyes filled with tears. My mouth hung open. Had she really just said that? "You know what, you stupid little cow?" I said, letting it all out. "I'm glad it happened to you. If this is the kind of person you are, you deserved to be tortured. I wish they'd killed you in there. Then, I wouldn't have had to deal with this."

"Ari, shut up," said Noah.

I wanted to stop, but I couldn't. It was as if something awful was coming loose from inside me, like a dragon had been chained down for too long and now it was breaking free.

"Seriously, Noah? You want to talk about anger? You've been holding back too, so come on, let's hear it."

"Fine!" he shouted. "You know what I think when I look at you? I wonder why I bothered saving such a selfish little brat! You were playing me and Josh for months, stringing us along. He's better off dead in that lake than being your little plaything, your puppet, there to make you feel good. You leeched off him, and you leeched off me, and every time I see your face, I remember that you killed my dad. He was awful, and I hated him, but I can't ever forgive you for killing him. You want the truth? There it is!"

His words hit me in the gut. I reeled, preparing a counterattack. Steeling my gaze, and blinking back my tears, I said quietly, and coldly. "I wish it was you in the lake, instead of Josh." I didn't mean it, but I knew it would hurt him the most.

Noah unleashed, and Rachel joined him, screaming abuse, hurling filth and anger, and I retaliated until the three of us were yelling hoarse, voices cracking with rage, wrists bleeding from pulling against our restraints.

"Guys?" said Hud from the corner. His voice rose to a yell. "Guys! Stop!"

We did, but glared at him for interrupting our fury.

"It's Wheeler," Hud said. "It's the tone. The thing he called the Pulse. Can't you still hear it?"

I shook my head. "No, there's too much static."

"It's still there," Hud replied. "I can feel it."

Noah spoke through gritted teeth. "The amygdalae produce joy, but they also regulate anger, remember?"

The rage still boiled in my stomach, but I nodded. "Maybe this is stage two, the thing that comes after that flying feeling. Maybe anger comes next."

Rachel was still breathing heavily, eyes filled with hate. She spat the words. "So, what comes after anger?"

Hud was strangely calm. "We end up as Zealots."

THIRTY-THREE

The thought was too awful. Me, becoming one of those *things*. Those angry, violent, wild things, eating dead animals, and people. Maybe, left alone in this cage, eventually we'd eat each other.

"We've got to get out of here," I said.

"No kidding," Rachel growled.

"The people in the morgue," said Noah. "He's been testing his effect for months. Those bodies were the early experiments, to see what happened when people started to change."

"That's why there was the spike in random violent crime," I figured. "Wheeler was doing test runs."

Rachel looked at me. "If he gets any stronger, somehow accelerates the Pulse…"

I swallowed. "The whole city will change, turn into Zealots, and every child in the city will become his private army, and eventually food for the Shadows."

"Did you see what happened to the Shadow when it fed on that kid?" Noah said. "I've never seen anything like it."

"Me neither," I replied. "But if the Kindred want it to happen, I'm betting it's a bad thing." I turned to Hud, who was sitting quietly with his eyes closed, probably trying to tune out the effects of Wheeler's Pulse. "You seem to have a connection to the Shadows, somehow. Are you getting anything? Do you know why it changed?"

Hud kept his eyes closed and shook his head. "All quiet for now. The Pulse might be blocking the connection."

"Either way, we need to escape. Now." I craned my neck, trying to search for a solution.

Eden returned and stood at the doorway. She wore a small metallic device that looked almost like headphones. A band ran across the top of her head, terminating just above her ears, where it morphed into two flat half-circles with a switch on one side. A small red glow emanated from the switch. From the middle of the metal band, two more bands led toward the front and back of her skull. They were both glowing red as well. Her ears themselves weren't covered by the device, but still the whole thing looked high-tech, like a costume for a robot-themed rave party, or too-small headphones on a really pretentious DJ. She held several more devices in her left hand, and her right hand carried a knife as big as her arm.

"I'm not supposed to wear one of these," she said. "It's not for us kids to try. But I overheard the adults saying it was clearing their thoughts and I want to be as clear-minded as I can when I cut your neck open with this." She brandished the knife.

I felt my pulse throbbing in my throat. "Wheeler said you're not supposed to hurt me yet. Not until he sees what I've become."

She took a step towards me. "I don't care. Wheeler's been good to me, but I'm not going to wait any longer."

Eden unlocked the cage.

If I could just break my arms free of the restraints, I could maybe overpower her and escape. I pulled at my wrists and winced as the cable-ties cut into them.

She smiled an awful smile, crawled into the cage, and placed one of the devices on my head, despite my thrashing around. She was strong for her size. Eden put one on each of the others, too, and then pressed the switch on each of them. The lights turned green, and suddenly the rage inside me subsided. My mind cleared, like it was coming out of a fog.

"Wheeler gave these to all the Kindred?" I asked.

She nodded. "Dampers. They block his signal. I haven't turned mine on yet. I don't want to be disconnected from the Pulse for too long." Her eyes lit up when she talked of it.

"Why put them on us?" asked Rachel from the corner.

Eden didn't bother turning to look at her. Instead, she kept her eyes fixed on me. "You'll see."

She left the cage for a moment, moving to a security panel by the door. She entered a code and pressed several more buttons before returning.

"I just turned the cameras off. I don't want Wheeler interrupting your death."

Now was my chance. With no cameras I could use my abilities, if the others were smart enough to look away. I tried to tune into the knife, to heat it up so she'd drop it, leaving her distracted enough for me to melt through my restraints.

Nothing happened. I couldn't hear anything, not even static. It was like my ability had been switched off. I tried again, but still, nothing.

Eden grinned. "I'm not an idiot. The dampers stop the Pulse, but they also stop our abilities from working. Wheeler said they disconnect the mind from environmental resonance or something. It means I can kill you without worrying about your abilities. I've heard you're pretty strong, but I guess not strong enough to get past the damper."

She came closer to me in the cage, just out of arm's reach. Her damper still glowed red. It was off. That was fine for now. When she switched it on, I might have a moment to do something before she killed me.

Eden held the knife out, grinning. "Anything you want to say before you die?"

I took a breath, trying to seem calm. "Eden, I'm sorry for what happened to your parents. I truly am. I wish I could take it back. I wish I could undo all the damage I've done, all the death I've caused. But more death isn't the answer. Killing me isn't going to take away the ache you're feeling, the emptiness in your heart."

She scoffed. "You sound like one of those awful shows that my parents used to watch, those talk show where they try to solve everyone's problems. Pathetic."

"Eden, please!" my voice rose. "You saw what Wheeler did to that boy. You saw what he's using you for. Can you honestly say you're okay with that? He's going to kill all those people. Your parents were Unseen, right? That means they fought *against* Wheeler. They were trying to stop people like him."

"And look where they ended up," she snapped, raising the knife to my throat. The others yelled out for her to stop.

"You're fighting on the wrong side, Eden, just like I was! I know you feel alone. I get that, I really do. I know that you've lost so much. But look at us all. Each one of us in here has lost everything. Noah lost his parents. Rachel, too. My mum was killed just after your parents were. Hud's mum died when he was little, and he can never see his dad again. Am I angry about all that? Sure. Do I wish it was different? Sure. But that doesn't mean things can't get better, as long as we keep fighting on the right side. You want to blame anyone for your parents' death? Blame the Kindred. It wasn't my fault. Blame the Kindred, they're the ones who started all of this."

I heard the words back in my head, and stopped for a moment, realising the weight of what I'd said. The Kindred *were* at fault in all this. I'd played my part, but everything had ultimately happened because of them. I had to stop blaming myself.

Eden shook her head. "You know what you sound like? Blah, blah, blah. I'm bored. Time for you to die."

She put her hand to the switch on the damper and turned it on. The lights glowed green, and she pressed the knife against my skin.

It cut into my neck, and I felt blood run down my chest.

"Eden, please," I begged.

She smiled. "This is going to be slow."

My heart raced, and my head felt light. I was going to pass out from the adrenaline before she killed me.

"This is for my parents," she snarled and pulled the knife back, ready to hack into my arteries.

The others pleaded for her to stop, and so did I. I begged for my life, and suddenly Eden stopped. Frowning, she looked at the knife and lowered it, keeping her eyes on the blade until it came to rest at her side.

"I'm sorry," she said. "I'm so, so sorry. I know it wasn't your fault. I know it was the Kindred."

"What?" I said quietly, almost not believing what I'd heard.

"My head—it's so much clearer now. I don't know what I was thinking. It was like Wheeler was in my mind, making me angry, twisting my thoughts around."

She stared at the red curtain, towards where the boy had died. "He killed Rory. He actually killed him and fed him to the Shadows. He's using all of us. He used me to bring you in."

Pausing, she started to cry. "I'm so sorry."

"Uh," said Noah from his corner. "What the hell's going on?"

"It's the damper," said Rachel. "It's blocking Wheeler's influence, his corruption of her mind."

"Cool," he replied. "So, can she let us out?"

Eden nodded through her tears. "I can't believe I was so stupid. I can't believe I let him get in my head."

"There'll be time for that later," I said. "But he'll be back any second." I paused, taking in the suddenly very vulnerable little girl in front of me. "Break us out of here, and we'll take you with us."

She nodded again, raising the knife once more, but this time she used it to cut me free, and then the others. Running to a cupboard, Eden took out our packs and threw them to us. "There's a back way out of here," she said. "But we'll need to move fast."

As if to punctuate her words, a shout came from just outside the door. We'd been seen.

We bolted toward the red curtain, ploughing through it to the front of the stage. There were three exits. One on the left, one on the right, and the large door at the back of the room, below where Hud and I had spied on the proceedings.

The boy's body was gone from the stage, which was kind of a relief.

Shouts came from behind us.

"Head for the door on the left," said Hud. "It's the quickest way out."

The five of us sprinted across the chamber as Kindred guards burst through the curtains. They all had dampers on now, which meant they couldn't use their abilities. There would be too much interference from the crowd even if they turned them off. There were dozens of them, though, so they could just beat us to death if they caught us.

Hud went through the door first, barging it open with his shoulder. The rest of us followed, and I stayed to shut the door behind me, pulling a large bolt across to lock it.

The others stopped for a moment. "Think that'll hold them?" asked Rachel.

"No chance," said Hud. "Leave it with me."

We looked away, and a rumbling filled the tunnel we were in. Then, a splintering crack, followed by loud clattering that skittered to a stop. I turned back. Hud had collapsed a section of the tunnel. If the Kindred were so reluctant to turn off their dampers, it would take them ages to get through there. He switched his damper back on.

"Good work, but let's leave the dampers on now. Who knows what will happen if you switch it off again." said Noah. "Let's go."

Eden took charge, leading the way through the maze of tunnels. "Keep an eye out," she said. "They could come from anywhere."

Footsteps echoed from ahead of us. A lone Kindred rounded the corner, not wearing his mask. He couldn't have been more than nineteen. He froze when he saw us, and he turned and ran, shouting to the others.

Behind us, a crowd of Kindred appeared, brandishing swords and clubs. Ahead, in the tunnel, another mob of Kindred approached. We were trapped.

"This way," said Eden, gesturing at us from an open access door on my right.

We piled in, and I locked the door.

"We need to split up," said Noah.

"Really?" I frowned. I'd just gotten them all back.

"Noah's right," said Rachel. "We need to draw them away, split their focus."

"Fine. I'll go with Eden and Hud. You and Noah stay together. We'll meet at Century Park Station." If I was being honest, I didn't want to be with either of them right now. Their words while under Wheeler's influence still stung. A lot.

Eden gave them directions for a back way, and we ran through the access tunnel as the door behind us burst open, Kindred piling through.

Noah and Rachel disappeared out a door to the left, and Hud, Eden and I went right.

We criss-crossed through the tunnels until we were far enough away from the Kindred to be confident we'd lost them. Then, slowing to a jog, we continued through the tunnels toward Century Park Station. Eden managed to keep up with Hud and I, which was impressive considering her legs had to move twice as fast as ours did. I still wasn't totally sure she wouldn't snap and kill me. Had all the anger really just been Wheeler's influence?

Soon, we were close to Century Park Station, and the shouts of the Kindred were just a memory. Still, I kept one eye out for them as we rounded the corner and entered the station to wait for the others.

THIRTY-FOUR

The fluorescent station lights were blinding compared to the pitch-black of the tunnels. Blinking, I cleared my eyes and motioned the others forward. Hud and Eden scurried out of the darkness and over to the platform edge. Hud boosted Eden and I, and then we gave him a hand to clamber onto the platform. Once up, we sat on a cold wooden bench for a moment to catch our breath. We were in Century Park Station, the place I'd encountered the snake man who had sung with Wheeler's strange, pulsing tone. The tone that was now rippling through the city even stronger than before. The clock said it was four-thirty in the morning. Soon, the city would wake up, and the tone would start to change them. I switched the damper off for a moment and immediately began to feel lighter. My heart calmed, and my breathing slowed. If I stayed here long enough, though, I'd begin to feel angry again, so I turned the damper back on. The calm faded away, and my mind started racing once more.

If we didn't stop Wheeler's tone, the whole city would turn on itself like we had turned on each other in the cages. Eventually, they'd become Zealots. The kids wouldn't, though. They'd be corrupted slowly. They'd end up brainwashed like Eden, trapped in a spiral of anger and pain and death, and finally become food for the Shadows, allowing them to turn into whatever I'd seen in the Apex.

Eden sat next to me on the bench. Her eyes were heavy, and she kept blinking them open. She had both legs drawn up to her chest, and was holding her arms around them tightly. She looked so small, so alone, and so very far from when I'd encountered her that night at the pier. Eden glanced my way and saw me looking at her. I smiled weakly, but she retreated into herself. She seemed broken. I shuffled over next to her and put my arm around her shoulders. She flinched at first but relaxed in under my arm. Laying her head on my shoulder, she closed her eyes.

I caught Hud's eye. He was frowning.

"What?" I asked quietly, so as not to disturb Eden.

Hud shook his head. "Nothing."

"It's not nothing. What are you thinking?"

Hud sighed. "I don't know if you have what it takes to end this. To kill Wheeler. To do what has to be done."

"What are you talking about?" I huffed. "I've always done what it took to protect everyone. To protect my family. You have no idea what I'm capable of. You didn't see what happened back at Ettney."

Hud glanced around the station for a moment. "You should have taken them all out when we had the chance. We could have brought the whole damn Apex down on their heads."

"Yeah, 'cause that plan ended really well," I snapped. Eden stirred on my shoulder, and I lowered my volume again. "There's a difference between doing what it takes and killing without reason. You should know that. Hud, you're better than this. You ran straight in to save those guys at the docks. You don't want people to die, not really."

"And look where it got me. Kidnapped, caged, scurrying around like a rat in those tunnels. No, I'm done with holding back. From now on, I'm going to do whatever I have to. You should too, or we're not going to survive this."

There was a darkness in Hud now, one that hadn't been there when I'd met him. This war really did change people, and not for the better.

I ignored his words and turned my thoughts back to the task at hand. "It's all well and good to say whatever it takes, but we need a plan forward."

"Alright then, what have you got?"

I thought for a moment. "Wheeler is strengthening his signal somehow, broadcasting it throughout the city. There is no way it's coming just from him. He's amplifying it somehow."

"I suppose that makes sense."

"How do you amplify natural resonance though?"

Hud gestured to the device on his head. "The dampers interrupt the signal using technology. Maybe he's amplifying the signal with tech as well."

I sat up straighter, and Eden stirred on my shoulder again. "The equipment they were loading at the docks. What if it was some sort of signal strengthener?"

"Like a radio broadcaster."

"Maybe. But I'm willing to bet that the signal gets stronger the closer we are to the source. If we spread out across the city and switch off our dampers, maybe we can work out where the signal is strongest and triangulate the source."

"Sounds dangerous," he frowned.

"Whatever it takes, right?"

Eden stirred, and opened her eyes, sitting up slowly. "I was kind of awake just then. You're right. The equipment from the docks was designed to boost his signal. I don't know where he's taken it, though. He kept that a secret."

"It's settled then," I said. "As soon as the others get here, we'll spread out across the city to find the source of the Pulse. We've got to stop him before Coleton falls apart."

Eden stared into the distance for a moment. "Ari, if we come across any of my friends…"

"We'll try to save them, I promise."

"No, not that." She looked straight into my eyes. "They'll try to kill us. Don't let them."

I swallowed. There was no way I could kill one of those kids. Any kid. They weren't responsible for how Wheeler had corrupted them. They could be saved. If Eden could, they all could.

My mind turned to Skye. Her and Dad would be waking up soon with Wheeler's signal pumping through their brains. I had to get them out of the city. There was no way they could be here when everything went to crap. The last thing Skye needed was more trauma. She was dealing with so much already.

How would I explain it to Dad, though? Maybe I'd have to come clean about the Unseen and tell him the whole story. Sometimes, I felt like he knew more than he was letting on. Not the truth, but maybe he suspected I wasn't being totally honest about what had happened back at Ettney.

I'd cross that bridge when I came to it. Maybe I could convince Skye and Dad to leave without having to explain why.

Maybe.

A police siren echoed through the tunnel from somewhere above ground. Then another. And another. Something was happening, and it wasn't good.

"We can't wait for the others," said Hud. "We've got to get moving. Sounds like things are changing fast up there."

Eden and I nodded. "I've still got static on my comm this far underground," I said, standing. No way to check from down here. Maybe if we head upstairs, we can make contact."

The others agreed, and we got off the bench and moved towards the exit. I glanced around the station, double checking there were no cameras down here. This was one of the older stations, so security hadn't been upgraded in a long time. No chance of the Kindred spotting us. I should have checked as soon as we'd arrived. That had been sloppy, but I was so incredibly tired and there was no chance of slowing down now. I couldn't stop until Wheeler was dealt with. We didn't have much time.

I jumped, as two figures leaped down the stairs. Noah and Rachel.

Noah paused halfway down the stairwell to catch his breath. "We came out at the wrong station and figured it was faster on the surface. But anyway, you guys really need to see this."

Noah led us up the subway stairs onto the street.

My mouth dropped open.

Wheeler's Pulse was already working.

THIRTY-FIVE

"It's too soon," I moaned. "It's happening way too fast."

Above, the clouds had started to lighten with the first lines of morning, the sun blaring through the tiny gap between ocean and grey to blaze red across the rippled sky. It bathed the street in apocalyptic red, glaring off windows and radiating onto the road below. Each window lit by the sky seemed on fire, like something terrible was blazing behind the glass. A few lights had flickered on inside, replacing the fire with the yellow glow of incandescent bulbs. I stood at the entrance to the subway, taking in the moment. On either side of the street, office buildings mingled with apartments, reaching ten or fifteen stories up, hunching over us, slowly coming to life as residents awoke from the noise. Sirens echoed across the city. Something was happening elsewhere, something requiring all the emergency services by the sound of it. Above us, four floors up on a balcony, a couple made out semi-clothed against their balcony railing. It wasn't romantic, though. The way they pawed each other was awful, primal, animal. They were high on Wheeler's tone.

Three apartments to the left, an elderly man with a huge moustache slid open the glass door to his balcony. He had a robe that hung loose around his ample stomach, but he didn't care. He raised both fists in the air, mouth wide, and let out a guttural whoop, then collapsed onto the metal railing, laughing hysterically like he was drunk.

Two floors above the kissing couple, a twenty-something blonde woman in silk pyjamas emerged from a curtained door. She grinned from ear to ear and waved at us. Her pyjamas had a cat on the front, and there was a small black one sleeping on a glass table that rested against the railing. She smiled again and climbed onto the table. The cat raised its head to stare at her for a moment, before settling back down to sleep. Standing on the table, the woman's head almost reached the bottom of the balcony above. She was right on the edge of the table, and watching her teetering there made my stomach turn. The woman stepped slowly forward, carefully stepping onto the top of the metal railing, balancing there with a huge smile on her face.

"Get back!" I called, trying to break her out of the trance, but there was nothing I could do. She waved again. "Time to fly!" she yelled to the blazing amber clouds. Before I could shout stop, she jumped, squealing with delight, pyjamas billowing in the wind, falling and tumbling floor after floor. I looked away just before she hit the pavement with a crack. Eden went green.

I turned her head to me. "Look away, Eden. Don't watch this. Don't watch any of this."

"The whole city will be awake soon," said Noah. "When that happens…"

Rachel nodded. "I don't want to be here when they reach the angry stage. We've got to shut this down before then."

We ducked back into the station to avoid the noise. Amidst the sirens blaring outside, I explained my plan to use the dampers to find the amplifier.

"Good idea," said Rachel. "Let's split the city up into quadrants. That'll be the fastest way to cover ground."

"You really think it's wise to split up?" asked Hud.

"We have no choice," Rachel replied, checking her watch. "We're running out of time."

"I'll keep Eden with me," I said. "And I'd like to take the eastern side. I need to check in on my family and tell them to leave the city."

Noah nodded. "I'll cover the west. Hud and Rachel, you guys decide where you want to go."

"I know north best," Rachel said. "It's near the warehouse. Hud, you take south."

"Done," Hud said.

"And keep your eyes wide open everyone," Rachel pointed up the stairs. "This place is going to fall apart fast. Everyone's comms still have battery?"

The others were okay, but mine was running a bit low.

"Keep them off for now to save battery," she said. "Turn them on in an hour when we're in position.

The street already seemed more chaotic as we returned above ground. The woman who'd jumped lay concealed behind a car, but a man was standing over her body, laughing hysterically at whatever mess was on the pavement. I shook my head slowly.

"Try to boost some transport while you're at it." Rachel glanced around the street. "We need to move fast, and I don't think anyone's going to care if we borrow their wheels right now." She walked toward the hysterical man, who'd stopped his small electric runabout to get out and gawk. He'd left his keys in the ignition and paid no attention when Rachel shut the door and drove off.

"Well," Noah said, "that was easy." He glanced around the street, which was mostly bare of other vehicles. "Guess we should find our own. I can drop you at your place to check on your dad and Skye, then head to my quadrant."

I shook my head. "It's okay, Eden and I will find some bikes or something. Don't waste your time ferrying us around."

"Ari, that's crazy. You don't want to be riding around the city when it's like this."

"I'm going to have to anyway, if I'm going to track down Wheeler. I can't drive yet, remember?"

"I've given you a few lessons. You could handle an auto."

"And get us killed? No thanks. Besides, if the streets get blocked, a bike will be the fastest way to get around."

"Ari, just—"

"I don't want to ride with you," I snapped. "I can barely look at you. After everything you said back there, you really think I'm okay to just get over it and move on?"

He went silent for a moment. "So, that's what this is about."

I nodded, swallowing the lump in my throat.

"Ari, I didn't mean anything I said back there. It was Wheeler's influence, nothing more."

"No, he just releases what's already there, in the deepest parts of our hearts, our minds. Everything we said… It can't be taken back."

"Ari, I—"

"I kept telling myself I didn't love you, and maybe I don't anymore. But you've been lying to yourself, too. You keep telling yourself you do love me, but I think you love the idea of me instead, not who I really am. I see that now, and it's not fair on either of us."

Noah went to speak again, but I cut him off.

"No, not now. We have to go save the city, remember? And to be honest, I don't know if I want to see you again after this. Maybe not ever."

"Ari, please."

But I was gone, marching up the street with Eden in tow. She stayed quiet, watching me, and I didn't bother turning around to see where Noah went. He could take care of himself, and I didn't much care if he did or not at this point.

I took a deep breath as I stepped over a crack in the pavement. I missed Josh more than anything right now. He'd never hated or resented me, even though I'd brought so much pain into his life.

A small hand pressed into mine, and I looked down to see Eden staring up at me.

"You'll be okay," she said, and I closed my eyes, pressing a tear out of each.

I had to be strong. I had to push on. I had to save my family, again, from the Kindred's plans.

I had to save the whole damn city.

THIRTY-SIX

We rounded the corner onto a larger street. There wasn't much traffic out yet, but the cars that were had come to a standstill. A crowd was scattered across the road, staggering in all directions, smiling and hugging and partying. They were mostly still in their pyjamas, having come out into the street from their apartments to join in the revelry. They shouted, and screamed, and whooped, and danced. One young guy tore his shirt completely from his body and stood up on the hood of a luxury sportscar. He screamed into the morning, raving about how he felt amazing, letting loose every swearword in the dictionary, and a few that weren't, before jumping up and down on the bright red hood.

"Come on, everyone!" he called. "Let's flip it!"

The others yelled their agreement, and a dozen of them gathered on the left side of the car. The man on top chanted, "Flip it, flip it, flip it!" and the crowd joined in. The group lifted the vehicle on one side, and as it rolled the shirtless man leaped off, scraping his bare torso on the asphalt. The car rolled onto its roof and started leaking fuel from somewhere underneath. The young man stood, yelling, arms in the air like he'd just won a football match. The crowd cheered, and applauded, and gathered round the car. Something sparked at the front of the vehicle, and flames built from the underside.

"Get away," I yelled. "Everyone get away!"

I tried to tune to the car, but it was no use. There were too many people staring at it, giggling, laughing, yelling, enjoying the flames. The fire on the underside grew higher.

"Get away!" I tried one more time, but no-one listened. They were mesmerised by the show. The young man jumped onto the underside of the vehicle, towards the back and away from the flames. He cheered again but was cut off as the fuel tank exploded. A fireball shot into the air, covering him completely and throwing the crowd to the ground. Their faces seared, but they didn't seem to care. They cheered again as the man dropped to the asphalt, skin smoking from the blast. He had stopped moving.

I turned to Eden. "We need transport through the city. They're not in the angry phase yet, but this place is still way too dangerous."

Eden nudged me and pointed to a rental bike rack that held ten bright yellow bicycles, lined up and ready to be borrowed.

"Awesome," I smiled, and ran to the bike rack that sat outside a closed fish-and-chip shop. "These'll do."

The bikes were locked by a security mechanism, and I didn't have money or a credit card to pay and unlock it.

"Can you face away for a moment?" I asked Eden. "I need to melt the lock."

Eden turned away, standing to block the crowd's interference. I switched off the damper for a moment, and the Pulse made me dizzy. Nevertheless, I tuned to the metal lock and raised its resonance. The lock melted, running down the side of the bike and onto the grey sidewalk. I melted a second one, and the locking bar fell clanging to the ground. We now had two bright yellow bikes ready to go.

"Not really camouflaged, are they," said Eden with a wry smile.

"No helmet?" I said, switching my damper back on.

"I'll be fine," Eden replied. "We've survived worse so far today."

"You're not wrong," I said grimly. "Let's go, before this crowd gets any wilder."

To punctuate my words, a window smashed behind me, followed by a cheer.

"Hey," said a low voice behind me. "Hey, you."

I turned to see a man a few years older than me. He had a dark smile on his face.

"Nice hat," he said gesturing to the damper. "You look like you know how to have fun. Want to join us?"

Guiding Eden behind me, I frowned and tried to look tough. "No, thanks."

"Come on, babe. We're all having such a great day. Don't spoil it for us by being a killjoy." He was tall, and strong, with black hair and dark brown eyes that scanned me up and down. The business suit somehow made him scarier.

"Not being a killjoy, I just have somewhere to be." I stepped slowly backwards, towards the bikes. "You go party, though. Seriously, it's fine."

"I don't want to go somewhere else. I want to be here. With you. I deserve that."

Two of his friends walked up behind him. This whole moment felt familiar, like the guys in the car the other night. Except these guys were under Wheeler's influence, instead of acting purely on their own. Maybe Wheeler was right about the dark parts of ourselves. These guys were just as bad as the ones who'd tried to approach me the other night. They were just as rotten inside. They were just better at hiding it during everyday life. They probably weren't cruising the street at night looking for girls to harass, but deep down they wanted to.

The three of them advanced slowly, smiling, without any fear of being seen by the crowd. With all three of them there, I couldn't use my abilities. I backed away and bumped into the bike rack, sending several clattering to the ground. The men looked at it for a moment, and I tried desperately to tune. I wasn't fast enough though, and my mind went to static as soon as they looked back. I glanced behind me. Where was Eden?

There was a crack, and the man at the back left fell to the concrete, legs crumpling like a ragdoll. The men turned, but too slow. A second crack and a third, and they both hit the pavement. All three of them, knocked unconscious by Eden, who was standing over them, grinning, holding the metal locking bar from the bike rack.

I surveyed the unconscious crew on the ground. "Wow. Well done."

"It was nothing," Eden said. "Actually, no. It was awesome. And really fun. Anyone else you want knocked out?"

Despite my heart still racing, I laughed. "Not right now. But it's good to know you're available."

I stopped for a moment, watching this short, scrawny girl in a hoodie wielding a three-foot metal bar with blood on the end. She looked seriously tough. "Maybe you don't need my protection after all," I said, smirking.

"I can handle myself. But I'm glad you've got my back."

"Seems you've got mine, too."

One of the men on the ground stirred. Eden readied the bar, but I held my hand out to stop her. "One more could kill him."

"So?"

"Let's avoid unnecessary civilian deaths for now. Even if they are creeps. Besides, we should get moving. This place is getting busier, and we've got to make it to my family as soon as possible."

We jumped on the bikes. My seat was a little too short for me, but Eden's bike fit her perfectly. I had to stand to pedal properly, but it would have to do.

Eden and I wove our way through parked cars and people, who were still mostly in the happy phase. Occasional cheers and shouts of joy echoed through the streets, and a few blocks away, smoke billowed out of an apartment building. The sirens were so omnipresent now, I barely noticed them.

A new sound ripped through the atmosphere, though. A harsh, blaring signal that wailed up and down.

"What's that?" Eden shouted over the din, pedalling beside me as we turned into an empty alleyway.

"I think it's the emergency warning system. They did a test a few months ago, and it sounded like this. It's meant to be for terrorists and tsunamis and stuff. Guess someone still has the presence of mind to realise something's wrong here."

A police car turned into the alley, lights and siren blaring.

Eden swore. "Are they after us?"

"Don't know. Let's pretend they're not."

We pumped our legs and jumped up onto the sidewalk, letting the cop car pass. They caught up to us, and the siren was deafening. There was a yell from an open window, and a policeman smiled at us, waving and laughing hysterically. The engine revved, and the tires screeched as the car skidded around the corner. The cop let out a final yell as the vehicle disappeared from view.

"Even the cops are whacked," said Eden. "Awesome."

Pretty soon there'd be no sane person left in the whole of Coleton. No-one except the Kindred, Wheeler, and us.

THIRTY-SEVEN

Dad's building was half an hour by bike, but a cycleway ran pretty much straight there, allowing us to duck off the main roads and out of immediate danger. The cycleway ran through a nature corridor, and it was weirdly quiet considering the chaos we'd just woven through. The emergency signal still wailed through the streets, but it wasn't nearly so loud, muffled by the trees, and the wind that had begun to pick up across the city. The clouds overhead had lost their red morning blush, and had instead grown dark green and billowing, preparing for a possible downpour, or maybe even a hail storm.

The wind made it hard to push the pedals, especially as the cycleway curved gently uphill. I didn't mind, though. Anything to be off the streets.

Paperbark trees lined the corridor on each side, losing strips of themselves from countless kids pulling off the thin bark over the years. They looked straggly and sad, but a few rows deeper the trees were thick and beautiful, forming a mottled layer of sandy brown that blurred as we sped past.

Eden's energy showed no signs of waning, and she easily kept pace with me.

"So, your dad, what's he like?" she asked.

"He's okay, I guess. Him and Mum used to fight a lot when I was little. It's one of the reasons they split up. He doesn't scream at us, though. I think he's trying to make up for everything that happened. Maybe Mum's death made him realise what he was missing. I dunno. It's all really awkward between us."

My mind went back to Dad's uncomfortable conversation with Josh and I on the lounge, and I swallowed and shook my head to clear it. Not now, Ari. Keep your mind on the mission.

"And your sister?"

"She's sweet, and wise beyond her age. I think she's had to grow up fast considering everything that happened. She's the reason I'm fighting, really. Keeping her safe is the most important thing in the world to me."

"That's nice," said Eden, "she must like having you as a big sister. I never had that. I guess I don't have anyone, now."

I turned to look at her pedalling furiously to keep up with me. "You've got us, Eden. You're not alone in this, and you never will be. Got it?"

She smiled back and said nothing.

The turnoff to Dad's place came up on the left, and we veered off the cycleway, through the exit, and into an empty side street to approach the back of Dad's apartment building.

The clouds overhead were moving fast, tossed by the wind which cut through my jacket. I'd find something warmer when we got inside, and maybe something for Eden too. Her teeth were chattering, despite the exercise.

I had no keys; they'd disappeared somewhere under the city. The intercom was up a short flight of stairs, and I buzzed Dad's number. The intercom rang once, twice, three times but no answer. I frowned and looked at Eden.

"Try it again?" she said. I dialled the number and pressed call once more. This time, Skye answered. She sounded weird.

"Hello?"

"Hey, Skye, it's me. Can you buzz me in?"

"Ari! You're back!"

The door beeped and the electric lock clicked. I pushed the door open and Eden followed me inside.

I pressed the elevator button, and waited, tapping my foot impatiently. A moment later, the doors opened, and I punched in the access code for floor ten. The doors closed, and the elevator thunked as it began its climb. As each floor number clicked over, I started to feel tense. The higher we went, the surer I was that I was heading into something awful.

Floor five… six…

Maybe Dad was dead. Maybe the Kindred had gotten to them. Skye had sounded weird over the intercom. Maybe it was a trap, and they were forcing her to lure us here.

Floor seven…eight…

I grabbed Eden's hand, palm sweating. We had to be ready to run or even fight if necessary.

Nine…

Ten.

The lift opened into the empty hallway. There were five doors in the corridor, two on each side with Dad's door at the end. From the first door on the left came muffled laughter. It was hysterical, almost insane. Something bad was happening in there. I took a step out of the elevator, walking slowly, trying not to draw the attention of anyone inside.

While the apartments were newly renovated, the building itself was old, made of timber and brick, and the floors in the hallway were creaky. The hall was lit only by wall lamps that radiated beams from the sconces, up the grey mottled walls and onto the ceiling. I passed the laughing apartment, and the noise stopped. A voice came from just behind the door.

"I can see you out there."

I knew the voice behind that door. I'd run into her a few times in the corridor and downstairs. Mrs Parker, an elderly lady who lived with her infirm husband. She had rounded glasses and swept back hair, and she always smiled at me and Skye when she saw us.

"Hello, Ari," she called again. There was a darkness in her voice. "Would you come inside? We're having tea. Well, I am. Max is dead, of course."

Her husband.

My shoe stuck to the carpet and I looked down. A red puddle pooled from under the door, seeping slowly out into the hallway.

No. No way.

It had started. The dark stage. The one where people's deepest impulses broke free. Mrs Parker had murdered her husband. If I didn't move, she might try to kill us too. A shadow shifted behind the peep-hole. She was watching us. I put my hand over the peep-hole, shoes still sticking in the puddle, and Eden looked away. I switched the damper off, ignoring the floating feeling, and melted Mrs Parker's door lock shut. Hopefully now she couldn't get to us.

If we didn't stop the Pulse soon, stuff like this would be happening all over the city. Wheeler had said the city would burn. He wasn't kidding.

Mrs Parker called from behind the door, and the doorknob rattled. "Ari? Where have you gone? I'd love for you to join us. Your friend, too. Max isn't much company, not now he's scattered all over the apartment." She chuckled. "He's waving at you right now... At least, his arm is." She laughed hysterically, and the doorknob rattled again.

I turned to Eden. "Let's go. Now."

"Ari?" Mrs Parker called again. "Ari?"

Hopefully the door would hold. Skye and Dad had to get out of here before they lost it too. I didn't want to know what Dad's darkest impulses were. Judging by the times he and Mum had fought, they were nothing good.

I wiped my shoes on the carpet to get the blood off, feeling sickened at the smell coming under Mrs Parker's door, and we hurried towards Dad's apartment at the end of the building. The door was unlocked.

Expecting a Kindred ambush, I pushed the door open slowly and stepped back. Red was splattered across the walls, the carpet, the furniture.

Blood.

THIRTY-EIGHT

"Ari?" said Skye from the kitchen. She was covered head to toe in red that had soaked her nightie and drenched her hair.

"Skye!" I ran to her, leaving Eden standing at the door taking in the scene.

"How cool is this!" Skye said, twirling in a puddle of blood in the middle of the kitchen.

I took her hand to stop her. "Skye, what happened? Are you hurt?"

"No," she grinned. "Do you like it?"

Her eyes were big, gleaming white beneath the red crust on her skin.

"I found this big tin of paint, and Dad opened it, and we painted the whole room!"

I spotted the empty tin of red paint on the bench. The stuff that soaked the room wasn't blood.

I let out a sigh, feeling the adrenaline drain from my system. Despite the situation, I started to laugh. Eden joined from the doorway, stepping inside and closing it behind her. Stewie barked from inside the bathroom. He was locked in there, which was a relief.

Skye stared at me with a huge grin. She was definitely in the happy stage. She put her hands in the air and twirled again, sending paint splattering off her dress and onto the kitchen cupboards.

"Skye, where's Dad?"

"In his bedroom. He's cranky, so he went to lie down."

Dad's bedroom door was shut. I walked to it, leaving Eden to supervise Skye. The doorknob refused to budge, so I knocked. "Dad? Hey Dad?"

"Go away!" came his voice from inside. "Don't open the door!"

"Dad," I called, "are you okay in there?"

"Ari, don't you dare open that door. It's for your own good. Take Skye and go!"

I looked at Eden, who shrugged.

Skye smiled and kept twirling.

Tuning to the doorknob, I lowered the resonance until ice condensed on the outside. I kept going, as far as I could, and the brass doorknob became brittle in the frame. Stepping back, I kicked the door as hard as I could, and the lock shattered, letting the door swing back to slam against the wall.

My mouth dropped open. Dad's grey bedspread was covered in red, but it wasn't just from the paint. Both his wrists were cable-tied to the bedframe, and they were bleeding where the plastic had cut into the skin.

"Ari!" he said. "Get away!"

I walked towards him, ready to free him from the restraints.

"Stay back!"

Stopping in place, scanned the room. I should have scanned for a Kindred ambush before I walked in.

Fortunately, there was no-one else here. "Dad, who did this to you?"

His eyes dropped, and his voice got quiet. "I did."

"You cable-tied yourself to the bed?"

Dad nodded, refusing to make eye contact. "It was the only way."

"The only way to what?"

He sighed, finally looking at me. "After me and your mum, you know...we were having problems. I used to get so angry. I used to lose control. When I moved to the city, I got counselling to deal with my anger. They taught me how to know when it was coming, how to manage it, to let it wash past me, strategies to stay calm, that sort of thing."

I stepped towards him again. He looked so broken, so ashamed. Telling his daughter about his failings couldn't have been easy, despite the fact that I was well aware of them already.

"I'd been going so well, but this morning after we painted the house, I started to get angry. Really angry. I started to lose control, and I couldn't stop it." His brow was furrowed, and his shoulders moved up and down in shallow movements as breath rasped heavy from his mouth. "There's something wrong with me, Ari. Something really, really wrong. I tied myself up here, so I wouldn't hurt Skye or you or anyone else."

"Oh, Dad."

He looked down again. "I'm sorry, little one."

"It's okay, the whole city's losing it. The only reason I'm alright is 'cause I'm wearing this thing on my head." I pointed to the damper.

"I'm not just sorry for this," he said, shaking his head. "I'm sorry for everything. For what happened with you and your mum. For what happened after. For not being there the last few years. It was me. That's all on me."

I opened my mouth to speak, but nothing came out. We'd never talked about this. Not really. It was always the giant elephant in the room, lurking in the corner. I'd never been game to bring it up, and he hadn't either. Looking at him now, he was a broken man. I wasn't ready to even consider forgiving him, but I still felt sorry for him, in a way. Leaving a family doesn't just hurt the ones you leave, it does something to your soul, tears out a piece of it that never quite comes back whether you realise it or not.

"If I'd been there," he sighed, "maybe your mum wouldn't have died."

I had to tell him. Tell him what was going on with him and why he felt so weird and angry. I should probably also tell him about my abilities and the war and Josh and what had really happened to us at Ettney, plus where I'd been for the last twelve hours. He hadn't even asked about that, but it was probably because of what was happening to his brain. If only we'd grabbed more dampers before we'd escaped, I could give them to Dad and Skye and stop the Pulse changing them. I would have given them mine, if I wasn't currently the city's last line of defence against the Kindred.

Dad sat on the bed, slumped, wrists tied to the middle of the metal bedhead, staring at the red that stained the blankets around him.

I took another step forward and sat on the edge of the bed, right at the end. "Dad, I—"

His head shot up, and his pupils had dilated. His irises looked completely black, same as the Zealots in the underground. He snarled and threw his head towards me.

I leaped off the bed and stepped back to the door.

"Come here," he hissed. "Come closer." His mouth curled, and his jaw clenched, and he snapped his teeth at me, pulling on the cable-ties which cut deeper into his wrists. Blood ran freely down his arm and dripped onto the bedspread. He screamed in anger, throwing himself towards me again and again and again.

Eden appeared at my side. "That doesn't look normal."

"It's not," I said. "He's turning fast. If I stay here, he's going to rip his hands off to try and get to me. After that…"

"Let's not find out."

I nodded.

"Want me to knock him out? I'm getting good at it."

Dad threw himself at us again, and the entire bed jumped our direction.

"No, don't do that. But we should find a way to lock this door. The window doesn't open far enough for him to get out, and it's reinforced glass. If we can fuse the door shut, it'll at least keep him contained."

Eden turned to the hall. "I'll find something. You keep watching him."

After a minute, Dad stopped thrashing, and his head dropped back down to stare at the bedspread once more. He went still, too still, like he was in a trance.

"Dad?" I ventured.

"You need to go," said Dad quietly. "The Unseen are going to need you, now more than ever."

THIRTY-NINE

I froze.

He kept staring at the bedspread. "Yes, I know about that. I know a lot of things I'd rather not. But we don't have time for that. Whatever's happening to me is happening fast, and if it's affected the whole city like you say, none of us are going to survive the next twenty-four hours. So please, leave me here, take Skye, and go."

"Dad, I—"

"Go!" His voice changed again, and his face contorted, and he was back to blind, unrepentant rage.

In shock, I stepped out of the bedroom and shut the door behind me. It hung open a fraction due to the missing lock, and Dad's psychotic screaming filtered through the crack.

How much did he know? And *how* did he know it?

Skye still twirled in the kitchen, and Eden returned with a bunch of cable ties.

"Found these in the cupboard. Useful?"

I thought for a moment. "Maybe."

I walked away from the door and looked around the loungeroom. In the corner, next to the television, was a lampstand made of polished steel. "That might help."

Bringing the lampstand back over to the doorway, I smashed the glass cover off it and unscrewed the base to remove the metal pole. I threaded the cable ties through the hole in the door where the lock had been, and then used more cable ties to connect them to the lamp pole. I tightened it all up, and let the pole lay at an angle to the ground. It protruded on both sides of the door, locking the door in place. Dad wouldn't be able to open the door from the inside, 'cause the metal bar would stop the door from opening.

"Clever," said Eden.

"Saw it on one of those survival shows once. Never thought I'd have to use it."

"Never thought I'd be helping Ari Carpenter lock her dad in his room, either."

I smiled despite the circumstances. "First time for everything, hey?"

Eden looked at Skye, who had grown tired of spinning and was now simply sitting in a paint puddle, splashing it over herself. "What do we do with her?"

"We're going to have to lock Skye in her room too. Now that she's affected, I don't think it's safe to move her out of the city, not with Dad out of action."

Dad's bedroom door slammed against the jamb. The metal barricade rattled in place. Dad was either off the bed or had somehow jumped it over to the doorway.

"Is that gonna hold?" Eden asked.

"Not sure."

She thought for a moment. "Got an idea. Stay here."

Eden left the apartment, returning later with the end of a fire hose. "Saw this outside when we came in."

"You're going to hose him down?"

She chuckled. "No. You lower the door's resonance, and I'll hit it with the hose."

Now it was my turn to be impressed. I switched off the damper, ignoring the floating feeling that began flowing through my mind, and tuned into the front of the door, lowering its temperature to freezing. Eden kept her eyes closed and turned the fire hose on to blast the door with water. As soon as the spray hit the door, it froze, building up a layer of ice that thickened as more water poured onto the top. After a minute, the whole doorway was frozen solid by a glacial mass.

I switched the damper back on, walked over, and tapped the ice. "Pretty solid."

Skye was next. I went into her room and removed everything she could hurt herself on when she went wild like Dad. I didn't want to cable-tie her to anything, though. Dad had lost blood, but he was bigger. Skye's tiny body probably wouldn't handle that. At least Skye's door opened outward, so it was much easier to seal when the time came.

"Hey, Skye," I said, coming out into the living area. She looked up from behind the kitchen bench, head bright red with paint that had started to dry and flake off in places.

"Yeah?"

"Want to play in your room for a while?"

"I guess so." She stood. "I feel weird inside."

I swallowed. It was starting. "I know, but you'll feel better in your room," I lied. I could ask for forgiveness later, once all this was over.

If she even turned back after Wheeler's tone had gone.

No, I couldn't think about that. Not now. Focus on the mission, Ari.

I led Skye to her room and walked in with her.

"Want to stay and play?" she said. "Everything in here is so beautiful."

"I'd love to," I said over the lump in my throat. "But right now, I have to go do something important."

Her eyes went dark. "You're leaving me?"

"Only for a while," I said, backing away a touch.

"You can't leave me. No-one can ever leave me. Not again. Not anymore."

"I'm sorry, but I have to go. I'll be back, I promise."

"No!" she screamed, pupils dilating. She ran at me with both arms out, latching on and scratching at my shoulders. "No! You can't leave me! You can't! You can't!"

I held her close, and her nails tore at my back, legs kicking wildly at my shins. It hurt bad, but still I held her close.

"Don't leave me!" she screamed. "I hate you! Don't go! You can't! Not after you killed mum! Not after everything that's happened to me. Everything that *you* did! If you go, I'll hate you forever!"

I took a breath and held her close again, ignoring the blood seeping out of the scratches on my shoulders, ignoring the bruising already appearing on my legs. She kicked and screamed again and again, over and over, and I let her because it was true. I deserved it. I deserved it for leaving her and for letting all this happen and for all the awful moments that had come into her life because of me. I'd mostly forgiven myself for what happened at Ettney, but I could never forgive myself for what my mistakes had done to Skye.

There was a hand on my shoulder. Eden, standing by with the fire hose, ready to seal the door.

I gave Skye one last squeeze as she screamed into my ear, and I pushed her off me and ran to the bedroom door, slamming it before she had a chance to react.

"Now!" I yelled at Eden, and I switched the damper off, tuning the door quickly as the water hit it, freezing it instantly and locking the door in place. Skye's screaming became muffled behind the milky surface, and soon it was almost inaudible.

Eden turned the water off, and I turned the damper on, taking two slow breaths to calm my racing heart.

"She'll forgive you," Eden said quietly.

"That wasn't all Wheeler," I said. "Some of that was her. That's how she really feels."

"Maybe. But give it time. If I had an older sister, I'd forgive her."

I smiled through my burning eyes, reached out and ruffled her hair. "Maybe you do."

She smiled. "They'll be safe here."

"At least until the ice melts."

"I'll turn on the air-con, make it really cold. That will help as long as the power stays on." She marched off to the control panel next to the front door.

I looked at the ice, already starting to drip water onto the carpet. "I don't know if that'll be enough."

Eden turned to face me. "I'll stay here then, keep adding layers when they melt."

"No, I can't ask you to do that."

She pointed to my bandaged right arm. "I cut you with a knife. Let me make up for it."

"What if Dad breaks free?"

"He won't. Besides, you've seen I can handle myself. Let me keep your family safe."

I wasn't going to convince her otherwise, so I agreed. "Okay, but keep the front door locked. Who knows what's going to happen out there today."

"Got it. Also, you might want to change."

I looked down, and my front was covered in red paint from holding Skye, not to mention blood from the creatures in the tunnels. If I went out like this, I'd draw attention to myself. Walking into my bedroom, I undressed and threw the dirty clothes in the corner of the room. I stood still for a moment, taking a deep breath, surveying the mess that was typical of my room. Dad and Skye hadn't painted in here, at least.

The full-length mirror on my wall showed a body that was a little worse for wear. Bandaged right arm, bruises all up and down my limbs, and scrapes on both my knees from scrambling through the tunnels. There was even a bite mark on my shoulder. I shrugged. At least my torso looked okay, despite the red stains and the black blotch on my stomach. I was almost used to it, now, the cold skin, the clammy feeling when I touched it. It was still smaller than my palm, and I put my hand over the top. For a moment, it was like it had disappeared. I saw my body without the blotch for the first time in months. I smiled at myself in the mirror, forcing my mouth to turn up at the edges, forcing myself to look like a relatively carefree teenage girl once more. Not that I was ever bubbly or particularly outgoing, but the stuff I was dealing with before the Unseen was nowhere near the intensity I was living at now. If that Ari, the one from before all this, could see me now, what would she say? Would she be impressed or horrified at the girl I'd evolved into?

Which One of You is Real?

I dropped my hand from my stomach, and I could see the blotch again. Time to get ready. The day was still cold outside, but I was going to have to do a lot of running before this was over. The jeans I'd been wearing had chafed my legs a bit; in the movies, people can run wearing anything. In reality, jeans were heavy and awkward.

Rummaging through my drawers, I pulled out a pair of black gym tights. They still fit, which was a relief considering I'd used them for literally anything but exercise. The long grey t-shirt I threw on reached halfway down my thighs, giving me a sense of modesty. Didn't want to run through an imploding city with my butt on display. White runners were the best choice of footwear, and I put on a grey hoodie to keep me warm and cover the glowing damper on my head. I looked back at the mirror. Hopefully, I'd look like I was just out for a run.

Yep, saving the world in my activewear.

That was a new one.

FORTY

Leaving Eden to barricade the door, I exited the apartment, stepping around the blood pool expanding from Mrs Parker's, and ignoring her pleas for company.

It was good timing. I had about five minutes before I was supposed to turn my comms on, which was just enough time to start scoping the source of the signal. On the street, I grabbed the bright yellow bike from where it was stashed next to the door, and quickly tapped the switch on the side of the damper. I didn't need to check if it was off; my heart slowed immediately, and I started to feel light inside. Time to work fast. I tuned into Wheeler's tone, hearing it loud and clear in my mind. It was pulsing and had grown even louder than before. Whatever amplifier Wheeler was using, it was effective.

Switching the damper back on, I jumped on the bike and rode north, up Dad's block, stopping at the lights. A car went screaming past filled with people, most of whom were naked and yelling incoherently. It didn't surprise me, but it was a bad sign. The city was falling apart.

Staring at the red light, it struck me that I probably didn't need to worry about road rules at the moment;

nobody else would be, and the police were probably just as messed up as everyone else in the city. Checking carefully for vehicles, I rode out against the red light. It felt transgressive, somehow, and gave me a bit of a rush.

The streets were quieter in this part of Coleton, which made the journey fast. The emergency alarm had stopped, too.

I didn't have a watch, but an open and abandoned car had a green clock shining from the dash which had just changed to six. Time to turn on my comms.

I put in the earpiece, running the cable under my hoodie so it didn't flap about when I moved. A muffled shriek came from the apartment building across the street, caused by goodness knows what awful thing. I ducked behind the gate of an upscale office building to avoid attracting attention.

The comm clicked as I turned the dial on, adjusting the volume so I could hear the others. These didn't have a button to talk, instead they switched the mic on automatically when we spoke.

"Hey guys," I said.

"*Ari?*" Rachel replied.

I nodded, then remembered she couldn't see me. "Yes."

"*The others aren't on yet. How's the signal where you are?*"

"Pretty strong near Dad's place. Eden stayed there to keep an eye on them. I've been heading north, I'll check the signal now." I turned the damper off and tuned to the gate next to my head. Wincing, I turned it back on. "It's strong here too, but weaker than at Dad's. The signal's coming from somewhere south of me."

Rachel's voice echoed, as if she was in an empty building. "*Not much my way, so the signal's probably in the south-east.*"

"Great. That narrows things down a bit. Hopefully the boys can clear it up even more."

There was silence, for a moment. Glass shattered inside the apartment building across the road, and something crunched into the car I'd checked a moment ago. I ducked my head around the gate to see the carnage. A double-width fridge had landed upside down on the roof of the car. The vehicle's windows had all blown out, scattering glass across the asphalt. Overhead on a balcony, two young women laughed hysterically. I ducked back behind the gate.

"*Hey, Ari?*" Rachel said, sheepishly.

"Yeah?"

"*I've been thinking about what you said to Eden.*"

"Which bit?"

"*All of it, to be honest.*" She took a deep breath. "*I've been blaming you for everything that happened to me at Ettney. The torture, the scars, everything I've had to deal with since. Flashbacks, night terrors, the whole damn psych textbook.*"

A small bird landed on the gate above me, brown and ruffled, looking like it had just woken up. It chirped, then flitted off into the sky, like everything was fine, like the city wasn't imploding around it.

"*Anyway,*" Rachel continued, "*I've been playing things back in my mind, and I honestly don't think I can be angry at you anymore. Not trusting you was what led to that whole mess. If I'd brought you in the loop sooner, if I hadn't been so paranoid, we could have avoided a whole lot of awful stuff.*"

I opened my mouth to speak, then closed it, silently.

"*I've been angry at you, but I think I was really angry at myself. I'm sorry.*"

Finally, I found some words. "It's okay, Rach. Seriously. You don't need to apologise. We've all done some pretty messed up stuff and made some huge mistakes. Me more than most. But I've been realising that, at the end of the day, the past is just a memory. It doesn't exist anymore. We have to live with the consequences, but whatever happened is gone forever. What we do moving forward is what counts, right?" I thought of Noah, and rage rose inside me. Maybe I didn't entirely believe what I was saying.

"Right. Good. Okay, then." There was a smile in Rachel's voice, one I hadn't heard in a long time. "You know, after we save the world, you'd make a pretty good motivational speaker."

I chuckled. "I dunno, I'd look pretty gross in a pant-suit."

"*What the heck are you guys talking about?*" said Noah over the comm.

"*Nothing, and nice of you to join us.*" Rachel said. "*Seems like the signal is south-east of the city. What do you think?*"

Instead of answering, Noah swore, and a colossal boom came over his intercom.

"*Noah?*" Rachel said. "*Noah, are you there?*"

There was a pause, and a second explosion. In the distance, towards Noah's position, smoke rose above the cityscape.

"What on earth was that?" I said, to no-one in particular.

"*Sorry guys,*" yelled Noah. "*I can't really hear you. My ears are ringing bad. A petrol station just blew up a block away. It's crazy out here right now, people everywhere. I just saw a guy run past, and his back was on fire, skin just melting off him. This city's really messed up.*"

"What about the signal?" asked Rachel.

"*The signal? I think it's south-east as well. It's not that strong where I am, but it was when we left Century Station.*" He was still yelling, and I turned down the volume on my comm a bit.

"Hey guys," came Hud's voice. *"What was that bang?"*

"Tell you later," I said. "How's the signal where you are?"

"I'm right near the docklands, and it's really strong. If I turn off the damper for even a second, I start to feel really weird. I think it's somewhere close."

It was right back where we started.

"Okay. Let's meet at the park near the docklands," said Rachel. "We'll keep checking the signal as we travel. And Hud, see if you can narrow down the exact spot he's broadcasting from."

I rose from my hiding spot behind the gate and picked up the bike.

"And everyone," Rachel added. *"Be careful."*

We mumbled acknowledgement and switched off our comms to save battery after agreeing to switch them on again in half an hour, when we were all closer to the docklands.

At the end of the street, a black van turned slowly around the corner. Other cars I'd seen this morning had been almost out of control, occupants affected by the high of stage one. This was different. Government, maybe? But why weren't they affected?

I caught a glimpse of a masked face behind the dark tinting.

They weren't government.

They were Kindred.

FORTY-ONE

The Kindred were out and about. Were they looking for us, their escapees, or were they just gloating over the citywide carnage they'd helped Wheeler cause? If I could see them, they could see me, but would they recognise me as the girl caged at the Apex gathering? I had changed my clothes and my hoodie covered most of my face. Maybe I'd be okay.

Still, my behaviour wasn't exactly in line with the rest of the city. Time to amp it up and convince them I was affected by the signal. Judging by the actions of the affected so far, there were two ways to go: break stuff, or take all my clothes off. I chose option one.

Screaming wildly, I kicked over a garbage bin, scattering debris over the road, and threw my hands in the air, making sure to keep my face turned away from the van. The engine hummed as it drew closer, cycling down a pitch. They were slowing. I had to take things up a notch, do something crazy that no sane person would do. The bin rolled slowly toward the curb, clattering as it bounced over a pot-hole. Still facing away from the van, I ran to the bin, collected it, and held it in front of my face. I charged towards the van's windscreen, and hurled the bin into the glass, turning at the last second so they couldn't see my face. The bin bounced off the windscreen; it was reinforced glass, but my actions had the desired effect. No-one trying to avoid detection would hurl objects directly at the vehicle searching for them. The engine revved, and the van picked up speed past me, continuing to the intersection.

I'd escaped for now, but if the Kindred were cruising across the city, getting to the docklands was going to be a lot harder. I waited for the van to disappear around the corner, then picked up the bike. I'd have to stick to side-streets if I was to avoid detection.

I was about to ride off when I heard tyres screech. The black van reversed back into the intersection, slamming on the brakes to stop in the middle. They were looking my way.

They'd recognised me.

The wheels skidded again as the van whipped around in an arc, lining me up in the windscreen, ready to run me down. There was nowhere for me to go on the bike; they'd be on me in a few seconds. No alleys on this street that I could duck down. I had to ditch the bike and lose them on foot.

Throwing the bike down, I ran up the stairs of the office building next to me. The van engine roared as it grew closer.

I switched the damper off and concentrated on the lock that closed the two large wooden doors. It melted in a moment, and I kicked the left one open as the van pulled up outside. Damper switched back on, the airy feeling faded back into nothing.

No time to barricade the door; I had to disappear fast. There was no chance I'd survive a direct confrontation. I needed to escape or take them down one by one.

The hall in front of me opened out into an enormous foyer, marbled floor stretching to an imposing teak reception desk that was engraved with the company name: *Blackwood Logistics*. The name rang a bell; they were a massive international corporation dealing in, well, logistics. Whatever that was. Either way they surely had enough money to repair what I'd done to their front door, and whatever damage was about to happen next.

My shoes echoed as they slapped the marble, sending thunderclaps ricocheting off the vaulted ceiling. Three elevators sat at the back of the foyer, screens all reading G for ground level. Taking them would be a dumb move. The Kindred team could just force the doors and melt the ropes of the elevator I was in, and I'd plummet to my death. I had to take the emergency stairwell to the right.

An alarm blared through the building as I made it to the stairwell. With the city melting down it was highly unlikely a security team would respond. The alarm covered my footsteps, but it would also cover any noise of the Kindred's approach.

Bursting through the stairwell door, I looked back. Three Kindred had entered the foyer and were heading my direction. They moved fast, almost cat-like. These guys were specialists. They'd swapped their regular masks for the combat kind, with blinders on each side to avoid interference from other team members. A green glow came from the dampers under their hoods.

I vaulted the stairs two at a time, throwing the door shut behind me. Nothing to barricade it with; I'd have to outrun them. The cut on my arm throbbed under the bandage, keeping time with my heart, which threatened to thump out of my body.

If I could make it to the roof, maybe I could move to the next building and lose them. I looked up through the middle of the stairwell. The building was twenty stories, at least. That was a lot of stairs to climb.

I reached the second floor no problem, but heard the door slam open on the ground floor below. They were coming.

No chance I could outrun them to the roof; I was already puffing, and my arm felt like it was on fire. I had to try this another way.

Reaching the eighth-floor door, I pulled it open, but continued to mount the stairs to level nine. Hopefully they'd take the bait and think I was on level eight. I let the ninth-floor door close quietly behind me and stopped for a moment to plan my next move. This floor was an open plan office. Not the best place to lose my pursuers if they figured out my decoy on the floor below. Cubicles ran the entire length of the room, dividers sitting just above head height. Around the outside of the space were meeting rooms walled entirely by glass. No chance of hiding in there.

Footsteps came from the stairwell. They'd figured out my distraction, and I was trapped; there was no way out of this office except the lifts behind me, and they wouldn't be here any time soon.

My legs pumped as I ran to the back of the office, hiding in the cubicle at the end. I turned my comm unit on to ask the others for backup. No light blinked on, and nothing appeared on the LCD screen. The battery was dead. I was on my own.

The three Kindred entered, puffing.

"See any more blood?" one of them asked.

I pulled up the sleeve of my hoodie and looked at my injured arm. Blood had soaked through the bandage and onto my hand, and it was dripping onto the carpet. I must have left a trail up the stairs, and it would lead them straight to me. Wiping my hand on my pants, I ducked under the desk. The cubicle was mostly enclosed, but a centre space under the desk had been left free for cables to run. It was just big enough. I squeezed into the gap, which ran the entire length of the cubicle space. If the Kindred didn't look here, I could make it to the stairwell.

"Guard the door," said a woman. "We'll flush her out."

Great.

"More blood, look," a youngish man said. "Follow the bloody brick road." He chuckled at his own joke, which wasn't at all clever, or even funny, despite the laugh from his companions.

I was hidden here in this part of the cable run, but if they came to the back of the room, they'd spot my escape route. Now they were guarding the door, too.

I wasn't getting out of here until all of them were dead.

FORTY-TWO

Through gaps in the cable run, I could see two Kindred walk slowly up to my end of the office, one taking each side. I crawled through the cable run about halfway, until they were almost level with me on each side.

"Should we turn off the dampers?" asked the younger man.

"Leave them for now," said the woman. "Don't want to get all happy when you're trying to kill. She's got hers on, too. Saw it when we came in."

I put my hand up to switch the damper off but stopped. If Wheeler's tone affected me too much, I'd lose my survival instinct and give myself away. They'd kill me on the spot. If theirs were on too, at least the playing field was even—as even as three on one could be, anyway.

No way I could take all three of them directly. My only shot was to divide and conquer.

Both the Kindred looking for me had moved further up the building, so I crawled through a gap in the cable run into one of the cubicles. It was sparse, almost military in its precision. No personal photos adorned the walls, but a pen-holder sat to the left of a laptop dock. Inside was a perfectly-polished silver pen. I grabbed it, transferring it to my left hand which was, for the moment, stronger than my right. This was risky, and I couldn't miss.

I coughed quietly, just enough for the Kindred on this side of the room to hear. Then I ducked back under the desk to hide behind a set of drawers.

Feet shuffled on the carpet, coming closer to where I hid.

The footsteps continued and feet came into view, stopping to face the desk I was under. I readied the pen in my hand.

The woman bent slowly down to look under the desk. Her eyes glowered underneath her mask. "Got you."

A hand grabbed my foot from the other side, and I swivelled to face it. The second fighter held my leg, having snuck up from behind. He brought his other hand up to secure his grip, and the Kindred woman grabbed at my hair. I lashed out and hit her in the neck with my fist. She swore and moved back for a moment. Mustering all my strength, I drove the pen into the hand on my leg. Blood sprayed out of the injury, and the man gasped, releasing me. I kicked hard with my now free leg and connected with his mask, driving it into his face. The woman had recovered and grabbed at my hair again, and I swung wildly with the pen, stabbing her wrist. The man was still reeling from the head-kick. He was my next move. His mask had shifted on his face, and he couldn't see out the eye-holes. I dove towards him as he straightened his mask, driving the pen into his throat. He gasped for a moment, and blood pumped out of an artery in his neck. I wriggled the pen around to make sure I'd really done the job, then withdrew it. He collapsed and gurgled for a moment, writhing on the ground. No way he'd survive that.

I should have felt sick, but adrenaline proved useful.

Realising I could handle myself, the woman changed her strategy, leaping over the cubicle and landing on the younger man, cracking something inside him. He went still.

"Need help?" called the Kindred guarding the door.

"I'm good," she called. "Gonna put this one down all by myself."

I scrambled backward to the other side of the desk. She had the upper hand, and I needed to regroup.

Staying low, I moved two cubicles down, hiding behind a filing cabinet. My hand felt empty, and I looked down. I'd lost the pen; it was slippery with blood and must have fallen from my grip when I scrambled under the table.

"Come out," called the woman. "There's no way you're going to survive this, let alone make it out there in the city. The whole town is burning, and a pretty young thing like you won't stand a chance once Coleton enters the Zealot stage."

The voice grew closer as she walked slowly my direction. There were clunks and scrapes as she checked behind furniture. I had nowhere good to hide, and no weapons. There were no pens on this desk, and if I left this cubicle, she'd see me straight away. I could go under again, but now they'd figured out my hiding place it wouldn't be safe for long. I had to make a stand now before the other Kindred near the door came searching.

The desk had a stapler, but I couldn't exactly staple her to anything. A small trash bin sat half-full to my right, black liner dotted with tiny paper circles from a hole-punch. Guess the cleaners hadn't made it here before the city fell apart.

"I'll kill you far quicker than a Zealot would," said the woman. "I hear they tear people apart with their teeth.

Who knows why. Maybe it's anger. Maybe it's desire. Pretty messed up, and I'm not saying I'm all on board, to be honest with you. Wheeler's creative, but his plan lacks finesse. We're a patient people; in no hurry to execute the Agenda. Why else do you think it's taken thousands of years to get this far?"

The woman was a talker, for sure, but it gave me time to formulate a plan. She was so close, I could see the edge of her robe. If she searched this cubicle, I was done. Reaching carefully to the desk with my left hand, I picked up the stapler. The woman was coming from behind me, and if I could get her to move to the next cubicle without looking back, I'd get the jump on her.

"Regardless, the Fathers want to try Wheeler's accelerated strategy, so here we are. I must say, despite the grisly nature of what's going on outside, it's honestly quite beautiful. Humanity at its most real, its most true. Breathtaking, really."

I hurled the stapler over the cubicle, hoping she didn't see me throw it.

The stapler clattered to the floor, and there was a smile in the woman's voice. "Clumsy little thing."

She leaped forward, expecting to catch me in the cubicle. But I wasn't there. I was coming up behind her with the black plastic liner from the trash can. She turned as I reached her, and she grunted as I forced the bag over her head, pulling it tight around her neck.

Her arms were free, though, and she reached up to tear a hole in the bag to breathe. She turned to face me, and I gathered up the spare plastic, pulling it even tighter around her neck like a scarf. She gagged, and scrambled for air, but the tightened bag constricted blood-flow through her neck as well as oxygen, and her eyes rolled back. She still wasn't out, though, so I twisted my arms and slammed her head on the desk. She finally stopped struggling and went limp. Once she was on the floor, I removed the woman's damper so that if she woke up, she'd be useless. A moment passed, and the final Kindred called out from near the door.

"Hey boss? You okay down there?"

Silence. I crept to the back of the building before he came looking.

"Boss? I know you said to guard the door, but I'm coming down anyway."

Leaving the exit free.

I ducked my head around the corner of the back cubicle. The door was clear.

"Boss!" yelled the man. He'd found my handiwork.

Keeping low, I ran for it. I wouldn't have to kill anyone else today.

But just before I made the door, the final Kindred barrelled in front of me, arms outstretched. He grabbed me, but my momentum carried us into the push-bar on the door, ploughing us both out into the stairwell. He hit the wall hard, which knocked the wind out of him for a moment, and he let go of me. He was huge, and strong, and there was no way I could take him down by myself. He was clearly fast, so I couldn't outrun him. He shook himself and stepped toward me.

I had to do something drastic. I ran up a flight of stairs with him directly behind. At the corner of the stairwell, I turned to face him. I had the height advantage here. When he reached the top step, I ran at him, catching him off-guard. He wasn't expecting a full-frontal attack from a seventeen-year-old girl. It was a dumb move — unless I'd already turned off my damper.

My momentum carried the man down the stairs, and he staggered backwards the whole way. I tuned into the concrete wall, hoping my mental picture of the layout was accurate. Cracks ripped through the wall on the landing, and I jammed him against it. The wall gave way and caught him by surprise. He let go of me and grasped at the sides of the hole which had now opened up behind him, but they crumbled too. He fell, in slow motion, framed by the cloudy sky outside and the cityscape beneath it. He screamed as he fell to his death out the side of the ninth-floor landing.

I stood at the hole, catching my breath, surveying the cityscape. It didn't look too bad, except for the smoke billowing from a number of buildings. Smirking, I considered offering my services to Blackwood Logistics as an office remodeller. The view was better here than from inside. I laughed out loud, despite that not being particularly funny, and realised I hadn't turned my damper back on yet. I corrected that immediately, and felt the euphoria drain away.

Something caught my eye out of the gap in the wall, just visible through the buildings in front of me. I had to go higher and get a better view.

I climbed the stairs to the top floor, level twenty-three, and up to the roof exit. The building had a beautifully manicured roof garden, with sun-lounges and even a small pool. Blackwood kept their employees very nicely indeed.

Clouds gathered overhead, and I stared closely at them, looking for the thing I'd seen down on level nine.

My heart thumped. A black shape slithered through the clouds, just visible amongst the grey. It was heading south towards the docklands. A Shadow. Small from down here, but just as terrifying. Another moved behind it, then another, and another. At least eight Shadows slinking through the clouds, all heading in the same direction. Hud's vision had come true; they were in the sky.

And they were heading toward my friends.

FORTY-THREE

I sped down the stairs and out of the lobby, grabbing my bike from where I'd ditched it in front of the building. More Kindred might be coming, and I had to warn the others. I'd been sidelined too long, and they'd be meeting at the park in the next ten minutes. With my comm dead, I had no way to warn them about the Shadows. And I wouldn't make it on time with a bike.

I stopped and stared at the black van the Kindred had left outside the office. It was empty, now.

Free ride.

I opened the drivers' side door to find the keys still in the ignition. Noah had given me four driving lessons, which he really shouldn't have done as he wasn't on his full license, but they might prove useful now. A look at the gearstick gave me some good news; it was an automatic.

From the corner of my eye, a face caught my attention. I started back, but it was just a Kindred mask. There were spare masks and robes in the back of the van. I put one on in case any Kindred saw me along the way.

Clipping in my seatbelt, I turned the keys and the engine roared to life.

"Okay, Noah," I said out loud. "Hope your lessons paid off."

I pushed the accelerator and the van lurched in place, engine whining.

Handbrake. Right.

Letting the handbrake go, I tried again. This time the van jumped forward, ramming the bin I'd thrown at it earlier. My bloody hands slipped on the steering wheel, and the van swerved. I hit the brake and wiped my hands on my pants, leaving dark handprints on the black fabric.

Grabbing the steering wheel again, I steadied myself, and this time gently pressed the accelerator. The van moved evenly, and I smiled. First time driving solo. Sweet.

A radio crackled on the dash.

"Unit six, report your status."

I slowed at an intersection. The light was red, but no other cars were around, so I sped on through.

"Unit six? Unit six, respond."

Silence. Maybe that was me. I pushed the button that said *Auto Talk*. "Ah, yeah, this is Unit Six. All good here."

"All good?"

A man staggered onto the road, shirt covered in blood. I swerved to avoid him and swore.

"Doesn't sound all good."

"Sorry, nearly hit someone. But we're okay."

"You were in pursuit of the Unseen girl. What happened?"

I looked in the rear-view mirror. The man was laying on the asphalt waving his arms and legs like he was making a snow angel. His skin was getting shredded on the road's surface, but he didn't seem to care.

"Uh, wasn't her. False alarm, sorry."

"Okay," said the voice, *"Keep an eye out, then. They can't stop this, but they can still hurt us."*

261

I smirked. "Really? The Unseen are just some pathetic kids. What can they really do?"

"Don't underestimate them. The girl, Ari something, you know what she did at Ettney? You know what they're calling her?"

"No?"

"Adiantempos."

Huh?

"Alright," I said over the intercom. "I'll keep an eye out for her, let you know if I see anything. Unit Six out."

I turned the radio off. They were calling me *Adiantempos*. That sounded like the First Language. I'd have to ask Noah what it meant when I saw him next.

Noah. Even though I hated him right now, I suddenly wanted to see him. Wanted to hold him. Wanted him to hold me. A little part of me wanted to repeat what I'd done in the shipping container, love him, attack him... whatever that was. I couldn't entirely blame the Pulse for that. A lot of what I felt was me.

Maybe I didn't hate Noah after all. Maybe I just hated the way he made me feel.

Driving through the city was an assault on my eyes. Men, women, and children staggered in the street, covered with blood and who knows what else. Fire spewed from shopfronts, tearing through stock and pouring smoke out of their broken windows. Ahead, the entire side of an apartment block was burning.

The crowds weren't happy now. They were starting to turn. Starting to get angry.

I slowed to navigate through a street crowded with abandoned cars. The van jolted as I clipped a red sedan, and I slowed even more. No use banging up the only transport I had.

There was a thump on the passenger window, and I turned to see a man plastered against the glass. His eyes were blackened, and his teeth dripped red. He yelled again, furious, and I hit the accelerator to lose him. The man disappeared behind me, a whirlwind of rage.

I jumped, as a second thump sounded at my window. Another dishevelled man screamed at me, bashing at the window with his fist. When that didn't break the glass, he hit his face against it, bashing his cheek into the glass again and again and again. I accelerated, but he held on to the side mirror, locking his feet above the wheel well. I turned to avoid a parked car, and he still held strong, smashing his face into the glass, trying to break through. His cheek was bloodied, and his jawbone was starting to poke through the skin. He didn't care. He just wanted in.

The glass spiderwebbed with cracks. It would smash completely soon, and then he could reach me.

I hit the accelerator again. There was a thick power pole ahead on my side of the road.

The window cracked, the safety glass shattering but staying in place. He peeled it away with one hand, and smiled, teeth visible not just through his lips but also the hole he'd smashed in his cheek.

I aimed the van at the power pole.

His hand reached out, scratching at my shoulder, pulling at my hair. Then there was a crunch, and he was gone, struck off the van by the pole I'd sideswiped to get rid of him.

My side view mirror was gone too, which was just as well; I didn't really want to see what I'd done to him.

The commotion had drawn a crowd, and now dozens of people spilled onto the streets. They weren't Zealots yet, not quite, but they ran at me with the same awful rage, throwing themselves against the van, then attacking each other when they got in the way.

One man hit the passenger door and went down hard, scraping along the asphalt. The crowd tracking me stopped and surrounded him.

I turned my eyes from the rear-view mirror as they ripped him apart.

At least they were distracted.

I floored the van as the road cleared ahead, suddenly void of parked cars, and rounded the corner onto the main highway into town. No-one was on this road, and I redlined the van, holding tight to the steering wheel so as not to kill myself. It was kind of a rush, driving so fast in the city, especially considering this was only my fifth time on the road. The van started to shake, and I lifted off the accelerator a little. No good dying before I got to the others; I'd be no use to them then.

In the rear-view mirror, as I sped away, Dad's apartment block flashed briefly between two larger buildings. My thoughts went to the man I'd wiped out on the power pole. If Skye and Dad got much worse, they might bash themselves to death trying to escape. Who knew what was happening back at the apartment. Hopefully Eden was okay and keeping an eye on them for me.

Still, if I didn't end this soon, Dad would end up a Zealot, and Skye—she'd become something else entirely.

FORTY-FOUR

I pulled up across from the park, removed the Kindred robes, and got out. The others, on seeing me, emerged from some thick bushes next to a skate ramp. First Rachel, then Noah and Hud.

"Where were you?" snapped Rachel, and then she stopped and took in the blood on my hands, hoodie, and gym shoes. "You look like you just came from one hell of a yoga class."

I smirked. "It's a long story, but I'm okay. My comm died, sorry."

"Never mind," she said, pulling out a new set from her pack. "I took the opportunity to duck into the warehouse to resupply. We've all got fresh comms, and I've stocked up on weapons."

"More tasers," said Hud. "Plus, guns."

I frowned. Guns were a bad idea against the Kindred. They could easily explode them in our hands.

Rachel saw my face. "The Kindred all have dampers. They won't be able to use their abilities without switching them off.

"What's stopping them?"

"Turn yours off for a moment."

I did, and I immediately lost control of my mind, floating up into the clouds, like my body was tiny, and nothing mattered any more. Nothing except freedom. My hands went to my jumper, desperate to strip it off. I suddenly wanted to be completely free, free of everything society imposed on me: words, reason, even clothing.

"Whoa there," said Rachel, swatting my hands from my jumper and switching my damper back on. "No need to do that."

Back in my right mind, my face went red hot. "Sorry, I—"

"It's okay," said Noah. "She pulled the same stunt on me, and let's just say these two know me a *lot* better now."

I snickered and felt a bit better. "The Pulse is really strong here."

"Exactly," said Rachel. "It acts almost immediately. The Kindred won't switch off their dampers now. And neither can we, or we'll lose all control. This is the one time in this war that guns are a *good* idea."

As if to punctuate her point, an elderly man ran past completely nude, hollering like he'd won the lottery. We all watched him for a moment, before looking away, embarrassed.

"Well, that's burned into my brain now," said Hud. He turned to me. "I was just telling these two, I narrowed down the exact direction the Pulse is coming from." He pointed west.

"That's toward Century Park," I said.

"Let's check there first, then," said Rachel, handing out belts that each carried a taser, handgun, and new comm unit. She pointed to the gun. "Know how to use this?"

I looked at Hud, who nodded. "I'm a country kid at heart; wouldn't be right if I hadn't gone pig hunting a few times on the back of a pickup."

"Me too," I said. "But I used a rifle, and I was a terrible shot."

"That'll have to do for now," said Rachel. "At least you know what to expect when you pull the trigger."

I frowned at the metal lump in my belt. It was heavy and promised nothing but death. What else was a gun for but killing? I'd done plenty of that today, but I didn't relish it. It made me feel awful, and empty, and cold, and I didn't like it at all. Killing doesn't just hurt the victim, it damages the killer. It does something to your soul.

My hand moved instinctively to my stomach, hovering over the black mark on my skin. I had to be okay with what needed to be done today. The city needed me. My friends needed me. My family needed me.

I wished they didn't need me to be a soldier.

A few more gear checks, and we were ready to move out.

"Guys?" said Noah.

Rachel raised one eyebrow.

"I've been thinking. The team should be here from Korea in about six hours. We could really use the backup if we're heading into a firefight with the Kindred. Wherever the signal is, it'll be well-defended, and they'll probably be expecting us."

I shook my head. "Before then everyone in this city will be either Zealots or dead. We can't wait that long. Plus, we have no more dampers. Even if the team arrives, they won't be able to enter the city."

"Ari's right," said Hud. "It's now or never."

Noah looked scared. Josh's death had really rattled him. I couldn't blame him. It had rattled me, too, but I was better at ignoring it, shoving that whole mess down into a little compartment like I'd been doing with everything else for the last six months.

Thinking of Josh made my pulse race. I pictured his face, so scared, as it was pulled under the water, eyes wide, mouth open—and I imagined what had happened next under the surface, his skin drying out, his heart stopping as the Shadow sucked everything from him. Strangely, it didn't make me sad. It should have made me sad, but it didn't. It made me angry. It made me want to kill every last one of the Kindred in this whole city, maybe even the world.

That anger must have shown on my face, because I caught Hud looking at me with approval. He was ready for a fight, too, but there was something else in his eyes. Something really dark. Getting captured by Wheeler had changed him. Whatever he'd seen in the Pulse, whatever Wheeler had done to him—he was different.

After a few moments, I spoke. "They might be expecting us, but they won't be expecting us to turn up in a Kindred van." I pointed to the black van behind me.

"That's Kindred?" Rachel said, nodding with a smile. "Nice work."

"And there are robes and masks in the back. We can get in the same way we broke into the Ettney Complex. Right under their noses."

Noah looked me in the eyes for the first time since I'd arrived. "Okay. That's actually a good plan."

"Don't sound so surprised," I snapped.

"Sorry," he backpedalled. "That's not what I meant."

"No time for your domestics, guys," said Rachel. "Gear up and get in the van."

We all hopped in the back of the van, which was empty except for two benches running either side under the windows. It was just like the one Hackman had driven when we went out to the farm to supposedly rescue Skye and Mum. For all I knew, it was the exact same one, which was a weird feeling.

Throwing the robes on over our clothes, we slipped the masks on.

"Whoa," said Hud, "it's really creepy looking at you three and seeing Kindred staring back."

"We're used to it," said Rachel. "Like Ari said, this is how we took down the Ettney complex."

"You guys are totally bad-ass." He sounded impressed.

His compliment jogged my memory.

"Hey, Noah," I said. Behind the mask his eyes registered surprise that I was talking to him. "I heard on the radio, they have a nickname for me. I think it's the First Language. Reckon you can translate?"

"Sure," he replied.

"They call me *Adiantempos.*"

Noah chuckled quietly.

"What?" I said, ready to be offended. "What does it mean?"

"It's actually pretty perfect," he said. "Loosely, it translates as 'The Approaching Storm.'"

Hud whistled. "That's a sweet nickname." He stepped backwards, kicking Rachel's pack which she'd placed on the floor.

"Hey, careful with that!" she yelled.

"What have you got in there, dynamite or something?" Hud laughed.

"Basically, yes," she replied. Hud's laugh drained away.

"I picked up a stack of grenades from the warehouse. I figured they might help us take down the transmitter.

Worst case scenario, we drive the whole van into the building with the grenade pins out, blow up the whole freaking thing."

"And ourselves in the process," said Noah.

"If that's what it takes," I said.

"Okay," said Hud. "Let me get this straight. We're driving a van, disguised as Kindred, into heavily protected territory with no backup, surrounded by a city that's literally ripping itself apart, with a backpack full of high explosives and a death wish."

"Pretty much, yeah," I said, smiling despite myself.

"The approaching storm indeed," said Hud. "These guys aren't gonna know what hit them."

FORTY-FIVE

Rachel did the driving to Century Park, while I caught the others up on what had happened in the Blackwood office.

"Blackwood Logistics," said Noah. "I've heard of them. They do all kinds of stuff, don't they?"

"Yeah," I replied, not looking at him directly. "Their office was massive. Hopefully they don't mind the bodies. And the giant hole I left in the wall."

"That was a pretty cool move," said Rachel. "I'm gonna remember that one. Hey, we're coming up on the park. Keep your eyes open.

Century Park was a killing field. The lawn was covered in bodies, grass stained red in the aftermath of whatever had happened here.

Rachel braked slowly and pulled up alongside the wrought iron entrance. None of us said anything. There was nothing we *could* say. Men, women, even a few children lay dead and dying. A middle-aged woman snarled at us from underneath a pile of bodies. She couldn't work her way free, which was the only thing keeping us safe from her. A hairy figure roamed at the other end of the park, moving from body to body doing who knows what.

"Zealots," I said, pointing the figure out to the others. "There must have been a whole lot of them through here. Look, there's a few dead on the ground amongst the other bodies."

Rachel kept driving, a slow circuit around Century Park. No-one stopped us; there was no-one left alive in this part of the city. On the next street, I caught a view of Downtown. It was empty, tents torn down, occupants scattered, or maybe lying dead in the dishevelled gardens.

I took a deep breath, remembering the night I'd come here less than four days ago.

Even before the Pulse, this town was angry, a seething mess of inequality and resentment. The lower classes hated the upper, the upper hated the lower, and the middle hated everyone. Everything happening in Coleton today had always been here, hidden under layers of propriety and fear of retribution.

I sighed. Wheeler's Pulse was the flashpoint, but the kindling was already piled high across the city. If it hadn't been Wheeler, it would have been something else. Some politician, profiteering off collective anger. Some businessman, leveraging instability and fear. People are smart by themselves, but pretty dumb in groups. They would have let themselves be riled up into violence, stirred up into riots, slaughtering each other in the streets just like the bloodbath we saw now. It wouldn't have been the first time that happened in history; the artefacts in Wheeler's basement testified to a long history of human self-destruction. We didn't need the Shadows to help us; we were quite capable of killing each other on our own. It was happening already in cities across the world, a collective anger threatening to tear us all apart. Maybe the Kindred were stirring things up, maybe they weren't, but in the end the only winners were the rich, the powerful, and the Shadows.

A thought hit me. The media. It was obvious, now that I turned it over in my mind. "I think I know where the transmitter is."

The others turned to me.

"Elements Gallery."

"Of course," said Noah. "I can't believe we didn't think of that before."

"I blame the exhaustion," I said, blinking my tired eyes, "and the Pulse. Anyway it's right near here. I guarantee that's where Wheeler's hiding. He's already got the basement set up like a bunker, and the building's right next door to the Channel Three studio.

"He didn't need to build his own transmitter," said Rachel. "He'll be piggybacking off their broadcast signal. The equipment he brought in must have been used to couple up to their network."

"It's our best bet," said Noah. "Let's go."

Two streets over, Rachel once again slowed the van to a crawl.

"What is it?" I asked.

"Look."

Ahead, two blocks up, was a mess of barbed wire and temporary fencing that blocked off the entire street. Dozens of Kindred stood guard in rows and each held an enormous blade, almost like the machete I'd found in Wheeler's basement.

"Look," said Noah pointing from the back. "The windows up top."

Several floors up in an apartment building on each side, two Kindred sat pointing enormous guns through the window at the street below. Snipers.

"Oh, come on," I said. "That's too easy; I can blow up those guns from here."

Rachel shook her head. "Remember what happened at the park? No chance you can turn off your damper, not this close to the signal. They're banking on that."

"Masks back on," said Noah. "We'll get in the old-fashioned way."

"Nothing old-fashioned about this," said Hud.

Rachel edged slowly towards the barricade. When she was less than a block away, one of the Kindred standing guard gestured for us to stop. We did, and he approached Rachel's window, the glass missing from when the man had smashed it out with his face on my way from Blackwood.

"This street's closed," he said. "You know that."

"Yeah," Rachel lied. "We got a bit turned around out there. Which way's the entrance, again?"

The man tilted his head slightly. "They're all closed. Total exclusion zone. Nobody in or out." His voice became threatening. "Which unit are you, anyway?"

"Um—" Rachel began.

"Six," I interjected, a little too loudly, keeping my head turned away so he wouldn't recognise my eyes through the mask. "Unit six."

"Wait here." He walked back to the others and talked with them for a moment.

"Should we go?" asked Noah, nervously.

"That'll blow our disguise completely," said Rachel. "Let's see how this plays out."

Hud sat forward. "We could ram them or use the grenades?"

"No way," I said. "Snipers, remember? Plus, we need the grenades for the transmitter."

The man began walking back. He looked casual.

A little too casual.

A red dot appeared on Rachel's chest. Then another.

"Hey Rach," I said. "Look down."

She did and swore under her breath.

"Okay, maybe you were right, Noah. New plan. Hud, grab a grenade, but move slowly."

He carefully removed one from the bag.

The man was almost at the van, and he shouted. "Take off your masks, now!"

Rachel shook her head. "What about anonymity, hey? Isn't that why we wear these?"

Quietly, she murmured to Hud, "Take out the pin, but keep the lever depressed."

"I know how to use a grenade," Hud said. "I've seen it in movies like a thousand times."

"Hope you're a good throw," she replied. The man outside was still shouting. He reached the window. "Remove your masks, Unseen scum."

"Hud," said Rachel. "Now."

Hud reached forward and threw the grenade out Rachel's window. The man paused for a moment, staring at the little black oval bouncing along the road. He yelped, then dove as the grenade exploded, lighting up the street and filling it with chunks of flying asphalt. Rachel slammed the van into reverse and the tyres squealed. The red dots had disappeared from her chest, the snipers' sightlines obscured by smoke and flame. Rachel turned the wheel, spun the van a hard right, threw the gearstick into drive, and floored it. Deafening cracks ripped through the air, and a hole appeared in the back of the van. Sniper fire.

"Anyone hit?" Noah yelled.

We checked ourselves. All okay.

The van squealed again as Rachel sped out of sight of the Kindred. Once it was clear we weren't being followed, she slowed the van a touch.

"Guess we can't get in that way."

"Maybe not," I said. "But we're heading toward the docklands. Might as well keep going."

We went silent for a moment.

"You want to take the tunnels?" asked Noah.

"I don't *want* to, but we have to. It's the only way in."

We were going back. Back to where we first ran into the Zealots.

Back to the place Josh died.

FORTY-SIX

The docklands were abandoned, and the tunnel entrance unguarded. That didn't mean we'd have a safe run the whole way, but it was something. The entrance sat as we'd left it; burned to scraps, with the forklift still parked on one side. No-one had cleaned up, or probably even reported it. The Kindred would have paid off the dock staff to keep our eventful evening quiet.

The van headlights lit the tunnel as we approached.

"If we can clear some of this debris, I could get the van in there," said Rachel.

"The tunnels are pretty wide, so as long as we keep the van centred on the tracks it should be okay," said Noah.

"Driving's definitely quicker than walking," I agreed. "I'd feel safer in a vehicle anyway; it's a faster getaway."

We jumped out of the van as Rachel pulled up, and we cleared the debris in front of the tunnel. The wood from the door was heavy, and it took all four of us to lift the larger pieces.

Once the tunnel was cleared, Rachel got back in the van. The rest of us stayed outside to guide her into the tunnel, before jumping back in. The tunnels looked different from inside the van; we were higher up than on foot, and the headlights lit it far better than our torches had.

"Where to?" she said.

"We shouldn't go directly to the gallery basement; that's bound to be guarded, especially 'cause they'll know we used it to get into the tunnels."

"What about Century Park Station? That's a few streets behind where the Kindred had the barricade; it's inside the exclusion zone."

"If you guys can get me near the lake, I can guide you to where I found Ari," said Hud.

"And then I can get us to the station," I said "I've got a pretty good idea of where we went after we escaped."

"That takes us out of the old section and into the main subway tunnels," said Noah. What about trains?"

"I doubt any of them are running today," said Rachel. "I think the drivers are probably all busy."

The trip was quiet, and the tunnels in this section were abandoned; although I jumped when we turned into the section where the animal corpses lay. There was no sign of any of the Zealots we'd killed; either the Kindred had cleaned them up, or the Zealots had done something unspeakable to their fallen brethren.

Noah pointed ahead. "Here's the spot where we turned to the lake," he said. "Hud, is this close enough?"

"Yeah," he replied. "I spent way too long down here by myself. Got a pretty good idea of where to go now."

Hud guided us further into the tunnel network, and despite a few wrong turns, we ended up where he'd found me in the dark.

Rachel slowed the van to a stop.

"Okay," I said. "I think I can get us to Century Park from here."

We veered right at a junction and the tunnels became better maintained; we were in the new section. A red light glowed ahead in the dark, signalling trains to stop. An alarm echoed; five beeps, and a recorded message telling us to evacuate the subway. It must have been activated with the emergency system I'd heard above ground. It was eerie, hearing the message echo through the tunnel over and over again.

Rachel drove slower now; as we grew closer to the exclusion zone there was more chance of encountering Kindred fighters.

A marker on the wall read *Century Park, 1km,* so Rachel stopped the van. "We should go on foot from here," she said. "Don't want the engine noise giving us away."

We got out of the van and began trudging down the tunnel, but not before Rachel swung the grenade-filled backpack over her shoulder and made sure each of us had a gun and taser in our belts. Honestly, they were hard to miss. The gun was heavy even though it was small, but I knew enough of guns to know I shouldn't underestimate its power. Last time I'd fired a rifle on a friend's farm, the kickback had nearly dislocated my shoulder.

The extra weight from the weapons was annoying. My legs were so sore they felt like they were going to drop off, but I shook them out and tried to count the railway sleepers to keep my mind off the pain. My arm was hurting, too, but not as much as before. It had become itchy, which was either a good or bad sign.

"I've been thinking," said Noah quietly as the recorded message ricocheted off the brick roof of the tunnel.

"About?" asked Hud.

"About what happens after today. If we take down Wheeler."

"When." I frowned. "*When* we take down Wheeler."

"Okay, when. There's still a Kindred army flooding the streets, and a swarm of Shadows flying around somewhere."

"A Swarm of Shadows," said Rachel, trying to laugh off Noah's concern. "Sounds like a fantasy book."

"He has a point, though," I replied, defending Noah even though I didn't want to. "When I was in Dad's apartment building there was an old woman, Mrs Parker. She'd murdered her husband. A lot of people have died today. A lot of people have become killers. Not to mention the slaughter we saw at the park. I can't get that image out of my mind, all those people torn to pieces. So much violence and anger and death. Even if everyone gets back into their right mind, I don't know if there's a way back from this. Not for Coleton."

Rachel stopped, and turned to us both, torchlight illuminating her face as it bounced off the ground, lighting up her chin and making her look severe. "There's always a way back," she said firmly. "Always. No matter how far gone we get. Look at me. The stuff I went through at Ettney—the things they did to me—I should be unable to function, I should be sitting in a chair staring off into space muttering to myself about who knows what. I did, for a while. But I made it back. I have a way to go, but I made it back."

In the distance, the emergency evacuation warning beeped again.

She looked me in the eyes, her pupils glinting in the torchlight. "The people of Coleton might need a lot of help, and it will take a lot of time, and a lot of anger and bitterness and tears, but eventually they'll make it back. Not all of them, but enough of them to make a difference. Enough of them to mean that what we're doing right now matters. This *matters*." Rachel turned to Noah. "And if you can't pull your mopey head out of your butt and get on with it, I'm gonna reach in there and do it for you."

I snorted at the image, and so did Hud. Turning, Rachel stalked off down the corridor, leaving us to catch up from behind.

Reaching the next junction, she slowed, holding out one hand to indicate we should stop. We did, leaving the last shuffle of our feet to echo through the tunnel. A signal box glowed red beside Rachel, flooding the tunnel with amber light and casting deep shadows on her face.

There was movement ahead, and murmuring sounds.

"Kindred," Rachel whispered as we crept toward her position. "Lots."

"The station's just around the corner. They've got it guarded," said Hud.

"We need a plan," I replied, stating the obvious.

"What about the van?" said Noah.

"The one we just left fifteen minutes back?" Rachel sighed.

He nodded. "We know they can't use their abilities, so they'll probably have guns. If we speed through fast enough, they might not be able to hit us, and we can draw them further into the tunnel. You can drive, and I can use a few grenades to take them out when they follow us."

"Well," Rachel replied, sounding impressed. "Seems you did manage to remove your head from your rectum. Either that, or you do real good thinking in there."

"Bit of both," he grinned.

"No way," I said. "That is the worst plan I've ever heard. Who do you two think you are? Action heroes? They'll either shoot you dead on sight, or the grenades will blow up the train tunnels and collapse the whole thing in on you."

"I'm willing to take the risk," said Noah. "Rachel was right. I've spent the last six months thinking I was invincible after Ettney. Thinking I could take on anything. I mean, we destroyed the entire complex. But what happened with Josh the other night—it broke that spell. I suddenly saw the stakes, I mean the real stakes. Any one of us could die here. And that rattled me. It got in my head, and I couldn't stomach the thought of anything else happening to any of you."

"So… you're feeling better because now you're okay with one of us dying?" said Hud.

"Yes." He saw my face. "I mean no, not just any of you. But Rachel's right. I had my head stuck up myself so far, I could see daylight. I thought I was too scared of dying. But I'm not. Not anymore. I'm okay with losing my life here today." He looked straight at me. "The thing that scares me most is losing you."

The last word hung in the air, swallowed up by the emergency warning blaring from a speaker overhead.

I opened my mouth to reply, but I had nothing to say. Not here. Not right now.

Rachel cut in to the silence. "We'd better get walking then. Noah and I will get the van and lead the Kindred blockade further into the tunnels. Hopefully they'll all follow, but if not, you and Hud can fight your way through the remainder."

"This is insane," Hud protested.

"You got a better plan?" Rachel snapped.

He thought for a moment, then shook his head. "No."

"Wait for our signal," she said, "then be ready."

"What's the signal?" I asked.

"A five-ton black van hurtling toward you down a train line."

I smirked. "I'll try not to miss it."

Rachel and Noah jogged off down the tunnel to the van, leaving Hud and I to get as close to the station as possible without being seen.

We crept forward, staying low to the ground, until we saw the lights of the station washing the tunnel in their green fluorescent glow. The Kindred couldn't spot us from here, but I could just see them. There were more than twenty cloaked Kindred spaced along the platform, staring various directions, keeping a lookout. None of them seemed to have night-vision equipment, which was a win for us. All of them held very big guns, though, and dampers glowed green under the hoods of their robes.

Hopefully most of them would follow the van. If not, I couldn't see how we were going to take them out in time.

A few minutes passed, waiting, watching, sweating, stressing, and then an engine roared in the distance behind us. They were here. Hud and I pressed to the side of the tunnel as headlights appeared in the dark, turning through the junction and blinding us both as they sped our way.

There was movement on the station platform. The Kindred knew something was up. Hopefully they'd take the bait. The engine noise was unbearably loud in the tunnel as Rachel redlined the van. It had almost reached us, but something was wrong. She started flashing the headlights, flicking to high beams again and again. Noah screamed at us from the window, but I couldn't make it out.

A bullet cracked through the air, whipping off the tunnel roof and sending dust down around my head.

The van reached level with us, and Noah screamed at me again from the open passenger window. "Run!" he yelled, face ashen, before the van sped past us and toward the station.

Behind the van, under the red light of the signal box, I saw why he was scared.

Zealots.

Dozens of them.

FORTY-SEVEN

The blood on their skin glistened in the red light from the tunnel, hair matted together, eyes wild and dark. Some of their clothes looked fresh. They were new Zealots, maybe only transformed today through Wheeler's broadcast. Probably locals who lived close to the transmitter source, and so their change had happened fastest.

Rachel didn't slow the van, and I didn't blame her. It rocketed toward Century Park Station to a hail of Kindred bullets, which cut through the air around us and shot off into the tunnel. Hud and I pressed close to the wall to avoid the gunfire.

The rear door of the van kicked open, and Noah hung out the back, small black object in hand. "This way!" he called to us, and we began to run. He pulled the pin out of the grenade and hurled it down the tunnel toward the Zealots. I didn't dare look back, but a few seconds later I was blown to the ground by the blast. My ears rang, and I rolled over, holding my leg, which was bleeding at the knee.

The grenade had blown apart several Zealots, who were lying in pieces across the tunnel floor. The remaining

Zealots were swarming the dead, doing things to them that would be burned into my skull for a long time.

The Kindred had seen the Zealots now, and hesitated between the van and the onslaught, not sure which to protect against first. As the van passed the station, Noah hurled a grenade at the Kindred standing on the platform. They had warning from the one he'd just used on the Zealots, and one of the Kindred kicked the grenade down in the tunnel as the rest took cover. Hud and I stayed flat as the explosion ripped through the train line. The skin on my neck blistered from the heat.

The van disappeared down the tunnel, and half the Kindred followed it, leaving the remaining ten to deal with the Zealots. We were caught between the Zealot pack and the guards, with no way out.

The creatures had finished with their fallen brethren and turned toward the source of the second explosion. They were coming our way. Gunfire ripped them apart as the Kindred let loose volleys of automatic fire. Not that I could hear it now. My ears were dulled from the grenades.

Mowing down the Zealots had the desired effect. When one of them fell, the others pounced on it, leaving them vulnerable to even more fire. Wheeler's creations were brutal, but dumb.

A bullet sparked off the wall next to my shoulder. The Kindred were shooting fish in a barrel, and if we didn't move soon, we'd catch a bullet ourselves.

Hud was mouthing something, but I couldn't hear him over the ringing in my ears. He pointed toward a recess in the wall a few steps away. The headlights and explosions had given us night-blindness, but my eyes were adjusting to the dark again, allowing me to see the hidden area for the first time.

Behind us, a Zealot raised his head from the remains of the fallen and looked our way. He'd worked out that staying put was probably a bad idea, and stood to make a run for us, before doubling over as he took a bullet in the stomach. A second hit him in the top of the head, and he fell forward, limp. There were only a handful of Zealots left, and they wouldn't work as a distraction much longer.

Hud ran for the recessed area ahead. I followed, and he pushed open the access door.

The gunfire became even quieter, dull thumps echoing through the passage. The lights were off, but I dared to switch a torch on to see where we were. A metal staircase beckoned, and Hud turned to me.

He pointed to his wrist, then his ears. Right. We should wait until our hearing returned before moving forward. There'd be no way to know if we were being followed. I nodded in agreement, and we stood together in the darkness. Hud frowned and pointed to my right ear. I put my hand to it, and it came away with blood on my fingers. That ear had been the one facing the first explosion. My eardrum was probably blown out. That explained the awful pain in my head. If we lived through this, it was fixable.

In the meantime, the ringing in my left ear began to subside, and I could talk to Hud without shouting, although there was still a constant screeching, like feedback from a microphone.

"Reckon this leads all the way to the surface?" I asked.

"Doubt it. It's probably an access point to the platform. We'll still have to take down the Kindred, if they're finished with the Zealots."

"I almost feel bad for the Zealots," I said. "I mean, I know they're murderous psychopaths and everything, but they didn't have a choice to become who they are."

"They're abominations," said Hud. "They deserved to die."

Hud's face was dark in the torch's ambient light. From this angle, his expression reminded me of someone, maybe Dad's face when he'd changed and gotten angry. Either way, I didn't like who this new Hud was becoming.

We slowly climbed the stairs to find Hud was right. There were only two flights, and then a short passageway. At the end of the passage was another metal door, and on the other side of that was likely the Century Park platform full of Kindred.

I hadn't thought about Rachel or Noah since they'd sped past in the tunnel. Hopefully, they were okay.

Gunfire rang out across the station. If the Kindred were still distracted by the Zealots, they might not notice us sneaking up the stairs behind them.

Hud cracked open the door and the gunshots grew louder again. I peeked through at the remaining Kindred standing on the platform, firing wildly into the darkness. From the screaming further in the tunnel, more Zealots had turned up; probably drawn here by all the noise.

Hud slipped out through the door, and I followed, making a bee-line for the stairs. None of the Kindred turned; they weren't expecting anyone to come from behind. We made it halfway up the stairs before one of them saw us, and he shouted at the others. Two of them twisted around to face us, raising their weapons to fire. There was no cover, and nowhere to run. I froze and took a breath, waiting for a bullet to rip through my chest.

The roof rumbled, and cracked, and shook, sending dust onto the platform and the Kindred facing us. One of them looked up as a chunk of the ceiling hit him in the face, crushing him instantly. The Kindred all stopped firing, staring at the ceiling as it splintered into shards. Zealots swarmed the platform behind them while the rail tunnel began to collapse next to the station.

"We need to go," I shouted at Hud, but he didn't respond. His forehead dripped with sweat as he stared at the ceiling, and his left hand held the damper. He'd taken it off to use his power.

"Hud, what are you doing?" I screamed. "The Pulse!"

"Shut up, Ari!" he shouted back.

Zealots and Kindred both ran now, heading for the stairs to escape the collapsing subway. Concrete boulders blocked their paths, and a water main burst, flooding pressurised water at the base of the stairs, making escape impossible.

A gas line broke, too, and flames billowed from the ceiling. Hud was bringing the entire structure down, and with it, whatever sat aboveground.

"Hud! Stop! That's enough! There's no chance they'll make it up here."

"They have to die," said Hud. "I can't let you die down here. You have to survive. It's the only way. You run, but I'm staying here until it's done."

His eyes were sharp, and he seemed unaffected by Wheeler's tone, which was definitely still rippling through the air. Hud was strong. Stronger than me. Stronger than any of us. He was taking the whole station down, and he didn't care who he took with him.

With one final scream, he broke the remaining steel supports, and a deafening crack tore through the underground.

"Time to go," he said, and pushed me up the stairs as the station filled with smoke. We reached the top and ran out onto the street. I gasped as I saw what Hud had done.

He'd vaporised the entire concrete reinforcement, which supported a twelve-storey apartment building that sat atop the subway. The entire building was coming down into the station, and no-one would be left alive. I stepped slowly backward as the building shuddered into the earth. The windows blew out of the first floor, then the second, then the third, as the structure collapsed into the cavern below.

The building tilted, now, and Hud grabbed my hand, snapping me out of my shock and leading me further down the street. As the apartments crashed toward the ground, a middle-aged man fell over the side of his balcony, plummeting to the pavement. From the hair on his arms, he had been turning Zealot anyway.

The apartment block hit the asphalt, shooting debris into the street and breaking the windows of the office block on the opposite side. The shockwave thumped me in the chest, and a fireball ripped through the air as a second gas line ruptured. A dust cloud joined it, kicked up by the rubble that had collapsed into the subway below.

I took a breath. "Hud, what did you do?"

"I did what I had to," he said, putting the damper back on and turning to face me.

"How did you stay immune to the signal?"

"No idea," he shrugged. "Now, where's this gallery?"

FORTY-EIGHT

Dust still drifted into the sky as we made our way toward the gallery. The brown haze swamped the air around us, too, filling my mouth, making me cough, and turning the streets ahead to mist, a mist made darker by a cloud of smoke that billowed throughout the city from countless fires. On the bright side, the dust and smoke helped conceal our progress from any watchful Kindred.

I tried to raise Noah or Rachel on the comms system, but there was no response. Hopefully that just meant they were still underground, and nothing worse had happened to them.

Up here in the exclusion zone the streets were eerily silent. The quiet wasn't peaceful. It was morbid like a cemetery. Most of the residents here were probably dead inside their apartments, the buildings now giant concrete tombs where they were free to rest. Not in peace, perhaps, but at least they weren't like the Zealots, who roamed beneath the city, for some reason seeking out darkness, perhaps because they couldn't stand to see themselves in the light. People seek out darkness when they want to hide who they are.

Hud was certainly turning into someone else. He stalked ahead of me now, making waves through the dust cloud. In some ways, he reminded me of myself at Ettney. Lost. Angry. Ready to hurt anyone or anything that got in the way of my goal, the black patch on my stomach spurring on my darkest impulse. Did Hud have one too? A mark, the Seed of Night as Hackman had called it? I stared at him closely for any signs of the mark but couldn't see anything on his hands or neck. If he had one, it was hidden under his clothing, and I wasn't about to start checking that right now.

I saw the Kindred pack before they saw us, and grabbed Hud, pulling him through a smashed storefront. He opened his mouth in protest, but I pointed down the street, and he saw the hooded figures emerge from the mist. Staying low behind the butcher's counter, I took deep breaths and tried to stay quiet. The sign on the back wall of the shop advertised sausages at half price. I couldn't see any on display, so either they'd all sold out, or the Zealots had gotten to them first.

"This way," said a male voice. "Century Park Station is up here."

"Damn dust is making it hard to navigate." said a woman, "Why are we even heading there? It's not like there'll be survivors."

"We're not looking for survivors," the man replied. "We're looking for the filth that took down an entire building. That kind of power is unheard of. We need to kill them before they do anything else."

Hud's eyebrow raised, and his mouth turned up in a small smirk. He was pleased with himself.

"Keep an eye out," the man continued. "They're not the only threat. You saw that crew get taken by the Zealots at the park. Don't let them get a jump on you."

The footsteps faded into the distance, and I waited until it was quiet to speak.

"Hud, thanks for saving us, but that was too much. Those people in the building—I don't even know how many were in there. You should have stopped."

"They were going to die anyway," Hud growled. "Better them than us."

I shook my head. "Down at the docklands you risked your life to save those workers."

"And look how that turned out. Kidnapped by Wheeler, and—" he stared into the distance.

"What did they do to you?"

He didn't answer.

I sighed. "Well you need to get past it, and fast. You can't just go bringing down residential blocks every time things get dangerous."

"Sure," he snapped. "Easy for you to say. You're the star of the show. The hero of the people. The Chosen One, the Child of Prophecy, the Approaching Storm, all that stuff. I'm just a sidekick who couldn't save his girlfriend."

"Seriously?" my mouth hung open. "You think I want all of this? You think I want *any* of this? You have no idea what I saw in the Chapel. No idea what I—what I saw myself become. You have no idea the darkness I have to carry. You're worse than Noah. Pull yourself together and stop making this all about you. Too many people have died today, and I'm not letting any more die just because you're sulking."

I stood and stormed out into the street, despite the threat of Kindred patrols. Rachel or Noah must have told him about the prophecy stuff, and I wished they hadn't.

Hud matched my pace and put one hand on my shoulder. It was awkward, like he wasn't quite sure what he was doing. "Ari?" he said, quietly.

"What?" I spat.

"Ari, I'm sorry. I lost it back there. And you're right. I was sulking."

I slowed and looked at him, smoke spiralling around us, whipped up by wind currents starting to pick up between the buildings. Overhead, the sky was barely visible, but it seemed to be glowing orange. We were nearing sunset.

"Hud, it's okay. But you've got to keep your eye on the ball. We've got to stop Wheeler before things get worse. The backup team will be here soon, but it won't matter as long as the Pulse is active."

He nodded. "Okay." He frowned for a moment. "Back there, you said you saw something in the Chapel. What do you mean?"

I took a deep breath, trying not to choke on the embers in the air. "The Chapel in the Ettney National Park, the one that felt wrong. You've heard of it?"

"The others told me, yeah."

Maybe it was time to tell someone. I hadn't spoken the vision out loud to a soul, but maybe Hud could take it. Maybe I could trust him with that.

"I had a vision. The Chapel—it showed me my future."

"The look on your face tells me it wasn't winning the lottery."

"No." I looked around, suddenly conscious that we were exposed on the street. "I saw a city drenched in blood. I saw Noah dying. And I saw myself, turning into one of the Shadow things, and I knew I was the reason everyone was dead."

Hud stepped back for a moment. "Whoa."

"I know. And I don't even know why I told you that, except that I'm terrified that this is it. That Coleton is the city I saw, and that somehow, if everyone in this city dies, I'm going to turn into a Shadow creature and end the entire world."

Hud shook his head. "No. I don't think that's it."

"What do you mean?"

"I don't think Coleton is the city you saw. Plus, Noah's not dead."

"You did just bring an entire apartment building down onto the tunnels. I've been trying not to think about what that could have done to him and Rachel."

"They were in a van. They would have been long gone by the time I brought that down. My point is, though, that you're not going to end the world today."

"How do you know?"

"Because I think this war still has a long way to go, and I think that future is still a long way off." His eyes were intense, but his voice was hopeful. It made me feel a little better.

That hope faded when we rounded the corner into the street where Elements Gallery sat. The front of the gallery was guarded by close to forty Kindred armed with automatic weapons and even a gun turret. No chance of us getting through there. Next door, the Channel Three studios sat quiet, and above it the transmission tower was barely visible through the smoke.

Look," said Hud, pointing. "I've never seen so many in one place."

The transmission tower was swarming with Shadows that flew in spirals around the antenna. They reminded me of sharks in a feeding frenzy, ducking and weaving and swirling, as if the smoke was deep water and the signal their prey.

Every now and then, one stopped for a moment, tendrils pulsing.

"It's like they're feeding off the signal," I said as Hud and I edged back around the corner and out of their sight line. "They're drawn to it."

"So what? Blow it up anyway, kill the signal, and they'll leave," he said.

"I've seen one stop a fire by drawing energy from the flames. Even if I get to the roof without them or the Kindred guard spotting me, they'll most likely suck the energy from the grenades before they do any real damage."

"So, now what?" asked Hud, peeking back around the corner.

"If we can't stop the transmitter, we have to cut the signal off at its source." I took a breath. "We have to kill Wheeler."

FORTY-NINE

We stopped at the edge of the alley that led to the back of Elements Gallery. At least a dozen Kindred stood armed with automatic weapons, guarding the alley on both sides. They didn't see us because we were crouched behind the wall, and the smoke concealed our movement, but we were going to have to sneak past them to get in. At least the back was less heavily fortified. If we could sneak in through the back of the Channel Three loading dock like last time, we could avoid them entirely.

"What do you think?" I asked Hud.

He switched off his damper.

"Hud, seriously. That's not a good idea. Turn it back on."

"I was fine last time. I can hear the signal, but it's not affecting me. They won't be expecting someone to use abilities, not this close to the Pulse."

"Hud, I—"

"Stay here." Hud ducked around the corner. A series of muffled explosions thumped the air, and then silence. Hud reappeared and motioned for me to follow him. I did, and gasped. The dozen Kindred guards were no longer there. Well, they were, but they were in bits. Hud had blown up the ammunition in their guns. All of them. At once.

"How did you do that?"

"Just good, I guess," he smirked, one corner of his mouth turning up at the edge.

"The Kindred thought I was powerful," I said, "but I've got nothing compared to you. You've got the strongest abilities I've ever seen."

"Guess I'm more useful than you thought, hey?"

I frowned. "I never said you weren't—"

"Never mind. They probably didn't hear that out the front, but let's not wait around and find out." Without waiting for me, he set off down the alley.

I followed, trying not to look at the mess of bodies on the ground. The smell rising from them was already awful, as their insides were now very much *not* inside.

The Channel Three loading dock was unlocked. People had probably turned up to work this morning as normal, not expecting that, instead of broadcasting the news, they would become the news. Perhaps, right now, news crews from around the world were heading to Coleton as the city unravelled. Although, and much more likely, nobody outside this city knew what was happening at all. The Kindred would have made sure of that.

I slipped inside, and the dock smelled musty and wet, rising damp staining the concrete edges. My breathing echoed through the space. I tried slowing it; I hadn't realised how fast I was panting. Stress, probably, not to mention the smoke clogging up the air outside. The *Blackwood Logistics* truck was still here from last time. Maybe it was an outside broadcast truck for on-the-ground reporters. Whatever it was, it brought back memories from inside Blackwood's offices. I shuddered and tried not to think about what I'd done to those Kindred on level nine.

The gallery was quiet, and unguarded. Wheeler had so much confidence in his Pulse, in the guards outside, he probably thought he was invincible. That worked in our favour.

I sidestepped the mirror this time, refusing to look at whatever was happening there. Right now, I had to take out Wheeler; freaky art could wait.

"Hey, guys?"

I jumped as Rachel's voice came through my earpiece. "Rachel?"

"The one and only. Glad to hear you're alright; not sure what happened to the train station, but once we lost the Zealots we turned around, and the tunnel was blocked completely. Only just made it above ground at City Station. Noah's here too. We're both okay."

I was about to tell her what Hud had done, but he shook his head; mouthing *please don't.*

He wasn't ready for the others to know what he was capable of. I kept my mouth shut for the time being. Now wasn't a great time anyway. "Hud and I are at the gallery. Couldn't blow up the antenna 'cause it's swarming with Shadows. I'm going after Wheeler."

Glass broke somewhere at the front of the gallery.

"Sounds like they're coming," said Hud. "I'll hold them off. You go after Wheeler." He moved toward the sound, disappearing behind the wall.

I nodded. "Hud's gonna need some backup outside. Can you guys get here?"

"There soon. Just found some of those awful yellow share bikes." Rachel was puffing, obviously pedalling hard.

"They look ridiculous," growled Noah. *"If I die riding one of these things, I'm going to haunt their headquarters."*

I chuckled. "Stay safe out there; Kindred patrols are roaming inside the exclusion zone."

Gunshots ripped through the air from the front of the gallery. Hud had engaged the guards.

I moved toward the basement entrance at the front desk. No guards here either. Pushing open the basement door, I was hit with a rush of damp air. It felt quiet down there. Maybe Wheeler wasn't here at all.

My concern was quickly shut down as I rounded the bottom of the stairs. At the back of the basement, in front of the entrance to Wheeler's artefact room, stood a line of children. Arms crossed, pupils black. None of them wore dampers; they didn't need to. Wheeler's Pulse had a different effect on these kids. They weren't transformed into Zealots. They were corrupted, changed on the inside, turned into cold, calculating murderers. And all ten of them were watching me.

A flare formed to my right, and I leaped out of the way. The oldest child stared at me with a wry smile on his face. None of them had moved, but they didn't have to. The Pulse had strengthened their abilities, allowed them to flare despite the interference from me and all the other kids.

More flares burst as the kids let loose, firing at me again and again, exploding the air around me. A flare hit my chest and burned. I swore and rolled behind one of the mattresses left on the ground, lifting it up to protect against their line of sight. If they couldn't see me, they couldn't flare at me.

The mattress caught fire, then blew apart in a burst of gas. One of them had vaped it.

Another flare burst next to my head, catching the end of my hair alight. I swatted at it, putting it out as a flare seared my left leg. If I stayed here much longer, they'd kill me.

I ran for the exit, stopping halfway up the stairs to see if I'd been followed. Nobody came after me. The kids were protecting Wheeler inside the artefact room.

The grenades were still in my pack. Thankfully none of the kids' flares had targeted it, or we'd all be burnt to dust. Which reminded me to take my gun from my belt too, so they couldn't blow me up with it like Hud had done to the Kindred. I'd forgotten the gun was even there, but it wasn't like I'd had a chance to use it.

I couldn't even think about using the grenades on the kids. It wasn't their fault they were like this; they were just like Eden. Lost, confused, and controlled by Wheeler's Pulse. I had to take them down without hurting them. Not seriously, anyway.

Hiding in the stairwell, I rummaged through the pack trying to find something useful. The taser on my belt was powerful, but only had a couple of uses. Not enough for ten kids.

There. A smoke grenade. If I could interrupt the kids' line of sight, they couldn't flare at me.

A plan formed in my mind, and I looked up at the sprinkler system on the roof, installed in case of fire.

This could work.

I snuck back down to the base of the stairs, took a deep breath, and threw the smoke grenade. There was a bang, and the room began to fill with smoke.

The kids started shouting obscenities. They knew I was coming.

The smoke reached the stairwell, and I took the chance, diving into the room and behind a mattress that sat against the wall to the left. A second later the sprinklers started, gushing water from the roof to put out the non-existent fire. The room was thick with smoke, and I choked on it, but it was time to make my move. I ran to the artefact room door hoping that the kids had left their posts. They hadn't, and one loomed out of the smoke at me as I neared the door. He was only a few years younger than me, but he was tall, and strong. He was trying to flare but couldn't in all the smoke and water; there was too much going on, even for his Pulse-enhanced abilities. He raised his right fist to punch me, but I ducked, driving the taser into his stomach. He dropped, and swore, convulsing in the pool of water collecting on the basement floor.

I was hit on the head from behind, and my vision blurred. A fist connected with my face, and I staggered back, head reeling. A smaller girl with blonde hair swung at me again. Her face was wild, her teeth bared as if she wanted to sink them into my neck. She came closer, and I dove forward under her punch, connecting the taser with her stomach. She went down like the older one, who was still twitching a few steps away. He glared at me, unable to control his limbs, or focus enough to use his abilities.

A face emerged from the smoke. Then another, and another. The remaining eight children surrounded me in a circle, all different heights and sizes, but there was no way I could take them all down before they overwhelmed me.

Unless...

I looked at the sprinkler directly over my head. They were all staring at me, but none of them were looking at the ceiling. The sprinkler arced water down around me like a dome. Eden's trick just might work, but it involved turning off the damper. This close to Wheeler, who knew what the effect would be, but I had to try.

I switched off the damper and my mind became blurry, swirling and tumbling, twisting between joy and anger, euphoria and fury. I tuned, and the water froze as it came out of the sprinkler, turning into shards of ice that clattered to the floor. I caught a large one as it fell, and threw it at the group, knocking three of the kids onto their backs. The remaining five rushed towards me, but the ice made them lose their footing and they slipped backwards into the growing puddle on the floor. Using the ice as a platform, I switched the taser to continuous mode, flicked the switch, and dropped it into the puddle just as they stood to attack again. All eight of them dropped to the floor, twitching.

My head spun, and I wanted to vomit, and lie down, and give up, and kill everyone in the room.

No. Get it together, Ari. I gritted my teeth and stared with laser focus on the water the children lay in, ignoring the hurricane in my brain.

Give up, Ari. Give up and die.

No!

I blinked and stared again at the water, my mind filling with blood and rage and death.

My mouth twisted into a scream as I blocked out the awful, terrifying things buffeting my mind.

I lowered the water's resonance until ice formed on the surface. It grew, and covered them, and soon all the water on the floor turned to ice, immobilising the children, encasing them like a cocoon. It stopped the taser from shocking them, too, which they were probably relieved about. None of them could see the ice that held them, as they were all stuck staring straight up. They wouldn't be able to break out of that in a hurry, or use their abilities to melt it. If they did, the taser would shock them again. They were trapped for now.

Water still poured from the sprinklers, though, and I didn't want them to drown, so I ran to the basement entrance and froze the water pipe solid. Then, I switched the damper back on. Immediately the awful thoughts subsided, my mind stopped spinning, and my breathing slowed. I sat for a moment, panting. The water stopped, dripping from the ceiling in bursts. The smoke was still thick in the air, making the room look almost like an Arctic lake covered in mist. It would almost have been beautiful, if it weren't for the ten angry children swearing at me from their ice prison on the floor.

I stood and walked toward the artefact room entrance, trying not to slip on the ice, and staying out of the sightline of the children in case they managed to flare.

Wheeler *had* to be here.

If the whole city felt like I had when I'd turned the damper off, no wonder it was such a bloodbath out there. Those kids on the floor must have had the same things running through their mind, too. Wheeler couldn't be allowed to continue this horror.

It was time for him to die.

FIFTY

The door creaked as I pushed it open, and the air inside was still. Suffocating. In the artefact room, everything lay as it was when we'd come through the night before.

Had it only been one night? Somehow the dark curtains felt even blacker, like the room had no edges, but continued as an infinite void, an endless space containing all the darkest moments of humanity.

I'd felt like this in the Sanctuary at Ettney: the horrible realisation that the Kindred had been working throughout history, that every time humanity was at its worst, the Shadows were there, orchestrating, lurking, consuming.

The rows of artefacts still sat on their plinths, illuminated by spotlights as tributes to the horror of war, the brutality of our kind, the violence and the darkness that stained our past, our present, and would likely stain our future.

At the end of the last row, movement.

Wheeler stepped toward a sword with an intricately carved hilt, his face lit by the spotlight bouncing off the plinth.

"You know, this sword drew the very first blood in the crusades." He smiled, running his hand along the edge of the blade. "Bit dull now, but still so beautiful."

I frowned. "You're a psychopath." I filled the words with as much venom as I could muster. "You're a psychopath, and I'm going to kill you."

Wheeler laughed, a deep belly laugh that filled the space, echoing around the room. "You don't get it, do you? After everything you've seen, after everything I've shown you."

He walked to the right, and I moved left, keeping as much distance between us as possible.

"Get what?"

"What I've been trying to teach you. What I've been trying to teach all of you." He ran his hand over a helmet with a crack in the middle but didn't bother to explain where it was from. "What you've seen out there; that's truth. *That's* freedom. Not the pathetic veneer of respectability, of supposed goodness, of *'society'*" He curved his fingers in air quotes as he said society, as if the very notion was ridiculous. "That out there is the truth!" he yelled. "That, out there; that is humanity revealed! Filthy, angry, brutal, and *honest*. This is who we really are." He shook his head, as if disappointed in me. "After everything you've seen you still don't get it."

Wheeler kept walking, touching each object on its plinth, revelling in its history. He stopped at a yellowing human skull. "This one is local. It belonged to the first white man to settle in this region. He shot and killed four First Nations men because he thought they were trying to attack his family. They were actually trying to warn him of a brown snake they'd seen crawling under his house.

Adam Cole, his name was. Hence, Coleton. This whole city is a tribute to a murderer."

"That's awful," I said quietly.

"That's humans," snapped Wheeler. "And you'd be a pathetic fool to think anything less." He pointed wildly at the roof. "Those people up there, they deserve this. They deserve all of it. You've seen what's truly in their hearts, what their deepest desires really are. It's not honour, or loyalty, or love." He picked up the skull for a moment, looking it in the eyes. "It's hate, isn't it, Adam? That's what made you shoot those men. Hatred. Arrogance. Fear."

"But you're the one making them do this," I replied, sidling to the left to keep away from Wheeler, who was steadily advancing toward me. "You're bringing it out of them."

"No," he shook his head. "You know that's not true. Deep down, you know. They deserve this."

I looked around at the artefacts, dozens of them giving testimony to what he said. I felt the blood cry out from the swords, heard the tears of the children at the end of the guns, saw the devastation unleashed by war and anger and hatred. Maybe Wheeler was right. Maybe we did deserve this.

Maybe we didn't deserve to be saved.

"You can feel it, can't you?" he smiled. "You know I'm right. And in a world where we no longer exist, the Shadows will remain. They'll be the truth of us. They'll be the testimony to our arrogance. Our greed. The Shadows are the truth of our world, and the truth of our humanity."

"Truth is freedom," I said.

"Precisely."

I felt the cold spot on my stomach burn again. The seed called to me, the darkness reaching out as it had in my bedroom, in the Chapel, in my darkest days since. So many nights I'd laid awake reliving the violence at Ettney, drawn into a spiral of fear and sadness and suffocating terror, feeling like a part of me wanted to surrender to it all.

If I was honest with myself, a part of me did agree with Wheeler. I'd spent the last days trying to save this city, despite that feeling. The guys who'd yelled at me from their car near Century Park, the anger seething in the suburbs, the media stirring up the mob, the politicians and bureaucrats hoarding wealth and bribes, the rage that was brewing everywhere we looked; Coleton was broken, and everybody knew it. Maybe it would be easier to start again.

There was a thrumming in my ears I hadn't noticed until now. It had started when I'd entered the room. Wheeler's Pulse. It had grown so strong that even the damper couldn't fully protect me.

I shook my head, clearing my mind of the thoughts he'd planted.

"No," I said. "We deserve to be saved. They deserve to be saved."

Wheeler scoffed, but I ignored him.

"Yes, there's darkness out there," I said. "Yes, we've done terrible, awful things. *I've* done terrible, awful things. But that doesn't mean I'm not worth saving. That doesn't mean this city, these people aren't worth saving. Nobody is too far gone. Nobody is so dark they can't make it back."

Wheeler laughed. "Tell that to your friend, Hud."

"What's he got to do with this?"

"You've seen what he's capable of. You haven't wondered why?"

I frowned at Wheeler.

"Never mind," he laughed. "You'll know soon enough."

"What you're doing out there; that isn't who those people really are. They might be hiding secrets, they might have dark impulses, but freedom isn't acting on the darkness, it's being free to choose the light."

Wheeler shook his head. "You're just a child," he said. "You know nothing of humanity."

"I know that I'm going to kill you," I said. "And whatever you've done to Hud, I'm going to stop it."

He shook his head, as if I was the dumbest girl on earth. "I've done nothing to him. But if you really want to kill me, do it." Wheeler stepped out into the middle of the room and got down on both knees.

"What are you doing?" I asked, staring at him.

"Do it. Kill me. It won't stop this. Nothing can stop this now. I've played my part. I've done my duty, and I'm ready."

"You're insane."

"All the more reason to kill me." His voice rose to a scream. "*Kill me*, you pathetic little bitch!"

Now was my chance. I ran for Wheeler, picking up a long, curved blade from its stand. He smiled as I ran for him, and he stretched out his arms, the same as Hackman had done at the Chapel when he burned. I reached Wheeler, and he didn't stop me, didn't try to run. He grinned again when I pressed the blade to his throat. A trickle of blood ran down his neck.

This close to him, looking him in the eyes, I hesitated. He was human, just like me. He was broken, just like I was, but maybe he could get better. Maybe he could be saved. I'd just given a big speech about redemption. If I really believed it, maybe he could —

Wheeler grabbed my hand and pressed the blade into his throat. It cut deep, and he smiled, coughing up blood that soaked his teeth.

"I deserve this," he choked out. "That's the truth, and this is *my* freedom."

Wheeler's eyes rolled back in his head, and I stood frozen, shocked at his confession. He fell, neck peeling away from the blade, and hit the floor dead.

That was it. It was over.

I switched off the damper, and immediately the tornado hit my mind.

The Pulse was still active. Wheeler was dead, but somehow his tone was still alive.

FIFTY-ONE

I turned my damper back on and stared at Wheeler's body, blood pooling from the wound in his neck. He wasn't breathing. He was definitely dead. So, why was the signal still throbbing through the city?

Through the open door back into the basement, I could hear the kids screaming. The city overhead would still be chaos. How was the Pulse still broadcasting?

It was strong in here, too, much stronger than outside the building.

At the back of the room, I noticed a shiny black piece of equipment pushed up against the wall, near the entrance to the tunnels. It was hard to see in the darkness, which was why I hadn't seen it before. I'd been too distracted by Wheeler.

I walked toward it. It was a big box with flashing lights and dials, and must have been what Wheeler had brought in through the docks. Cables led from the back of the box up through a hole in the roof, probably running all the way to the Channel Three antenna. I found the power cord coming out the back and followed it to a power point hidden behind the curtains to the left of the carved doors.

Taking a deep breath, I pulled the plug. A spark arced from the power point, and the lights went out in the artefact room, plunging the space into darkness. The unit didn't turn off, though. It was still running, and the signal was still visible on the dials, which hummed with the Pulse energy.

The next step was the cables leading to the antenna. I still held the sword that had killed Wheeler, so I wrapped my leather utility belt around the handle, and hacked them to pieces. Blue sparks flew from the back of the unit and the cords.

The Pulse still hummed through the air.

I took the sword to the unit now, cutting through the plastic sides, hacking the broadcaster into bits. The sword was still sharp considering how old it must have been, and before long the unit was in parts on the floor, sparking and hissing and flashing its lights even though it had been destroyed.

The Pulse was still there.

Somehow, it was still broadcasting. Something was sending a signal to this unit, keeping it going, reaching the antennae even without electricity or a physical connection. The Pulse was so strong it didn't need equipment anymore. It was sustaining itself.

From out on the street came a muffled explosion. The others were fighting the Kindred, and they'd need my help. I'd completed my mission to end Wheeler. We could work out the next step together.

I ran through the basement, ignoring the kids spewing filth my direction. They were still trapped in the ice, although for how much longer I wasn't sure. The smoke was finally clearing, now, and they'd break out soon. Mounting the stairs, I jammed the basement door shut with a chair from behind the front desk. It wouldn't do much against their power, but it was something.

A scream came from outside. I heard Rachel shouting at Noah to take cover. The front window had shattered, but not broken, and I saw Hud through the spiderwebbed glass, holding off two Kindred who had taken cover behind a wall of sandbags.

The signal was stronger up here than it had been in the basement. Without Wheeler's broadcast of the Pulse, I could feel the secondary source. I looked at the three outside: Noah, Hud, and Rachel. They'd have to wait. The Pulse took priority.

I walked carefully through the gallery, keeping an eye out for rogue Kindred. More screams split the air from outside.

The signal was stronger towards the back of the gallery, in the hall I'd first entered.

It was so intense, I could almost see it in the air, waves of resonance rippling through the hall and out into the city. What if Wheeler had just been a conduit? What if something else had been using him, sending the signal through him like a puppet? Maybe he really did regret what he'd done. Maybe, like he'd said, he really was free now. Free of its control.

I stopped behind the mirror, feeling the Pulse run through the floor, the air, so strong it was almost electric. The hair on the back of my neck stood up.

The Pulse was coming from the mirror.

The whole time, it had been the mirror. I'd literally looked straight at it without knowing.

Which One of You is Real?

The text glared at me now, as I moved slowly around to the front of the artwork. I'd thought it meant the me out here or the reflection in the mirror, the girl who'd twisted and morphed into a Shadow creature.

But maybe it wasn't asking whether me or mirror-me were real. It was asking which version of myself was true. Who I was inside, whether I was good or evil. Which one was the truth? Which one would I set free?

Truth and freedom.

I shook my head. I should have seen it. I should have recognised the connection, but I was so focussed on the human enemy I'd forgotten the reality. This war wasn't just about people. The Shadows were in charge of it all.

As I came around the front of the mirror, I stepped back. The mirror no longer reflected anything at all. Nothing was visible inside; it was a void. An impossible black. Almost like a doorway.

I held my hand up, expecting to be met by glass. Instead, my hand lengthened, stretching impossibly into the distance, fingers reaching into the depths of the void.

I tried to withdraw it, but I couldn't. My hand wouldn't come out. The more I pulled, the further my hand seemed to stretch. Bracing my other hand on the mirror frame, I counted to three, then pulled as hard as I could.

The world tilted and seemed to fold in on itself, corners pressing into corners, reality twisting around my head.

And I fell, screaming, into nothing.

FIFTY-TWO

It took a moment for my eyes to get used to the dark. When had I stopped falling? I didn't remember the impact of landing, but I seemed to be okay. I picked myself up off the cold ground and tried to work out where I was. The mirror, the void, the doorway; it had taken me somewhere.

Somewhere that felt eerily familiar.

As my eyes adjusted, I saw I was on a thin bridge made of black rock. It stretched as far as I could see in both directions. I was in some kind of chamber, an enormous cavern that was so huge I couldn't see the bottom. If I fell off this bridge, I'd have a long time to regret it before I hit the ground.

The air was cold and smelled of death. Echoes rippled around the cavern, sounds which had no source. Whispers, mostly, coming from everywhere, and nowhere. Occasionally, a clicking sound came from overhead, almost as if there was something on the ceiling.

The Pulse was gone, which was good, because I was no longer wearing the damper. I'd somehow lost it on the way here.

I needed a better look around to assess my situation, so I focussed on the air around me, lighting a small flare that burned in an orb above my head.

My mouth dropped.

The cavern roof wasn't made of rock. It was made of tendrils, giant, pulsing tendrils that rippled across the ceiling, shifting and turning and writhing like intestines. Some were enormous, like tree trunks, and reached from the roof all the way down into the void below. I still couldn't see the bottom. The impression was of being in an enormous, cavernous forest, but instead of leaves, the trees were filled with snakes.

Ari.

My eyes darted around. Who'd called me?

There was no-one here. Nobody on the bridge and nobody above.

Still, I had the sudden feeling I was not alone. Something was watching me from the void below. Something enormous. Something impossible. Something awful.

I had to get moving, figure a way out of this place. Perhaps I was deep under Coleton, even deeper than the tunnels. The mirror had taken me there.

Surely that was it.

Both directions of the bridge stretched off into the darkness, further than I could see. I set off in the direction I was facing.

Ari.

I shivered, and wished I had a thicker jumper on. It was a damp cold, like being in a cave, and it was cutting right through my clothes.

The patch on my stomach was like ice, too. I could tell, somehow, that it wanted to be here.

I walked carefully, so as not to lose my balance and plummet into the abyss below. As I did, the trunk-like intestines shimmered in the flare-light. Normally, I wouldn't have been able to sustain such a long flare, but for some reason, here it felt easy.

Little by little, I became aware of a thumping, a low galloping sound that was almost too low to hear. Perhaps it was my own heartbeat in my ears.

Something breathed on the back of my neck, and I whipped around, expecting to see a Shadow.

There was nothing. This place was toying with me. Teasing me.

It was impossible, but I felt the void below me smile.

I kept walking. There was nothing else to do. It was either walk or lay down and die, and I wasn't giving up just yet.

Maybe I *had* died, and this was hell. Maybe I was never, ever leaving. Maybe I'd be trapped here for eternity, walking along an endless bridge alone while I slowly lost my mind.

Ari.

"What?" I screamed into the cavern. "What do you want?"

My voice echoed around the space, coming back to me a second later, but distorted, like it was in reverse.

"You want me? Come and get me!"

Nothing. The tendrils on the roof ignored my screams. The void below said nothing.

A shriek. An ear-piercing shriek that filled the entire cavern, deafening and inhuman. I covered my ears, but it didn't matter. The shriek was inside my mind.

"Stop!" I screamed. "Stop it! I'm sorry! Make it stop!"

The noise faded, and I realised I was on my knees, head to the ground.

My flare had gone, too, no longer sustained by my focus. But a new source of light had entered the cavern. It came from the trunk-tendrils themselves. Distorted ripples of light twisted inside the trunks, which I now saw were translucent, bumpy like the Shadow's tendrils, but filled with distorted shapes.

I stared, and my hands clenched when I recognised the shapes in one of the trunks.

Six bodies, strung up inside a sandstone room.

The Chapel. I was looking at the Chapel. The image shifted and distorted, but it was undeniable. I could see the Chapel in the forest at Ettney.

Inside another trunk, hooded faces held up flaming torches. In another, an empty cave flickered with electric lights. There were more scenes, many more, likely from across the world.

Rachel's face loomed at me from another trunk. Her voice came through as an echo, barely audible, as it rippled through the space.

"What do you think it is?" she asked, as Noah joined her.

"I don't know," he replied, "But we can worry about that after we've found Ari."

I held my hands to my mouth and shouted at the trunk. "Guys! I'm here! Something happened with the mirror!"

They didn't hear me, instead shaking their heads and leaving to try and find me. At least they were safe.

A breath once again warmed the back of my neck, and I turned to see a shape fade into the darkness like smoke.

I backed away, keeping my eye on it, and re-lit my flare.

I tried to slow my breathing, but my whole body was pumped with adrenaline. My hands tingled, and my heart raced.

Ari.

The voice was close behind. I screamed and turned around, falling backwards and scuffing my hands on the rocky ground.

Ari, it's me.

I couldn't find the source of the voice, but I knew it. "Hud? Is that you?"

Sort of.

I reached into the darkness, as if I could touch him somehow, prove he was real. His voice was echoing through the cavern, like an aftershock, like a remnant. He was speaking, but he wasn't really here. "Are you a ghost?" I shouted into the dark. "Are we dead?"

No. At least, I don't think so.

"Did you touch the mirror too? Why can't I see you?" The trunk that reflected Coleton rippled again, and a pulse of smoky light spread through it and up into the tendrils on the roof.

The last thing I remember was running through the tunnels under Coleton, Hud's voice whispered. *I escaped from Wheeler, then ended up at this weird underground lake. I tried to cross the water, and something happened. I think... I think I was caught by a Shadow.*

"Hang on. We've spent the last day fighting together. You brought down a building. You don't remember any of that?"

That wasn't me, Ari. I've been trapped here since I saw the Shadow. It took me, and I remember screaming a lot, and then I was here.

"Where's here exactly?"

I'm not sure, but there's something down there in the darkness. Something awful. And it knows me. It's been calling me since I was a child. It's been calling out to me, and I don't know how to stop it.

I looked at the trunk where I'd seen Noah and Rachel, the one that showed the inside of the gallery. Hud walked past, looking at the mirror. He stopped, stared at it for a moment, and smiled.

You can't trust him, Ari. He's using me. He's...

He trailed off. I looked around the cavern, trying to find him once more. "Hud?"

You need to run. You need to run now. It's coming, Ari. It's coming for you.

The room pulsed, as if responding to the urgency in Hud's voice. A hum echoed from deep below, coursing up from the void. It was enormous, and terrible, and I could tell it wanted me.

Ari, run!

"How do I get out of here?"

I don't know. I'm trapped here too, but you have to run. It's coming, Ari! It's coming!

The cavern vibrated with a mammoth evil, a presence impossibly old, and incredibly powerful. I began to run. My flare was snuffed out by the thing in the void, and I ran in the darkness, path lit only by the lights glowing from the trunks. It was as if the whole cavern was alive with power. Tendrils peeled from the roof, and the floor shook like an earthquake. Rocks cracked off the sides of the bridge.

And suddenly, a warmth. A beautiful warmth like nothing I'd ever felt before, like light was exploding on the inside of me. Despite the horror emerging from the depths, I felt safe. Warm. Protected.

Then, just as quickly as the feeling came, it went, leaving me with one, inescapable, all-consuming thought.

I just *knew* that the only way out was down.

I took a deep breath and leapt into the abyss.

FIFTY-THREE

I stood in front of the mirror, staring into the darkness once again.

Had I even left the gallery? No, the others had come past here and hadn't seen me. The damper was back on my head, switched on.

"Ari!" yelled Rachel, spotting me from near the front of the gallery. "Ari, where the hell were you?"

"Hell pretty much covers it."

Noah joined her, holding a baseball bat in one hand. The end was red with blood. "Are you okay? He asked. "You look sick."

I felt sick, too. Something about the thing in the void still lingered, but even worse; Hud stood behind them both, looking at me. I wanted to expose him then and there, whoever he was, but I had to play it smart. I'd seen how strong he was. If he wanted, he could use his abilities to tear the three of us apart in a second. Now was not the time to confront him. Not yet.

"The Kindred out front are dead," Rachel said, "mostly thanks to Hud here. A couple fell back to regroup, so we've got a few minutes before they return with reinforcements. We found Wheeler dead in the basement. Well done." She held up the backpack I'd discarded on the basement stairwell. "I used the gas knockout grenade in here to shut those kids up. They'll wake in an hour or so."

"Knockout grenade?" I asked, incredulous. "Seriously? It would have been nice to know that was in there. Would have made the whole thing a lot less complicated!"

She looked remorseful, screwing her face up with a shrug. "Sorry about that. Didn't think we were going to get separated. Should have mentioned it in the tunnels."

"Never mind that," said Noah. "Nice work with the ice move. Haven't seen someone pull that before."

I ignored him. "Regardless," I said, "You probably noticed the Pulse is still going." The others nodded, and I continued. "I know where it's coming from."

"The mirror?" Rachel said, as if she'd already worked it out.

"Exactly."

"Easily fixed," said Noah, swinging the baseball bat at the mirror before I had time to stop him.

It didn't connect with the glass, instead it stretched out impossibly, like my hand had earlier, spiralling into the dark.

"Let go!" I yelled. Noah did, and the bat was sucked into the mirror, disappearing a second later.

Noah stepped back. "What the actual—"

"Yeah, there's a creepy abyss bridge that's about to get a new baseball bat," I said.

"What is this thing?" asked Noah, quietly.

"Well, when I was inside there," I said. "I saw tendrils that reflected different places in the world. I saw here, and the Chapel, and a bunch of other spots, probably Kindred locations. I think this is a doorway to wherever the Shadows come from. I think there are doorways across the world, connecting that place to ours, allowing them to come through. The Pulse is coming from the mirror, but it's true source is in there." I pointed into the abyss.

"Maybe the grenades will take it out," said Rachel, swinging the backpack off her shoulder and rifling through the contents. "There aren't heaps left, but there's enough."

"Worth a shot," I said.

Hud remained silent, standing back and observing. He creeped me out, now. I'd thought he was just traumatised from whatever had happened at the hands of Wheeler, but this was so much worse. He wasn't even here anymore; it was like something was using his skin, wearing him like a costume. I wanted to throw one of the grenades at him and blow him to pieces, but I didn't know what it would do to the real Hud trapped in the cavern. Maybe this was still Hud's body, and we'd need it to get him back.

Rachel handed two grenades to each of us, leaving the pack empty. "Okay, guys, a few of these are Thermite, which pack one heck of a punch. Still, it's not like the movies. We can't just throw one in and let it blow up the others. Doesn't work that way. We've got to pull all the pins, release the safety levers, then drop them and run for the loading dock. We won't have long before they do their thing."

I could tell she was enjoying this.

"You all ready?" she asked.

"Not really," said Noah.

We pulled the pins, and Rachel counted. "Three. Two."

My legs tensed to run.

"One."

We dropped the grenades and ran for it, sprinting to the loading dock, slamming the door shut behind us.

There was a colossal bang, and the floor shook. The door flew open, shooting flame above my head, and sending chunks of concrete and smoke flying into the lower dock.

The flames cleared, and we came back into the gallery to inspect the damage.

Nothing. The mirror stood exactly as it was, although there was an enormous hole in the blackened floor, and the plaster walls of the hall were mostly gone.

Rachel swore. "That should have worked."

"It's giving off intense resonance," I said. "Maybe we need a powered solution."

"Use our abilities to destroy the mirror?" Noah asked.

"Why not?" I shrugged.

"For one thing," he said. "The interference would be massive." He pointed to his head. "Not to mention as soon as I turn off this damper, I'm probably going to try and kill you all."

I looked toward the basement. "The Pulse gave Wheeler's kids incredible power," I said. "They overrode interference completely. If we can overcome the mental effects of the Pulse, maybe it will supercharge our abilities, make us strong enough to break through the interference from the Pulse, and each other, and vape the mirror from existence."

Rachel stepped forward. "It seems to be working for Hud," she said. I didn't take that as encouragement, though, knowing what I knew. He had other reasons for being so powerful, and I suspected they had nothing to do with the Pulse.

"I'm in," said Hud, frowning as he noticed me looking at him. This was the first time he'd talked since I'd left the mirror. The others probably just thought he was tired from the fight out front. "We should spread out, each take an angle."

Ari.

I stared at the mirror. Hud's voice was in my head. The real Hud. He was speaking to me through the mirror. If we destroyed it, we'd lose our chance at getting him back unless we could find another doorway.

Ari, it's coming. It's coming through. It knows the doorway is under attack. You need to destroy the mirror. You need to destroy it now!

It was almost imperceptible, but something shifted in the dark, in the void of space within the mirror.

"Guys," I said. "We need to do this now. There's something awful coming. Maybe it's using the Pulse to cross over. Either way, we don't have much time."

I could feel the thing from the abyss. It was watching me through the trunk tendrils, through the doorway, and it was coming.

"On it," said Rachel.

We spread to all four corners of the mirror.

The dark rippled, shifting in time with the Pulse.

"Switch off the dampers in five," she counted.

I put my finger over the switch.

"Four."

Taking a deep breath, I prepared for the onslaught of thoughts that would spiral through my mind.

"Three."

In the void of the mirror, a tendril appeared, stretching toward me. This one was different, though. It was scaly, not like the Shadows. A thousand tiny tendrils splintered off it, looking like a mass of bloodworms tied together, like an anemone reaching out in all directions.

"Screw counting, go now!" I yelled and switched off my damper.

The Pulse hit my brain like a tsunami, crashing into my focus, flooding my sanity, turning around and around, until there was nothing in my mind but death. Blood. Anger.

No.

I shook my head and focussed on the mirror, ignoring the horrifying images spiralling in my brain, the memories I'd been trying so hard to forget. I saw Skye, suspended in her bed by Shadow tendrils. Noah, dying in a street soaked with blood. Mum, falling forward with smoke pouring from her lungs. Elijah, the Unseen operative I'd killed, lying broken at my hand. I saw Rachel, back ripped to pieces by the Kindred torturer. And Josh, screaming, before the Shadow sucked him into the water.

"I'm sorry, everyone," I said. My vision blurred as my eyes filled with tears. "I'm sorry. Please, forgive me."

I sobbed it as a mantra, over and over and over again as the tendril reached for me from the mirror, as the others screamed and shouted and faced their demons, faced the awful visions blasting through their minds. Rachel yelled at an invisible tormentor, pleading with him to stop. Noah held his throat, as if his lungs were on fire once again, and I pled for forgiveness, begging the people in my mind to let me go, to set me free, to let me heal.

Hud stood still. Calm. Unaffected.

The mirror began to shudder. Despite our torment, it was working. I wiped my eyes and redoubled my efforts, screaming louder now, not out of sorrow, but of rage. I let it fill every part of me, flood my mind until there was nothing left. My scream was primal. Unceasing. Consuming. The tendril withdrew, sensing the doorway begin to close.

With one final push, I raised the resonance of the mirror, as high as it could go, then pushed it further, way past the point a normal mirror would have disappeared. The mirror shuddered, and flickered, and let out a bone-crunching screech, then blew apart into a cloud of dust with a shockwave that threw me to the ground.

The dust settled.

The Pulse stopped.

We had won.

I sat on the ground, panting for a moment, picking up the pieces of my broken mind. Noah and Rachel lay unconscious on the floor. Hud stood, gazing at the mirror, confident in our victory.

And suddenly, like that, I recognised him. I knew who Hud really was. Standing at just the right angle, with a half-smile etched onto his face, a fanatical blaze in his eyes like I'd seen in the Chapel just before it burned. It was impossible, but it was him. He turned, and caught me staring, raising one eyebrow as if he knew what I was about to say.

"It's you, isn't it?" I whispered.

He knew I'd worked it out. "Say it," he demanded.

I took a breath. "Hackman."

FIFTY-FOUR

Hud chuckled, a low, ominous chuckle that didn't suit him.

"Well done," he smiled. "But how did you know?"

I stood, struggling to my feet to face him. I had no weapon handy. It didn't matter; his abilities were too strong, and I felt mine fade now that the Pulse was no longer enhancing them. "The real Hud, he was in there." I pointed to where the mirror once stood.

He frowned. "The Echo Chamber? Interesting."

"The Echo Chamber?"

"The place where echoes of the world are seen. The place where *it* watches. Where it waits. You called the mirror a doorway, but the word 'tether' would be more accurate. It holds that world to this one."

I looked over at Noah and Rachel, willing them to wake. "What is that world?" I asked. Hackman had always been a talker. If I could keep him yapping till the others woke, maybe we could overpower him.

"You'll know soon enough." He stepped toward me. The windows behind him were dark, now that night had fallen. There would be no way of knowing if a Kindred assault was here.

"How?" I said. "How are you here? I saw you die. I saw you burn to death."

"*Peah cwalu sunis consumptei*," he said, speaking the First Language.

"That's from the Chapel," I replied. "It means 'through death we are consumed.'"

Hud-Hackman smiled again, as if he was proud of me. It made me sick. "Clever girl. You remember."

"Don't patronise me," I snapped.

"I'm not. But if you're clever enough to work that out, you might be able to work out what I am. What I became the night I died. How about a little hint?"

Smoke trickled from his mouth, edging its way out. His eyes went completely black.

"No." I said. "No way. It's not possible."

"It is, though," he said, voice deepening, distorting. "You know because you've seen it. You know what you become. I'm so glad you told me what you saw in the Chapel. I didn't think I'd get it out of you, but it was easy. You trust this boy."

I'd been such an idiot. I shouldn't have told him what I saw. Still, I couldn't admit to myself what he'd become. What I might become.

"I have to say," he kept talking, voice deep and strange, "He is an unusual child. He shouldn't have survived the feeding; but I felt a link, a tether, almost, from him into the Echo Chamber. I couldn't feed on him. Not properly. He refused to die. Instead, I found I could control him. It took hours of experimenting, playing, figuring it out before I could become him."

I pictured Hud trapped in the tunnels, fed on over and over and over while Hackman made him his puppet. It was awful.

"Why do it? Why not let him go?"

He laughed, an awful, guttural laugh. But it was bitter, too.

"All of us, the eldership, those who become powerful enough are promised ascension. This—state—it's a gateway. It's our path to immortality. Once we become Shadow, our bodies cease to be, at least in this world. We sustain ourselves through feeding."

Why was he telling me this? Maybe he knew he was going to kill me, so it didn't matter. Either way, I had to keep him talking. Noah stirred on the floor.

"The child in the Apex," I said. "The Shadow fed on him, and then it became almost solid."

"What they don't tell us, my dear, is that this state is excruciating. When I ascended in the fire outside the Chapel, I became trapped between worlds, unable to exist fully in either, and ripped apart by both."

My stomach turned. I'd always thought the tendrils coming from the Shadows looked like intestines, like something had been pulled inside out. Now I knew why. They were. The Shadows were literally being ripped apart every moment of their lives, if life was even the right word to use. They were in unbelievable agony. In a way, that was satisfying. It also made them incredibly dangerous. People will do anything to stop pain. Anything. When the Shadow fed on the child, it came back together as if the tendrils had literally sucked inside its body.

That was why they were corrupting the city. For some reason, the more corrupted someone had become, the more effective the feeding was.

"That's the Agenda," I said, and the entire history of the Kindred made sense. "To corrupt the world, to make them so dark inside that when you feed off them, you stop being torn between worlds."

"And exist forever," he said, eyes still black. "As long as there are humans, there will be food to sustain us. As long as you keep killing each other, destroying each other, as long as you keep pulsing with that beautiful, dark energy, we will survive."

It was too terrible to even think about. The whole planet as a factory farm for evil, humanity tormented and violent just like Coleton, used to sustain these disgusting, selfish abominations. "You're sick," I said, putting as much venom into my voice as I could.

"Maybe," he said. "But at this point I don't much care. I'm trapped, and every moment outside this body is agony. Using Hud, I feel whole. And I'll never let him go, not until the Agenda is fully realised."

One thing didn't make sense. "Why help us? Why destroy the mirror? Aren't the Shadows using the Kindred to make the Agenda happen? You've just destroyed the biggest weapon they've ever used."

He shook his head. "Wheeler was an idiot. His accelerated plan was never going to work, not properly. Although, I have to hand it to him; the children were a masterstroke. That avenue's certainly worth further exploration. Still, he had to be stopped, for reasons far bigger than you could understand right now."

"You also killed a bunch of Kindred."

He laughed. "The Kindred are nothing. The Unseen, too. Pathetic, tiny, mortal worms whose only purpose is to die. My plans are bigger than the Unseen. Bigger than the Kindred. You can't begin to imagine what's coming. You're all just pawns in this game."

He paused, then his eyes returned to normal, the smoke sucked back inside his mouth. He looked at me with softness. "All except for you, of course. You, the three of you," he gestured to the others. "You're all far more important than you know."

"Ever since the tunnels you've been pushing me to violence," I said. "You tried to make me destroy the Apex and kill all those people. You're trying to make me just like you."

He said nothing, just smiled.

"I'm going to kill you," I said, glaring at Hud-Hackman.

"That's the beauty of this," he grinned. "You can't. Ever."

Looking over his shoulder, he frowned. "More Kindred are coming. You should leave, now. I'll stay here and hold them off. Wake up the others and take the back lane out of here. Now that the Pulse is gone, the Kindred can use their abilities again. Stay out of sight and go west."

With that, he walked toward the front door and out into the night.

I ran to Noah and Rachel. "Guys, wake up. We have to go, now."

They stirred and sat upright, holding their heads. "What happened?"

"Long story, but we need to leave."

Rachel looked around. "Where's Hud?"

"Gone. I'll explain later. Right now, run."

They got up, and the three of us, so central to the Shadows' plan, ran back into the loading dock, through the alley, and out into the broken city.

FIFTY-FIVE

I stood on my balcony, overlooking the city lights glowing in the dark. There were less of them, now. So many buildings left empty or destroyed by fire. Still, the sounds of a party echoed through the night, rising from the restaurant across the street. Even after so much death, people still managed to drink. Perhaps they needed to.

Either way, the world was a darker place now.

Snatches of news echoed from the television inside, covering the NATO declaration of war against Russia. To cover up the truth, the Kindred had fabricated a story blaming Russia for a chemical attack that had affected Coleton. Nation after nation joined in the condemnation, and things had been tense even before the Pulse. Five days in, the war had officially begun.

Eden joined me on the balcony. She'd been living with us since the night of the Pulse. When I'd returned home, she was still faithfully watching the doors, ensuring Dad and Skye couldn't escape and hurt themselves. Skye was alright, but Dad had lost too much blood. I rushed him to an overwhelmed emergency department, where he remained, more than a week later, in a medically induced coma. I couldn't ask him how he knew about the Unseen, but there would be a lot of questions when he finally woke up.

The Kindred had changed, too. From what I'd seen in the Apex and across the city, the true nature of the Kindred had been revealed to the entire organisation. Even the low-level Kindred couldn't deny what they were really up to. Until now, the truth had been reserved for the upper levels of power. Now, the whole cult moved as one. They all knew the truth, and that made them all so much worse.

Noah had visited on the second day, to help clean the paint that had been splattered around the house. We didn't talk much, mostly forced phrases that enhanced the awkwardness, rather than helping. I hadn't seen him since, although he'd kept me updated on his search for Wheeler's kids, and his attempts to reunite them with their families. Eden was invaluable in finding them all, and Noah even managed to return the baby to her mother, who had thankfully escaped the massacre at Downtown. There was another baby who Eden seemed particularly interested in - apparently she'd rescued her from something awful the night she met Wheeler. I made sure the baby found a good home, and hoped she wouldn't remember anything that happened to her.

I sighed, staring out across a city that would never be the same, realising that, once again, my life had irreversibly changed.

Eden sighed, too. "What are you doing?" she asked.

"Thinking. Keeping watch. Hoping there aren't any more Zealots out there, hiding in the tunnels."

"The team from Korea got them all. At least that's what they said."

The cavalry had arrived, although late. They'd cleared out the tunnels in the days after the Pulse, wiping out the Zealots entirely. The Kindred abandoned the city once they saw the Pulse had ended, so the Korean team was left to mop up their mess.

In the clean-up, they'd found Josh's body in the lake, sunk to the bottom. I didn't want to see him. I wanted to imagine that maybe he'd survived, like Noah, or Hud, that he'd eventually come walking back in the door wearing that silly grin on his face. Or that he was trapped in the Echo Chamber with Hud, and one day he'd escape.

I didn't want to see him, but eventually I did. They had him laid out on a cold metal table in the Kindred safehouse, like the bodies we'd seen at the morgue. It was so awful, so impersonal. He deserved much more. His parents had been told he'd died during the Russian gas attack on Coleton. They'd never know he had died a hero, saving me and, by extension, this entire city.

Despite how grey his body was, his drawn face, his eyes still frozen open with terror, I went to him, and held him close, and cried.

"The world won't ever be the same, will it?" asked Eden, interrupting my thoughts.

"I don't think so. Not after this. Not now there's a war. There are some moments where you know history has changed, where you know you're living through something that will transform the world. This is one of those times."

"Well, at least we're on the same side now," she smiled. She could be difficult, and temperamental, and moody, but she had no-one else. I was her family now, and despite the still-healing wound on my arm, I didn't blame her for her anger. She reminded me of myself just after

Ettney. Lost and desperate and confused and looking for someone to blame. But if I could put myself back together, so could she.

Because despite all the awful things I've seen there's one thing I try to keep in mind. One thing that gives me courage in all this mess, one tiny, scrap of truth I'm holding on to. It's proven by the dark around me, by the chaos in Coleton, by the death I've seen way, way too many times. This truth is deeper than anything Wheeler thought was real: if there was death, that means there was a life, a beautiful, meaningful, powerful life. Death isn't possible unless life exists. If we know night, it's because we've seen the day. And that feeling I had in the Echo Chamber hasn't gone away, that feeling like something… someone else was there. Looking after me. Watching over me.

I've still got the dark spot on my stomach, but now I've got something else inside me too. Hope. Hope despite everything I've seen. Hope despite the war the world is hurtling towards. Hope despite the awful things I've done.

Because if there's a shadow, that means there has to be a light.

AFTER

Three weeks after the Pulse, I was woken by a knock at the door. I looked at the clock with bleary eyes. It was past two in the morning. Who the heck would be bothering me this early? Maybe Rachel needed something. Maybe a new attack was coming.

I swung the door open and jumped back as four black-clad men stood in the hall.

"Maria Carpenter?"

I scowled. "Who's asking?"

"The eyes—it's her," said the one at the back.

Before I could focus my abilities, they shoved a bag over my head. Then I felt a sharp pain in my neck.

And the world went dark.

I came to in a haze. The bag was still over my head, and my wrists were tied to the chair I was sitting in. I felt weird, and sluggish, probably because I'd been drugged.

"Hey!" I yelled through a parched throat. "Where am I? Let me go!"

A door clicked and hissed as it opened.

"Ari Carpenter," said a woman's voice. "It's nice to finally meet you. Welcome to Blackwood."

Ari will return in
THE TRUTH UNSEEN
BOOK THREE OF THE UNSEEN

No allies. No powers. No escape.

FROM THE AUTHOR

I hope you enjoyed The City Unseen!
If you did, it would be incredibly valuable if you would leave a review on the book's Amazon or Goodreads page. Reviews are the lifeblood of an indie author's sales, and each positive review can help others want to read the book, and help fund more books in the future. Even a short line or two makes a huge difference.

- Andrew C. Jaxson

Get your free Unseen starter library today!

Did you know you can get two extra instalments in the Unseen series for free?

The Unseen starter library contains the prequel to the series, *The Dark Unseen*, as well as a short story that bridges the events of The Fire Unseen and the City Unseen. PLUS you'll get further free short stories and novellas in the series as they're released.

You can get the stories with zero cost or obligation by signing up to the Andrew C. Jaxson readers' club here: andrewjaxson.com/free

Ad-blockers may make the sign-up form disappear, so be sure to switch it off if the sign-up form doesn't show.

ALSO IN

THE DARK UNSEEN
THE PREQUEL TO THE UNSEEN SERIES

The Shadows are coming, and they know my name.

Hud and his friends are camping in the mountains to celebrate finally finishing school. Tonight, he can finally make his move on the girl he's been in love with for four long years. But something lurks in the darkness, something Hud has encountered before and can't quite remember. When tragedy strikes the night turns to chaos, and Hud makes a terrifying and world-shattering discovery. As the teens run for their lives, old memories resurface, and an impossible evil will reveal itself.

"Tense and unnerving. Incredibly eerie." - Sarah Campbell, bookhookednook
"Thanks for the nightmares!" - Shanna
"If you adore on the edge of your seat suspense, you will love this." - Linda
"I am a HUGE Dean Koontz fan and I'm always looking for someone who may do something similar... I'm a fan!" - Christine

Available FREE at andrewjaxson.com

THE FIRE UNSEEN
BOOK ONE OF THE UNSEEN

Every town has secrets.
This one could end the world.

Nothing is as it seems in the tiny town of Ettney, Australia. Sixteen-year-old Ari Carpenter just survived a brutal accident, and now she's being stalked by shadows, and hunted by an impossible evil. As the conspiracy unfolds, Ari is thrown into a secret war fought with extraordinary powers that threatens not only everyone she loves, but the future of the world itself. This small-town girl might just save us all.

Packed with twists, action, romance ... and a few good scares. You don't want to miss this brand new young adult supernatural thriller series that is leaving readers breathless. If you are a fan of *The Hunger Games* and *The Maze Runner*, then The Unseen Series is a must read!

What reviews are saying:

"Frighteningly good...totally bad ass! The eerie world building was incredible." - *Sarah Campbell, bookhookednook*

What readers are saying:

"Andrew C. Jaxson has written an amazing book...very suspenseful, filled with action, and at times horrifying in the best way possible... Trust me, you will not be disappointed. I honestly believe Jaxson has written the next best thing." - *Josh*

"Riveting novel that is a superior thriller! Keeps you on the edge of your seat and coming back for more... A MUST READ!" - *Christine*

"An action packed page turner that will not disappoint. I could not put it down, so many twist and turns with every page turned... a fantastic read!" - *Megra*

Available now worldwide at andrewjaxson.com/fire